# Raptor Red

## Robert T. Bakker

Bantam Books
New York  Toronto  London  Sydney  Auckland

Raptor Red

A Bantam Book

PUBLISHING HISTORY
Bantam hardcover edition published October 1995
Bantam paperback edition / September 1996

Maps and interior illustrations drawn by the author

ISBN 0-553-57561-9

*Published simultaneously in the United States and Canada*

Bantam Books are published by Bantam Books, a division of Bantam
Doubleday Dell Publishing Group, Inc. Its trademark, consisting of
the words "Bantam Books" and the portrayal of a rooster, is
Registered in U.S. Patent and Trademark Office and in other
countries. Marca Registrada. Bantam Books, 1540 Broadway, New
York, New York 10036.

PRINTED IN THE UNITED STATES OF AMERICA

OPM    0  9  8  7  6  5  4  3  2  1

# List of Illustrations

| | | | |
|---|---|---|---|
| Astrodon | 7 | Aegi | 140 |
| Lungfish | 19 | Segnosaur | 145 |
| Iguanodon Feeding | 32 | Tro-odon | 154 |
| Mother Croc | 41 | Kronos | 161 |
| Trinity Turtle | 52 | Ammonite | 171 |
| Iguanodon Fighting | 62 | Acro | 177 |
| Gaston | 73 | Segno | 189 |
| *Utahraptor* Scent Post | 82 | Whip-Tail | 202 |
| *Utahraptor* Resting | 86 | Acrocanthosaurs | 211 |
| Multi | 100 | Flying Dactyl | 220 |
| Dactyl | 110 | *Utahraptor* | 229 |
| Raptor Red | 122 | Thumb Claw | 241 |
| Ostrich-Dino Hen | 128 | Dramatis Personae | 252 |

*This book is dedicated to all the amateur fossil-hunters who donate their weekends and vacations to enlarging our appreciation of the past. In Wyoming we call them the "Jurassic Irregulars." They work long hours without museum salaries, without government grants, and all too often without appreciation from the Ph.D.'s, and yet these amateurs are discovering new dinosaur species every summer.*

*Most of the time they pay for their own gas and drive their own pickups into the badlands. When we open up a new quarry, they contribute bags of plaster and bundles of burlap. Those of us fortunate enough to work full-time in small western museums rely on volunteers at every stage in the exacting process of cleaning the fossils, interpreting the anatomical facts, and clothing the bones with flesh and skin.*

*I started thinking about Raptor Red when I heard that a veteran amateur fossil-hunter had discovered a remarkable dinosaur. Raptor Red has come back to life thanks to such people.*

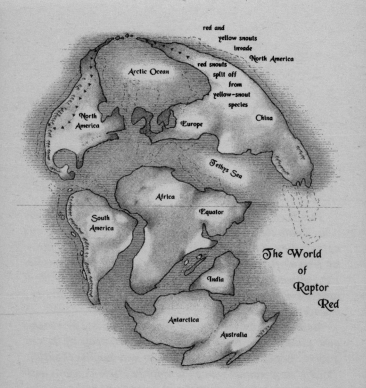

red and
yellow snouts
invade
North America

red snouts
split off
from
yellow-snout
species

North America

Arctic Ocean

Europe

China

North
America

Tethys Sea

Africa

Equator

South
America

India

The World
of
Raptor
Red

Antarctica

Australia

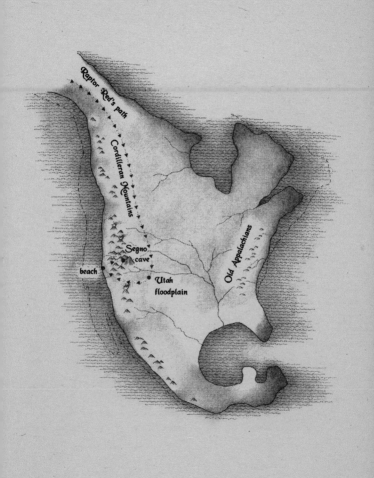

# Raptor Red

# Preface

*"Call her* Utahraptor.*"*

*That's what I suggested to my colleague, Dr. James Kirkland of the Dinamation Society, over the phone on a January afternoon in 1992. Jim was ecstatic about a giant fossil claw just dug up by a talented amateur, Bob Gaston, in red-gray rocks of Early Cretaceous Age. It was a raptor claw.*

*The bone bed was in Utah, a state with a glorious history of dino-discoveries, so the name* Utahraptor *popped into my head. And for some reason I automatically thought of the beast as a female.*

*"Why don't you call her* Utahraptor*? You know, 'The Hunter of Ancient Utah.' " He did.*

*I knew raptors well. When I was a freshman at college,*

*back in 1964, I helped excavate a raptor pod in Montana—
four skeletons intertwined in death, each animal about nine
feet long and maybe 120 pounds weight when alive. Raptors
were bantamweight dinosaurs, small and compact in the
body but equipped with weapons of exceptional deadliness.
They were kick-boxers. One claw on each hindfoot was trans-
formed into a big curved knife that could disembowel prey
with a single stroke.*

*These Montana creatures were named* Deinonychus—
*"terrible claw." Speed and agility were other raptor charac-
teristics. The first raptor species ever found was the
"Mongolian speedy raptor,"* Velociraptor mongoliensis, *excavated from the fossil sand dunes of the Gobi Desert in the
1920s.* Velociraptor *was even smaller than the deinonychs,
only fifty pounds or less. But* Velociraptor *shins and ankles
were long and strong, a design specification that ensured
high running speed. And all the raptor species had tails that
ended in elongated stiff rods, balancing poles that let the
animal engage in all sorts of nimble acrobatics.*

*It became customary in some paleontological circles to use
"velociraptor" for all the species in the family. Or just simply
"raptor."*

*All raptor species were masters of martial arts. They
could twist and turn while running at high speed, and they
had the capacity to jump while changing direction in midair.
Raptor hands were powerful and supple too—the combination of hand claws for grabbing and hindclaws for kicking
was formidable.*

*The raptor family was exceptional among the Dinosauria
for yet another reason: These were smart carnivores. In the
1960s, anatomists probed the inside of raptor braincase
bones and found to their surprise that the raptor's brain was
as large for its body weight as it is in many modern ground-
running birds.*

*Finding any raptor bone is a treat for us bone-diggers. But*

*what Gaston and Kirkland had just identified in their work-
shop was something so spectacular, no scientist had ever
dreamed of it. They had found the first giant raptor. Their
claw was from a beast twice the size of any other member of
the family and must have been carried by a body five hundred
to a thousand pounds—eight times heavier than a deinonych. It was the find of a lifetime.*

"The claw we've got—it's huge!" I could hear Jim jumping up and down at the other end of the line, and I started
jumping up and down too, because I knew something he
didn't. "Jim, Jim—Jim!" I yelled. "You just found Spielberg's
raptor."

"Huh?"

"You just found the giant raptor Spielberg made up for his
movie, you know—Jurassic Park."

Jim thought I was daft. He didn't know about the other
phone call I had gotten about giant raptors that morning. It
was from one of the special-effects artists working in the Jurassic Park skunk works, the studio where the movie monsters for Spielberg's film were being fabricated in hush-hush
conditions. The artists were suffering secret anxiety about
what was to become the star of the movie—a raptor species of
a size that had never been documented by a real fossil.

No one outside the studio besides me knew about the problem with Spielberg's giant raptor. No professional di-
nosaurologist was aware of the supersize raptor being
manufactured for the movie.

The special-effects artists were superb dino-anatomists.
It's funny how some of the best thinking about dinosaur shape
and dinosaur movement has come from movie artists. Even
the 1933 King Kong had some brontosaur sequences that
were a generation ahead of the dinosaurian dogma taught at
the time in universities. The artists doing Jurassic Park
wanted the latest info on all the species they were reconstruct-
ing. They wanted everything to be right. They'd been calling

*me once a week for months, checking on teeth of* T. rex *and skin of* Triceratops. *I'd sent them dozens of pages of dino-details.*

*The artists were up to date in their raptor knowledge. They knew that deinonychs were the largest, and that no raptor was bulkier than the average adult male human. Just before Jim called, I'd listened to one artist complain that Spielberg had invented a raptor that didn't exist. Apparently Spielberg wasn't happy with the small size of "real" raptors— he wanted something bigger for his movie. He wanted a raptor twice as big as* Deinonychus.

*I'd tried to calm the artist's misgivings. "You know, evolution can change size real fast. It's not impossible that a giant raptor could evolve in a geological instant. So maybe, theoretically, Spielberg's oversize raptor could have happened."*

*The artist wasn't impressed with my learned argument. He wanted hard facts, fossil data. "Yeah, a giant raptor's possible—theoretically. But you don't have any bones."*

*But now Jim's* Utahraptor *gave him the bones. The fossil beast from Utah turned out to be almost exactly the same size as the biggest raptor in the movie, an animal referred to in the script as the "big female."*

*Jim got back to work at the quarry, assisted by Don Burge, director of the museum at Price, Utah. Soon Don and Jim's crews had hand bones, foot bones, backbone, shinbones, and parts of the muzzle of their superraptor. They made a quick sketch of the entire critter, nose to tail. Not only was the* Utahraptor *huge by raptor standards, but it carried the most lethal weapons in its hands. The foreclaws had much sharper edges and worked like a set of six recurved carving knives.*

*In a few weeks Utah's giant raptor made the front page of* The New York Times. *And* Utahraptor *penetrated the worldwide community of dinosaur lovers—within a few days of the announcement, kids and adults all over the world knew the name. The giant raptor was fast becoming the sec-*

ond most famous dinosaurian meat-eater. The first, of course, is still Tyrannosaurus rex.

When the movie Jurassic Park came out at the beginning of the summer of 1993, it became the biggest blockbuster ever and made Velociraptor a household word. A significant percentage of the moviegoing public knew that the true star was more accurately called Utahraptor.

This book is the story of Utahraptor, told through the experiences of an individual raptor, a young adult female. Her story is pieced together from the fossil remains of Utahraptor and from clues about her world locked up in Early Cretaceous sediments.

Bones and rocks are eloquent storytellers, if you know how to listen to them. When you pick up a raptor shinbone, you can feel the rough-textured zones that mark the attachment sites of the muscles that gave power to the leg when it was part of a living animal. You can run your finger around the smooth surfaces at the upper and lower ends of the bone—the areas that formed the joints and that allowed quick, controlled movement.

Bones, muscles, and joints tell us much about the life and times of the superraptor from Utah—and we can learn even more from living species who have raptor characteristics today. Dinosaurs weren't the slow, stupid, overgrown lizards that museum displays showed in the 1950s. All dinosaurs show at least some of the adaptive hallmarks of the bird class. Raptors are especially close. In all details of their body construction—hips, knees, ankles, feet and hands, eyes and brain—raptors are designed like ground-running superhawks.

If you want to imagine the courtship behavior of Utahraptors or how they raised their young, don't think "lizard"—think "bird."

The rocks of Utah are full of clues as to what sort of landscape played host to Utahraptor. Fossils of water-loving turtles, crocs, and clams map out the size of rivers and ponds and swamps of the Early Cretaceous. Petrified tree trunks and shale beds with leaf imprints give snapshots of the flora. The very same sand beds and floodplain silts that entomb Utahraptor bones tell of floods that covered the lowlands during spring rainy seasons and of terrible droughts that turned lakes into briny salt flats.

Even such lowly creatures as earthworms and beetle grubs, the subterranean supporting cast of landscape evolution, left behind fossilized burrows that show up as bright green zones in the brown and red mud rock. When you sit in a dinosaur quarry in Utah, taking a break from chiseling out raptor bones, you can almost hear the gentle rustling of Cretaceous soil creatures, churning around the tangled roots of conifer seedlings.

We can learn from Utahraptor's story. Hers was a beautifully alert and sentient species. By looking through her eyes, we can see the evolutionary forces that were changing the natural world during the Early Cretaceous. Our own human ancestors were being created by the invisible hand of natural selection, as were the beginnings of the other animals and plants that enjoy supremacy in today's world. Utahraptor's story is part of our story.

The story begins with an invasion, an ambush, and a death.

---

The time is a hundred and twenty million years ago. On the flat, featureless floodplains that were central Utah, an evolutionary event is about to occur that will shock the ecological community of dinosaurs. The event is the arrival of a new superpredator.

# Raptor Attack!

A pair of fierce but beautiful eyes look out from the dull green undergrowth of conifers and ferns that bound the edges of mud flats and riverbeds. The eyes follow every movement among the great herd of plant-eating dinosaurs that mills around in the open meadows, feeding high in the trees, and sniffing the air for danger. The eyes belong to a young adult *Utahraptor*, a female who has not yet reproduced.

The female *Utahraptor* moves her twenty-foot-long body quietly through the ferns, walking in long, slow strides on her muscular hindlegs. She stops every few steps, rotates her elongate head, surveys the plant-eaters. Her eyes move back and forth, executing the rapid scanning of a hunter who is thinking about everything she sees. She is an intelligent killer. She watches the pattern made by the huge herbivorous dinosaurs. She evaluates each individual as a potential victim.

If she could put her thoughts into a human language, they might be: *That cow over there is too alert—she travels with two near full-grown calves. They're too strong, too dangerous to attack.*

*And that young bull is part of a bachelor-pack, five adolescent males who are aggressive and inquisitive. We can't kill them today.*

The *Utahraptor* moves her muzzle slightly to the left. She searches the treeline for another pair of eyes.

*There!* She exhales in a short, barely audible grunt. Her eyes meet those of another *Utahraptor*, a young male. He has the same stocky, compact torso she has, the same long, low head, the same neck held in an S-curve, the same long arms and fingers tipped with cruel-looking claws.

She is half of a mated pair, locked together in Darwinian monogamy for the last three years. Their mutual attraction is evolution's way of giving both male and female the best possible chance to get their genes into the next *Utahraptor* generations. In nature, nothing else matters.

As the days have lengthened in the early spring, the female *Utahraptor* has been responding to a powerful shift in her own internal chemistry. During the winter she was hunting for herself and for her mate. But now, subconsciously, she's aware of a new responsibility. She is hunting for the next generation. Soon they must build a nest and they must raise chicks.

The female and male exchange glances again, and she nods to him. It's a message that means, *In the next few minutes our lives will depend upon each other. I'm with you.*

The raptor pair-bond is held together by these shared

risks. If they're efficient as a pair—and lucky—they'll be uninjured and well fed at the breeding season. Then and only then will there be a brief interval for copulation.

This is the most dangerous season for raptors. Mating and rearing young exposes both parents to the highest risk of injury and death they'll face all year. Hunting alone isn't good enough. A pair of raptors hunting together is four or five times more successful than a solitary predator.

The raptor pair have another reason to be anxious. They are newcomers to the Utah ecosystem, an immigrant species whose original home is thousands of miles away in northern Asia. The native prey species of North America have strange habits and may be equipped with defenses the new predators have never seen.

The female *Utahraptor* sniffs the dung heaps left by the plant-eaters at the edge of the treeline. She's searching for identification chemicals, clues to the nature of the animals she and her mate are stalking. She's reluctant to risk an attack on a herbivore whom she has never met. But she's optimistic today—the dung-aroma seems familiar.

She has learned that she and her mate often have the advantage in the new land—sometimes the native prey species haven't had time to evolve special countermeasures against the foreign hunters. Invading predators may hit new territory like a Darwinian blitzkrieg.

The female raptor sticks her narrow snout out between the dried fronds of a tree fern. The dull brown-red hue of the fronds matches her own body color. She sniffs the air, testing the prey's chemical signature—she trusts identification by smell more than by sight.

*I know this one. We've hunted it before. We can do it if we're careful.* Her thought processes click through her predatory options. She knows her mate is smart. She trusts that he knows what she knows.

*There. That one. That male acting alone, bullying the*

*cows. He's not paying attention—we can kill him.* The female raptor silently selects the target, wordlessly evaluating the bull's vulnerability.

Her thigh muscles begin to twitch. It's almost time. They're almost close enough.

She pauses one last moment, sitting up inside a clump of tall tree ferns. She looks back again at her mate. They're too close to their prey to exchange nods, but just looking at each other is reassurance enough.

Her target is the biggest of the herbivores in the Utah ecosystem, an *Astrodon* ("star tooth"), a brontosaurian species with a long neck, a long tail, and a torso built like a ten-ton elephant's.

Giant size confers a certain ecological arrogance, and astros have a swaggering disdain for predators. In the astro's mind, any carnivore would be foolish to attack. Millions of years of evolution have built into their brains the comforting knowledge that they face hardly any real threat from meat-eaters. The only giant carnivore species is the ridge-backed acro, *Acrocanthosaurus*, but these three-ton hunters are very rare.

Even if a full-grown acro did try to attack an astrodon herd, the combined defenses of a dozen astros, totaling more than a hundred tons of enraged vegetarians, would be impregnable.

As the astro herd ambles easily around the edges of the salt-lake bed, their big cushioned paws churning up the briny mud, brains routinely check sensory input for danger. No scents are alarming. They pick up the hint of a raptor a hundred yards away, but this is an eighty-pound predator that wouldn't dare challenge a twenty-thousand-pound bull astro. The resident raptor species is the commonest predator in the astros' world, and the big plant-eaters see or smell them every day. All the raptors are tiny compared with the star-toothed brontosaurs.

Never would the biggest native raptor, a 150-pounder, even dream of attacking astros, unless it was lucky enough to find an unguarded newborn calf.

There *is* a raptor pack ahead, chewing up the carcass of a five-hundred-pound plant-eater (an iguanodont species), but they slink away when a cow astro makes a mock-charge in their direction.

The astro brains go down their genetically programmed checklist for sounds. There's no cause for alarm coming from this sensory system either. A low undertone of crunching can be made out to the left, under some conifer trees, where a one-ton armor-plated nodosaur is feeding placidly on seedlings. No threat here—the nodosaur moves away when a young bull astro pushes through the trees to investigate.

The big astro eyes, built like hawks' eyes, the size of dinner plates, make rhythmic sweeps of the landscape, stopping to focus in on any movement. Yes, there is a second group of raptors two hundred yards to the right. A different species. But at a hundred pounds, still too small to worry about.

It's spring, the time when big bull astros start to joust with each other to impress the females. Dull thuds punctuate the hot still air as the bulls swing their necks, giraffe style, like flexible clubs, aiming blows at each other's heads.

And it's a time of new danger for the astros: There's a newcomer to the resident fauna, a species who has reached Utah after coming across the North Pacific land bridges from its Central Asian homeland.

The bull astrodons pick up the novel scent—the unmistakable aroma of a raptor species, just a little different from the three species the astros are used to. Strange odors usually jingle alarm in any animal's brain. A strange odor means a creature never met before, a creature whose danger potential hasn't been evaluated through experience.

But the bull astrodons ignore the new scent. Their danger signal is overridden by their sexual competitiveness, their springtime drive to get the most desirable mate. Hormones are kicking in, actuated by their internal clocks.

Astros have no genetically coded alarm for raptor odor, and the foreign species is giving off merely a new variant of raptorine smell. Millions of years of evolution have built into astro psyches a disdain for these puny predators. Darwinian processes can never prepare any animal for a totally new danger—natural selection gives it only the best response to dangers faced by its ancestors. And not once in their pedigree have adult astrodons suffered a serious loss from a raptor attack.

That evolutionary rule is about to be broken. The cow astros, always more cautious than the bulls, begin to bunch up, surrounding their yearling calves and stretching their necks to catch a glimpse of the raptor that is emitting the strange scent. Cows take no chances with their young, their genetic investment for the next generation.

Two bulls neck-wrestle with wild abandon, clunking each other about the eyes and ears. They don't pay any heed whatsoever to the new raptor scent, which has now grown very strong. They don't notice that they are far from the main herd. Their brains are pounding out the same message again and again: *Beat this bull, beat this bull, beat this bull, get a cow.* In the Darwinian game, bulls must take chances. The females reject most suitors, choosing only the strongest and most vigorous, so a bull will literally risk life and limb to impress a desirable mate.

The cows stop looking at the bull contest. All the cow eyes focus in the direction of the foreign smell. Their minds have switched over to calf-protection behavior. And the cows see what the young bulls don't. The cows see the attack coming across the lake bed.

The cow eyes follow the light glistening over the broad scales on the thighs and calves of the giant raptors running noiselessly over the hard mud. The bulls still are totally absorbed with their sparring. They don't see the foreign raptors until the horrible hand claws cut long gashes through their skin and muscle.

Messages of pain jump from the bull astros' skin to their brains. They experience the disconcerting sensation of their own blood dripping down the skin of their stomachs. Now at last the switches flip over in their brains. Switched off are all thoughts of mating. Switched on is terror of an attack more vicious than any they have ever experienced before.

One bull manages to break away in a terrified running walk. He screeches high-pitched notes through the sound-making chamber that bulges around the nostrils on his snout. The cow herd screeches in response. The matriarchs bellow in deep warning tones and swoosh their tails from side to side.

The other bull stares at its attackers—a pair of raptors ten times heavier than he has ever seen before. The bull can see and smell his own blood on the three hooked claws carried on each raptor forepaw. Conflicting impulses flood his brain: flee, counterattack, run, or try to crush these new horrors with his front feet.

The raptors attack again from either side. Their long forearms extend outward, and their claws catch the bull's skin. As soon as a raptor feels its recurved claw tip penetrate the skin, the hand muscles contract instinctively, driving the claw-knives four inches deep into the flesh. Biceps and pectoral muscles flex to the max, pulling the claws through the prey's body, ripping channels a yard long.

The bull stands stupefied. Pain from two dozen long claw gashes on right and left flanks is overwhelming the normal feedback loops in his central nervous system. No one cut is life-threatening. But the cumulative effect drains his strength.

Again the two giant raptors attack. But this time the bull charges, hurtling his huge bulk forward, whipping his tail right and left. The raptors sidestep the counterattack. They reach out and slap their forepaws against the bull as he stumbles past, leaving a new set of bright red lines on his hide.

The bull is confused. He had won battles the year before with a one-ton ridge-backed acro. But that meat-eater was slow and clumsy compared to these quick-footed giant raptors. The ridge-backed acro had lunged at the bull, grabbing at the bull's shoulder, trying to hold on with foreclaws shaped like grappling hooks. The bull had shaken off the acro and crushed it to death by pressing it against the ground.

The anti-acro tactics don't work now. These giant raptors don't try to grapple and hold on. Their foreclaws act like curved blades, cutting through hide and flesh. And the giant raptors don't even try to bite: Each new attack is a quick dash and slash, a fast run-up to the bull and then a quick blow by the Ginsu-knife claws.

And there's another frightening difference about this attack. These giant raptors are smart.

The bull astro has a brain much too small to form the concept of "smart." And yet, in an instinctive way he realizes that the two raptors are attacking as one unified enemy. Each fresh attack is coordinated. As one raptor slashes at the right shoulder, distracting the bull, the other raptor strikes from the left side.

The astro brain clicks over to the last-ditch defense tactic: panic and headlong retreat.

The bull bellows. His legs crack through the hard, white salt-crusts lying over the deeper parts of the lake bed. He stumbles, falling to his knees. The stinky sulfurous black mud below the salt-crust oozes up his calves. Up again on his feet, he smashes through the pterodactyl nests clumped together at the lake bed's center. The air becomes a crimson, fluttering curtain as a thousand red-winged pterodactyls take off, screaming and pecking at the bull as they leave their eggs.

A possibility of escape—a feeling of hope—develops in the bull's brain. The center of the lake bed is covered by five feet of dark odoriferous mud, sediment stained by the slow decay of dead leaves, dead clams, and dead fish. It's mud that clings to your feet and sucks your legs down. Surely the raptors will hesitate to follow.

The bull sloshes into the deepest part of the lake bed and looks around—the raptors are gone. His body weight presses his legs further into the muck. He has a hard time lifting his hindpaws up because they support most of his weight. He can move his forepaws, but he can't turn.

Calm settles onto his astro brain. Five minutes elapse. The pterodactyls begin to return. They are quiet as they float back down onto their nests.

Pink-tinged pterodactyl bodies surround the astro. Another five minutes go by. A gentle rustling from behind draws his attention. Some creature is carefully threading its way among the nests. When a pterodactyl snaps its beak and wigwags its wings in protest, the creature freezes.

Another creature is walking slowly into the lake from the other direction. It too stops each time the pterodactyls erupt in a screeching commotion.

The bull tries hard to make out the scent. But the aroma of the fetid black mud overwhelms the olfactory bulbs in his brain.

One of the creatures jumps up onto some abandoned pterodactyl nests, perching atop the yard-high structure of hardened mud. It's a giant raptor. It's only a dozen yards away.

The other raptor hops onto another nest, five yards away.

The two raptors stare at the bull. They are silent and still, a slight tremor visible in their calf muscles.

The fatal attack comes in slow motion. On both sides the giant raptors step carefully from one dry pterodactyl nest to another. They converge toward the front of the bull astro, where he can't reach them with blows from his tail. The predators pause, rock gently side to side, and leap.

The bull shudders under the weight—both raptors are clinging to the top of his shoulder blades. He roars and tries to bite them, but his neck won't twist around far enough.

The fatal strokes don't come from the raptors' hands. The killing blows come from the inner toe of the hindleg, a claw shaped like a Gurkha dagger. The raptors drive their hindclaws deep into the bull's side, carefully placing the claw tips between his ribs. The entire hindquarters of the raptors tense up as the thigh, calf, and back muscles generate immense tension, then explode in a spasmodic contraction.

The sharp-edged hindclaws slice deeply through the body wall of the bull, powered by nearly the entire muscle mass of the raptors. Gaping wounds five feet long expose his vital organs to the outside. The raptors strike again and again, carving up the still-living mass.

Down onto his knees and wrists, the bull collapses. Shock and trauma close down his central nervous system. The bull dies slowly, as the raptors watch from their perch on the edges of his hip bones.

The raptors wait. They've seen supposedly dead prey

suddenly come back to life. The astro is too large for them to take chances, so the predators watch to be sure the breathing has stopped in the body below their feet. Then they start to feed, plunging their long snouts into the warm carcass, pulling out hunks of liver.

Only a half hour elapses before both raptors are gorged. They squat down onto a pterodactyl nest, right next to the astro carcass. They catch the scent of small raptor species circling at a safe distance, hoping for a chance to rush in and steal part of the kill.

The male *Utahraptor* stands up to growl at a little predator. That is the first mistake the giant raptors have made all day.

The dead astro, still lying upright on its elbows and knees, falls over onto its side. The inert mass of the torso pins the male raptor's tail in the black muck. For the first time since they attacked the astro, the raptors are frightened and disoriented. The fallen raptor thrashes about but succeeds only in dislocating a hip and sinking further into the mire.

The female raptor shrieks and grabs his hand in her mouth, trying to pull her mate by the arm. But that action fails too—it rolls him onto his side. His face is smothered by mud. He tries to clear his nostrils but can't.

The desperate struggles exhaust the trapped raptor— he can barely keep his mouth above the surface of the suffocating mud. His mate cries piteously. She tries to dig out the mud from underneath his head. It's hopeless. Her sharp claws cut through the mud but can't shovel it out.

Her own hindfeet are beginning to sink through the surface of the mud flat, now churned up and liquefied by the frantic actions of the dinosaurs' feet. She doesn't know what to do. Nothing works. Nothing in her learned experience is helpful; nothing in her instinctive repertoire.

Finally her sense of self-preservation overcomes the

pair-bond, and she retreats to a bit of high ground. In ten more minutes the trapped raptor is dead, his body totally submerged in the dark sediment.

The female raptor sits stunned for hours—she has just lost the mate she had chosen for life. They had hunted together successfully hundreds of times. They made countless kills without either raptor being injured in the slightest. She does not know what to do.

# Raptor Red

The female *Utahraptor* doesn't have a name for herself. Her brain doesn't operate with words, not even with silent, unspoken syllables. It works with images, colorful bursts of memory that make up a dreamlike history the brain constantly updates. Every day new experiences and new associations from her senses rearrange the symbolic registry.

In her own brain the raptor identifies herself with the symbols she learned as a chick: *me . . . raptor . . . red*.

We can call her Raptor Red, because that's how she labels herself in her own mental imagery.

Ever since she was very young, eight years ago, a chick in her mother's nest, she has learned to recognize the sound and scent and—most impoitant—the color of her own kind. Before she opened her eyes for the first time— as she struggled inside the egg, trying to break free of the camouflaged shell—her nostrils sucked in the first breath of air, air filled with the heavy, close-in scent of mother and father, sisters and brothers.

That first invasion of airborne particles traveled down her nostril tubes and into the olfactory chambers built into her skull, right in front of her eyes. The airborne particles were caught like microscopic bugs on the sticky flypaper of her sensory membranes. Biochemical detector cells were galvanized into action as soon as the particles dissolved in the thin mucous lining. Electrical discharges, a thousand each millisecond, lit up the nerve pathways leading from the olfactory chamber to the massive olfactory stalk of her brain.

She hatched with the eyes of an eagle and the snout of a wolf. And her brain was already prepared to receive the imprint of its parent-smell and parent-color that defined "me."

The imprinting impulse was hardwired into her hatchling brain. No thought was necessary—it was automatic. First came the scent. *This smell—my kind—safety—food* was the essence of the message recorded.

From that moment on the female raptor could lift her snout, sniff the incoming breeze, and detect the exciting presence of "my kind" from as far away as two miles.

Then came sight. She opened her huge, clear eyes on the third day after hatching. A blurred image of a snout filled her visual field. The snout had a delicate strip of meat hanging from it. The rank odor triggered a quick response from the raptor chick.

She squeaked in delight, snatched the meat, and gurgled it down. This was the first time she saw what she had been eating for the previous forty-eight hours. The color of meat was now recorded in her brain, along with the odor of meat, and would stay that way for the rest of her life.

Another color too was recorded. Her mother's snout had a bright crimson streak running aft from the nostril. When the raptor chick's eyes gradually became focused, she stared long and hard at that streak. *Red-snout . . . mother.*

The raptor chick knew that two different adults, each with a very different scent-identity, had been offering her meat from the moment she had hatched. *Mother* smelled very different from *the other.*

She was raised equally by her mother and father. When the raptor mother left the nest for a day-long hunt, the "other" took her place. The raptor chick's sense of smell told her that the "other" was a raptor parent who was, in some incomprehensible way, fundamentally foreign. Later in her life she would come to understand that this foreign property was maleness.

Ghurk-snurg-GULP.

The raptor chick glommed onto a thick hunk of meat hanging from her father's jaws. As she swallowed, she saw the bright red streak on his snout—wider, more vivid than her mother's: *red-snout . . . my kind too.* Another vital bit of information was added to the hard disk of her mental computer.

The chick sensed that her own individuality came from both parents—she could smell herself, she could smell her own shed skin, her own droppings, and they all smelled like a combination of mother and father. She had a concept that mother was "half of me" and father was "half of me."

The double bond between chick and father and chick and mother was the only social union Raptor Red enjoyed for four months. The other raptor chicks in the nest were only annoyances and competitors. Her three brothers and sisters (it was a big brood by raptor standards) were greedy eating machines, always trying to steal scraps of meat.

Most raptor chicks die before they are a year old. The concept of sharing does not exist in the chicks' brains—at least not in the first few months. *Grab NOW!* is the only action-provoking thought.

It has to be that way. Life expectancy is so dismal that only the most aggressive, most selfish chicks survive to leave the nest. Without this childhood cruelty, raptors would cease to evolve, cease to adapt, cease to exist.

Raptor Red was the most successfully selfish chick in her brood. She snatched the most food. She grew faster than her sibs. She was first out of the nest, first to join mother and father on a hunt. A sister was next. Once they were out of the nest, much of the chick-chick rivalry evaporated. She played with her sister, and the two bossed the male chicks around.

Each brother and sister had its own unique scent-signature, and Raptor Red learned every one so well that the slightest whiff from a hundred feet away would tell her who was there. Her sense of smell told her that her siblings shared her identity, just as her parents did—in her mind, brothers and sisters were "half of me."

For her first four and a half years, all her loyalty was to those who were "half of me." For all this time Raptor Red would flee any *Utahraptor* who did not smell like family. She joined her parents in hissing at strangers. She and her sister would chase away chicks from neighboring packs when they got too close.

Family was everything until the young male came, a stranger who courted her. Raptor Red felt her fear of foreigners melt away as she watched him perform the courtship ritual. He smelled completely un-family—"not part of me." And she knew that was right for her mate.

She had been adult in body form, full grown, for five years when she and her mate attacked the astro on the Utah floodplain. They had been mated for three years. But prey had been so scarce each breeding season that the pair did not dare to produce chicks.

Now as she sits in the mud next to her dead mate and the enormous inert hulk of the *Astrodon*, she experiences feelings that are new: despair and loneliness. Raptors are social beings. They need the companionship of their own kind. They feel a deadly unease when alone.

And there is a form of sorrow. She doesn't eat any part of the dead *Astrodon*. But she does stay next to the crumpled body of her mate for thirty-six hours. On the morning of the second day, huge, sickle-shaped shadows pass over her body. Instinctively she looks up and hisses loudly.

Shadows like these generated her first sensation of fear when she was a chick. She didn't have to learn to hate shadows from the sky. Nearly all dinosaurs are born with the same preprogrammed response. Those that are unfortunate enough to hatch with a mutant gene that eliminates the shadow-fear don't survive longer than a week. They are snatched from the nest by jaws from above.

Raptor Red hisses again, flexes her legs, and leaps as high as she can, her jaws snapping shut three times in rapid-fire succession. The dactyl leaves.

Another dactyl, younger and more foolish, soars in low, behind the raptor's back, and stabs at her with his spike-toothed jaws.

She jumps. Tiny dots of red show where the dactyl teeth pricked her. One dactyl she can handle. But the sight of the dead *Astrodon* is a visual lure attracting six, then twelve, then two dozen of the aerial monsters with twenty-foot wingspans. All are young, hungry, and over-confident.

The dactyls, a species of *Ornithocheirus*, are beautiful. All their undersurfaces are brilliant shades of pale brown and white. The noontime sunlight makes their body covering of fine, hairlike scales glisten. Iridescent green marks the beaks of the males; blue denotes the females.

Their long, narrow, recurved wings are under the control of an exquisite apparatus of tendons, ligaments, skin, and muscle. Slight twitches of thigh and knee adjust the tension of the wing membrane held between forelimb and hindlimb. Leading-edge flaps, moved by a special prong-like bone attached to the wrist, are constantly expanding and contracting to maximize the efficiency of airflow over the wing.

Even when the dactyls fly so slowly that it seems impossible they could stay aloft, the wing machinery works flawlessly. When airspeed falls as a dactyl goes into a slow climb, the wrist bones open up a slot in the leading edge, letting some of the air rush through the hole and preventing a stall that would cause the wing to lose its lift.

But to Raptor Red the dactyls are targets for venting her anger. For a moment she forgets that her mate is dead. She dances up and down in a murderous frenzy, snapping and snarling, *Kill them—protect my kind, my family—kill them!*

She flips her tail right and makes a 180-degree turn left just as a young dactyl with a blue mark on its head swoops in for another peck at her backside. Her jaws clamp down on the extreme wingtip, just for a second.

That is enough. The dactyl stalls out and turns a cartwheel sideways in the air. Its wingtip strikes the mud. The graceful flying machine becomes a tangle of fingers, toes, neck, and wing membrane. Now, as mud splatters over the body, the brilliant pelage becomes oily and greasy and disfigured.

The dactyl cries loudly, once. Another cry answers from a hundred feet above.

Raptor Red leaps on top of the dactyl's torso, breaking its back in two places. The dactyl feels the loss of sensation from the shoulders back.

Savagely she slashes at the dactyl's neck with her teeth and foreclaws. She shreds its neck muscles and severs its head.

She grabs the torso, trots quickly to the edge of the mire, and sits down under the shade of a luxuriant conifer tree. Killing the dactyl has shaken her out of her depression. She knows her mate is gone, lifeless. She knows she will never see him again. She eats half the dactyl noisily, waits till the cool late afternoon showers begin, then starts to walk away.

The dactyl swarm—now more than a hundred—descends on the *Astrodon*. They peck holes in its belly skin. They reach in with their long snouts and yank out yards of soft entrails. They are happy—there is enough viscera and soft meat to fill their bellies, and enough left over to fill the pouches under their jaws.

One dactyl has a grace that distinguishes all his movements. He dominates the carrion-gorging assembly, choosing for himself the best bits of viscera. He finishes feeding before the others, spreads his green-topped wings, and follows the female *Utahraptor*.

An hour and a half later, the rest of the dactyl swarm starts leaving, taking off with difficulty because of their load of flesh. One by one they ascend on the afternoon updrafts.

Raptor Red sees the dactyl squadrons stretching in a long line to the south, to a grove of tall trees. Dactyls begin to arrive home, and they make awkward approaches to their treetop nests—it's only during take-off and landing that *Ornithocheirus* loses its aerial grace.

Each dactyl is greeted by a high-pitched chorus of squeaks and a pair of little dactyl snouts. Parent dactyls open their mouths wide. Globs of meat fall, regurgitated, hot and steamy, as dactyl chicks stuff their craws, then lean back on their haunches, bellies full, minds peaceful.

One dactyl is slow to return: a green-beaked young male who continues to circle the astro carcass after the others have left. He's looking for his mate. His huge eyes scan the mud, churned up by the struggles of *Astrodon* and raptor. He sees a battered, sorry mass at the perimeter of the swamp. He dives. He isn't sure he recognizes it. He must come close to identify the dead creature.

His weak sense of smell will not tell him who the winged victim is. But he must know. The lone dactyl makes a swooping pass at the mangled remains on the ground, and then he sees, in his peripheral vision, a bit of blue on what seems to be a head lying near the astro. The young male sees the identification marks on the head, and he knows the truth. His mate is gone, her body dismembered.

———

For four days Raptor Red travels during all the daylight hours, walking morning and afternoon, avoiding the midday heat. During the nights she crouches under the upturned roots of fallen trees. Even though the days are hot, she shivers most evenings. It rains just before sundown every day. The nighttime wind blowing across her rainwet hide sucks out her body heat at a terrible rate.

But the metabolic furnace within her body is up to the thermal challenge. Waves of shivering spread through her

muscles, and her heat production goes up by another fac-
tor of four, keeping all her vital organs at an optimum
temperature of 100 degrees Fahrenheit.

Still, shivering eats up heat calories so fast that by day
two of her trek, Raptor Red is ravenously hungry. She has
to find meat—fuel for her hot-blooded body. She sniffs
along the fern-tangled bank of a creek, now swollen with
rainwater. She has learned from experience that meaty
tidbits can be found washed up in just such locales.

She thrusts her snout into a clump of horsetail reeds.

"Yeech!" Her olfactory chambers are choked by the
suffocating aroma of half-rotten lungfish.

More carefully now, she investigates the three-
hundred-pound fish. Only half is totally disgusting. The
rear half is edible. She cuts the offending front end off
with her sharp foreclaws.

Gulp-chunk-chug. A hundred pounds of fish disappear
down her gullet.

An hour later her careful streamside search is rewarded again: a dead turtle, twenty-five pounds, with its
head bitten off—probably by a crocodile. One gulp and it's
gone, shell and all.

Raptors evolved as group hunters of big game. Raptor
Red killed dozens of multi-ton dinosaurs when she hunted
as part of a pair, first with a sibling, later with her mate.
But evolution rewards flexibility too. A lone raptor is like a
lone wolf—a meat-eater who must be able to forage for
small fry.

Raptor Red is surviving by herself, picking through the
zoological garbage thrown up by the overflowing creek.
She's lucky. It's an unusually wet spring. The turbid mix-
ing of river, pond, and stream waters carries a rich hoard
of dead and dying aquatic creatures. Her powerful olfactory sense serves her well in discovering carrion trea-

sures hidden in places even the keenest eyes would never discover.

Raptor Red realizes that she is now following a faint scent-trail. Her olfactory nerves can just barely detect the presence, far upstream, of warm dinosaur bodies—raptor bodies—and the prospect of rejoining her own kind raises her spirits.

As she climbs over a logjam of conifer trunks, she stops and stares and sniffs, raises her snout as high as it will go, sniffs again loudly, and stares.

There are raptors, five of them, three hundred yards away.

But something is wrong. She gets a big dose of scent, and her olfactory senses are overwhelmed with biochemical clues. Raptor scent, definitely. But her brain evaluates the scent-rich air and concludes: *Raptors—but not MY KIND!*

She's suddenly angry and afraid, confronted by a raptor so close to her own scent and yet so distinctly wrong.

Two of the foreign raptors approach slowly, holding their heads low in a submissive, nonthreatening posture.

She sniffs loudly. These are not small raptors. Too big to be *Deinonychus*, and the scent is wrong for *Deinonychus*.

Now she detects maleness in the two approaching raptors. They bob their heads in a greeting that's almost like the way her mate used to greet her.

But there's something wrong in their head-bobbing dance too. These foreign males don't do it right, and their flawed choreography makes her even more agitated.

*My kind . . . not my kind . . .* Her brain struggles with the mixed signals.

Now she can see the color band on their snouts. It's not red. It's yellow. She has never been with a family member with a yellow snout patch.

She thinks to herself. Images of self-recognition express, *My kind, red snout—my kind, Raptor—Red.*
*HsssscreeeeEEEEEEECH!!!!*

Her brain can't stand it anymore. She attacks, making huge arcs with her deadliest claw. She kicks up dust. She swooshes her tail from side to side.

The two foreign males freeze for a second, then bound away in full-speed retreat.

Then Raptor Red turns and runs away too.

She has no conscious way of understanding what has just happened. Deep inside her brain, the thought of being courted by Yellow Snouts is hateful.

The most important task she has had to perform, all through her life, ever since hatching, has been to identify "my kind." To Raptor Red, the Yellow Snouts are hideous liars and impostors. They have most of the correct signals for "my kind," yet they distort proper *Utahraptor* language and use foreign movements, and they give out the wrong scent.

Raptor Red snarls to herself, paces back and forth, and flexes her killing-claw in angry spasms. She's sure she has saved herself from some horrible, unknown fate. And she has. If she had mated with a Yellow Snout, he would have abandoned her. And she would have been cursed with chicks born dead or deformed or sterile.

Raptor Red doesn't know that this hatred is what has kept her species alive. It's her hate of Yellow Snouts that protects her own reproductive hopes. Any Red Snout attracted to a Yellow Snout mate would condemn her own genes to death. The hybrid chicks would never survive to a healthy adulthood. Natural selection has to be ruthless—genes that encourage such lethal unions are weeded out by death and infertility.

Raptor Red's inborn horror of Yellow Snouts is reinforced by dim memories from childhood. She saw her kind, her parents, drive them away. Back in her homeland in Asia, Yellow Snouts were distant neighbors who hunted in the densely forested highlands. Raptor Red's species preferred the more open low country. When members of the two species met, they fled, or they attacked.

Even when she was a chick, Raptor Red's nose told her that Yellow Snouts were almost "my kind." Her nose told the truth. Yellow Snouts are her ancestors.

Fifty thousand years before, the two species had been one and the same, a mountain-loving yellow-muzzled predator. Yellow Snouts kept to the ancestral habitats of dense forests, but a small part of the ancestral population became isolated on the far side of a huge river. That small population evolved different hunting techniques, different recognition colors, and different courtship dances. It became a new *Utahraptor* species, Raptor Red's species.

When the red-snouted *Utahraptors* finally met their yellow-snouted kin, their genes could no longer mix.

Raptor Red's species is lucky to be alive. New species are evolutionary experiments that usually turn out to be inferior to the parent species. And parent species usually exterminate their daughters.

But not the Red Snouts. Their adaptive equipment proved superior to their ancestor's, and when the two met, Red Snouts usually pushed out Yellow Snouts, the daughter species exterminating the parent species like Darwinian Lizzie Bordens.

Here and there the two can coexist, wherever especially dense cover permits the Yellow Snouts to escape their more aggressive red-snouted kin.

Raptor Red moves away at a quick pace, still agitated from her meeting with her near relations. If she were with her family, she'd attack. But she's alone, and she wants to get away, so she descends into a low series of dry lake beds that offer ground more to her liking than the coniferous woodland where the Yellow Snout pack is staking out their hunting territory.

Here she stays for a week. She is searching for a *Utahraptor* of her kind.

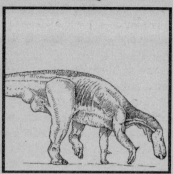

# Too Skinny for Parenthood (and too full of ticks)

Raptor Red knows she's too skinny. She looks at her thigh, pokes at it with her snout, and looks again. It's muscular but very lean. Two weeks on her own have been hard on her diet. A single *Utahraptor* is not an efficient predator, and she has subsisted on the equivalent of raptor finger food—a dead croc here, a half-decayed lungfish there, a dried-up iguanodon carcass in between.

Male *Utahraptors* prefer plump, well-fed females.

Raptor Red doesn't think this through. She doesn't have to. She was born with the same mate-search image that males of her species have. Her genes encode high standards, and in her first breeding season she sought a tall male filled out with muscle. All the young unattached females looked for the strongest males with the plumpest thighs.

Raptor Red's mother was a well-muscled raptor too, and this image reinforced the inborn standard of *Utahraptor* beauty.

Plump thighs are an outward sign of good hunters and good genes. Since father and mother *Utahraptors* share the burden of nest-making and chick-feeding nearly equally, young males and females scrutinize every potential mate. Skepticism rules courtship. Toward each potential mate, the undercurrent of thought in Raptor Red's mind was *I'll risk myself in reproduction with you only if you can convince me that you're healthy, smart, and trustworthy.*

Raptor Red didn't give even a second look to scrawny males during that first courtship season. But when a thickly muscled male bounced over to her and initiated a most vigorous mating dance, her courtship incredulity was overcome.

Now she's lost her mate, and she's skinny. Too skinny, she suspects, to be attractive.

She nuzzles the base of her tail. It's also too thin. Males and females check out each other's tails carefully during courtship—the tail base is supposed to be plump and well filled out, with fat layers over the muscle. When a raptor isn't eating well, the tail fat is the first layer to disappear.

Raptor Red stares hard at a crimson spot she sees near the tip of her tail. This spot is even more worrisome. Persistent wounds, even little ones, automatically disqualify a raptor from the ranks of the most desirable. She scrapes at the mark with her foreclaws, then licks it. It's not a scab— just a bit of dried lungfish meat that got stuck to her skin at her last meal.

Raptor Red carries out her sign-marking chores in the final minutes of daylight. She finds a suitable tree, tall, straight, with a thick trunk. She reaches high and scratches long claw marks on the bark, releasing sweet-smelling sap. Then she rubs her throat on the tree, leaving her telltale signature from glands on the underside of her jaws.

She pauses and adds the strongest signal of her gender and species—a dung pile. No raptor of the wrong species will miss the message now: *I'm an adult* Utahraptor *of the Red Snout species. If you're a healthy Red Snout male, consider ME. All others, LEAVE ME ALONE!*

That's all she can do now. The evening breeze will carry the scent-marks to any red-snouted *Utahraptor* within a five-mile radius. She has advertised herself. Now she must wait.

————

The sunset is glorious, illuminating Raptor Red's temporary nest with crimson and turning the dried bracken into incandescent lace. She's feeling better. Beautiful colors always lift her spirits. She begins to drift off to sleep.

*Bing.* A little alarm bell goes off in her head, triggered by her olfactory sense. A stream of molecules has entered her nostrils and hit special sensors inside her muzzle.

*Bing—wake up—bing—male alert—male alert.*

Raptor Red jumps to her feet, every muscle tensed. She sniffs deeply at the evening air. Yes, that's male scent, and it's her species. She raises her body and weaves her head back and forth, staring upwind. There *is* somebody out there.

"Snff . . . snff . . . SNFFFF!" *Utahraptor* male. "SNFFFF!" *Red Snout. My kind.*

A tall figure walks out of the shadows, walking with exaggerated strides. His head dips down and up in a deep bow. Raptor Red dips her head just a bit. She's hopeful—but suspicious. Raptor courtships are supposed to begin in the morning and go on all day, to give both sides ample opportunity to evaluate every move, every body part, every scent. She's lonely and unhappy with her lot as a single hunter. But she's not desperate.

"Snff!" Good. He's Red Snout, but not close kin. Her scent-evaluation centers automatically go through their checklist. Raptor Red's instincts won't let her accept courtship from family.

The male moves closer, bowing every few steps. Raptor Red moves out away from the bracken and into a little clearing where she can see better. The tall male comes to the edge of the open space but then stops. His graceful bows become awkward.

Raptor Red's heart sinks. She begins to think that the tall male is hiding something. If he followed the rules, he'd come up close.

She stamps her left foot: "GrrrrrKK!"

He stops, bows, and takes a half step. Raptor Red sees his body contours highlighted by the warm afterglow of the sun. *He is very tall—and muscular too*. She's beginning to hope that he's just shy.

They circle each other. Raptor Red becomes defensive—she thinks he's staring at her thin tail. And he is. He backs away, forcing her to follow and take the initiative in the dance.

*Don't go away—don't go away—don't go away*, Raptor Red thinks as she tries her hardest to appear graceful and strong and healthy.

The male turns broadside to her, a gesture that conveys indecision.

Raptor Red begins to feel uneasy about some of the male's moves. He's rushing the courtship preliminaries, violating *Utahraptor* etiquette. Now he walks beside her and tries to place his flank against hers. It's a clumsy attempt to apply the leaning gesture, where one raptor applies gentle pressure through its torso and the other raptor is supposed to respond with a slight push in the opposite direction.

It's an intimate form of physical contact, usually reserved for raptor pairs who know and trust each other. Raptor Red used to spend hours leaning against her sister when they were youngsters, and she and her mate enjoyed the lean in the early evening, after they had hunted and fed together.

She has missed this type of contact terribly over the last few days. But she feels her skin flinch when it touches his. She doesn't like the way he presses his hide against her shoulder. It is a dishonest touch.

Raptor Red stands still and makes a huge, sweeping bow—and at the bottom of her courtship curtsey, she sees the marks on the male's throat.

*SPOTS!* her brain screams. *HE'S GOT SPOTS!*

Raptor Red thrusts her snout under the tall male's chin. He pulls his head away, but not before Raptor Red gets a good look.

*Ticks—the red spots are ticks.* Raptor Red knows well the telltale sign of parasite infestation. She was born with a horror of little red spots. She has seen raptor chicks and raptor adults slowly succumb to tick disease, losing vigor every day.

She grabs the male's neck and looks very carefully. Small black dots are moving around inside the red marks.

*He's got bugs!*

Raptor Red jumps backward three steps, raises her head, and screams a mixture of threat and alarm. The male looks perplexed.

She lunges at him with all six foreclaws slashing circles through the air.

He gets the message. He slinks off into the darkness. In a few minutes his fading scent assures her that he's in full retreat.

If Raptor Red's thoughts could be put into language, they'd be, *Males are such liars. I'm a bit underweight—but I don't cover up my parasites. That bug-bitten loser is lucky I didn't slice him into little pieces.*

She goes back to her nest, fluffs up the bed of dry ferns, plops herself down, and nibbles furiously at an iguanodon leg she stored there. Then she goes to sleep.

———————

Raptor Red wakes up slowly, as is her custom. Before her conscious brain is alert, her senses have been scanning the air for sounds and smells. There are faint, distant scents from deinonychs and from some yellow-nosed raptors. And there is something else too, a scent that makes her eyes pop open. It's close and it's very familiar. It's almost like her mother's scent. Almost but not quite. But it's definitely Raptor Red-Kind scent.

*My kind . . . my family.* The scent leads Raptor Red to a steep bank in a dried-up riverbed.

Two tiny *Utahraptors*, only three weeks old, and an older chick stumble out from a burrow. They squeak and sniff at Raptor Red. She sniffs back. Their scent is like an imperfect memory of her own childhood. She cocks her head and stares. Her mother? Her father?

*Not father . . . not mother . . . but still part of myself—but less than half of me.*

No. The chicks aren't anyone she has met before. But Raptor Red's olfactory computer gives her a galvanic message: *One half of one half . . . These chicks are one half of one half of myself . . . They are my sister's children!*

Raptor Red backs up and sits down. The chicks approach with hesitating steps, sniffing, running back, coming forward, sniffing again. Their noses tell them this is their aunt.

"SsssssSSSSSSSS." A loud threat comes from the burrow. A big raptor head comes out, teeth bared. The head abruptly stops hissing.

Raptor Red sniffs loudly. This scent jolts her brain. *One half of me . . . this adult female is one half of me.*

*I KNOW YOU!*

The last time she smelled this scent was three years ago, on a cold day in Canada, the last day she was with her siblings. Before she and her mate began their invasion of the new southern lands.

Raptor Red dances a wild jig of greeting. She hops from one foot to another, going "eeep-eeep-eeep" like an overgrown chick.

It *is* her sister.

———

Early the following morning, a one-ton iguanodon is making contented leaf-munching noises as she feeds on lowgrowing cycad fronds. She clomps down on the tough palmlike leaves with her sharp beak. The saw-edged beak tip slices easily through the tough plant tissue. Her tongue automatically rolls the bitten-off pieces into a ball that is coated with saliva. With a gentle, efficient rhythm the plant-balls are transferred rearward to the chewing compartment, the oral cavity between the massive rows of molar teeth.

A low grinding sound, like a huge coffee mill, comes from within the iguanodon's cheeks. Twice a second the mighty molars come together. Twice a second the jagged edges of enamel from a hundred tightly packed teeth slide past each other, trapping plant parts and shredding them. Twice a minute the tongue balls up the ground mass of food and pushes it to the rear of the mouth. Once a minute a lump can be seen in the throat. The lump passes down toward the stomach in a slow, smooth movement.

It's the finest vegetarian food-processor in the Early

Cretaceous, a system that can start with dry, hard, dust-covered cycad foliage and convert it into easily digested plant pulp.

The iguanodon has modest powers of self-awareness. She *feels* happy and complacent and content. She *feels* efficient, in a vague "I'm doing what I should be doing and I'm doing it well" sort of way.

Still the iguanodon is alert. Her sense of smell is superb. She keeps track of the rest of the herd a few hundred yards upwind. Her large, clear blue eyes sweep a full 360 degrees every second or two. Her eye sockets project outward from her forehead, like cow eyes or deer eyes, so right and left visual fields can cover a zone in front, to the side, and dead ahead.

A faint crack in the bush makes her stop chewing. She focuses her eyes and ears forward. It's totally silent now. She can't detect a scent—the sound came from the left downwind. She starts backing away, toward her herd.

There's another crack of dried twigs being stepped on.

She hears a soft patter of feet on wet meadow, coming from the right, obliquely downwind, between herself and her herd. She tries to turn.

Whummp! A half-ton weight, moving fast, hits her body high on the right side. She falls. Another heavy weight falls on her neck, pinning her to the ground.

The two *Utahraptors* kill their victim efficiently, cleanly, with a flurry of slashes, hindclaws and foreclaws together.

Raptor Red stands up and makes sure that the rest of the iguanodon herd isn't massing for a counterattack. Iguanodons sometimes charge a hundred strong and try to trample raptors.

Not this time. A few iguanodons stand tall and sniff and stare. But then the herd begins to wander off in the opposite direction.

Raptor Red's sister begins to remove meat and pieces of liver.

The iguanodons' brains record the fact that a new hunting pack of *Utahraptor* is on the scene. Since a pack of two is much more dangerous than two independent raptors, the iguanodons will be extra cautious in the near future.

In the evening Raptor Red huddles close to her sister's chicks, keeping them warm and dry in a den in the brush. She sits up most of the night, alert, guarding her kin.

The evening is unpleasant, with a light drizzle and enough breeze to make Raptor Red shiver now and then. But it doesn't matter. She's enjoying a sound she hasn't heard for a long time. Her sister's snoring.

The youngsters and their mother fall asleep right away, aligned one next to another, heads and tails facing the same direction. Raptor Red lowers herself carefully between her sister and one of the youngsters, gently displacing the row of chicks. They make gurking noises but don't wake up. Raptor Red leans just a little bit against her sister's flank, which twitches several times. Her sister growls, opens one eye so she can see what woke her up, growls again, shifts her weight around, closes her eye tight, and resumes snoring.

That's exactly the way Raptor Red remembers her.

# The Computer of Sisterhood

Scratch, scratch, wiggle, scratch, scratch.

The *Utahraptor* chicks wake up scratching.

Oooomph—skunsh—SCRATCH.

Raptor Red and her sister wake up scratching too. The itchy feeling makes their spirits sag.

Both adults know what they're scratching at.

Ticks. Tiny green and brown ticks. Ticks that thrive in the underbrush made damp by spring rains. Ticks that have a narcotic saliva so they can bore a hole with their snout straight through a raptor's hide without the raptor knowing it. Ticks that are nearly impossible to scratch out once they have embedded themselves.

The adult *Utahraptors* fear ticks more than an angry

herd of iguanodons, because ticks cause pain and disease and death.

Ordinarily the raptors would roll in soda mud to smother skin parasites. Back when she was growing up in Mongolia, Raptor Red followed her parents into a mud bath in a soda lake every other day in the spring. It usually worked adequately. The Mongolian ticks—most of them— would drop off after being coated in soda mud. Some would stay bored in, suck blood, drop off later on, and hatch their tick babies under a moist bush somewhere.

The native Mongolian ticks rarely debilitated their raptor hosts. These Utah ticks are different. Their borings into the skin cause nasty swelling. When the raptors scratch with their paws or rub against a rough-barked tree, the swellings get much worse. The *Utahraptor*'s internal defense—the immune system—seems unable to cope with the side effects of the Utah ticks.

The two raptor sisters and the three chicks walk over to the iguanodon and eat their fill. The two adults fidget and scratch and look at all the low trees nearby. They want to find a very special little animal, a species that raptors view as a friend.

No luck. The pack wanders over to the riverbank to drink. Raptor Red is much more nervous now than when she was alone. She is anxious for her sister's chicks. Built into her mental processes is a computer that evaluates kinship. Her eyes and ears and especially her nose can detect another raptor who is close kin. Every breath she takes in company with her sister affirms their close blood bond. Her subconscious computer has a hard-and-fast rule: *Take care of your own chicks first; each one is one half of yourself. Take care of your sister's chicks next. Don't waste time on any other blood relative.*

Raptor Red has failed to bring her own chicks into the world, and so the strong hand of instinct encourages her to devote herself to her sister's chicks. Those chicks carry a share of her own genetic individuality. Saving her sister's chicks is saving herself.

A gentle swirl of the water's surface betrays the presence of a four-foot-long crocodile, a *Bernissartia*. Too small to attack an adult raptor. But crocs are clever opportunists. As a chick, Raptor Red saw another sister disappear into a turbid Mongolian river, only to reappear minutes later in the jaws of a croc.

Raptor Red splashes out a few yards and hisses at the croc, who submerges without a sound.

The pack drinks. The chicks play, making too much noise for Raptor Red's peace of mind. They jump on Raptor Red's back, then jump down into the water where it is a foot deep, throwing up a muddy fountain.

The adults have had enough. Raptor Red picks up one chick gently but firmly in her jaws and carries it back onto the meadow. Her sister picks up another. The third chick instantly loses its playful courage and darts back to the rest of the family.

The crocodile lies motionless, five feet under the surface. She's neither angry nor afraid. She thinks her slow, repetitive croc-thoughts: *Wait, wait, wait, wait.* She's a perfectionist at waiting. She's only a tenth as heavy as Raptor Red, but she's much older—she hatched thirty-four years ago. And she's the best croc mother in all of Utah.

Over the last twenty-two years she has successfully brooded twenty clutches of croc eggs, each with eight to twenty hatchlings. Two years were too dry to lay eggs. She's a fiercely protective croc-mom—she's never hesitated to rush from the water, openmouthed, at any dinosaur or male croc that got too close to her progeny. This threat, accompanied by extravagant splashing, always worked.

Now there are hundreds of adult or near-adult crocs in

Utah who are her children. And there is even a brood of her grandchildren. Her croc genes will take over her species in the next dozen generations. She is a gold medalist in mothering.

Crocodile motherhood depends on patience. The croc mother can wait two weeks for her next meal, because her metabolism per pound of her body weight is very low. She can stay underwater for an hour, not breathing, because she can shut down her internal metabolic furnace nearly completely. Her present wisdom comes from the slow, deliberate way the croc-race lives out its life-cycle.

She grew very slowly, learning much every year, not reaching breeding size until she was twelve. The croc-mother wasn't rushed into adulthood the way the raptor sisters were. Their hot-blooded growth rate propelled them into sexual maturity at the age of four or five. They had to learn fast, take chances, and live in the metabolic fast lane.

So the croc mother sits and waits and waits. Her tail tip is missing, and she has long scars across her back—reminders of her youth, when she tried to ambush dinosaurs too big to drag easily into the water. She hasn't made another such a mistake in a decade, and she never will. She'll die slowly of old age when she passes sixty, when thousands of her offspring will have colonized every river system in North America.

When she dies, her bones will bleach to dust on a riverbank. But her multitude of progeny will spread and proliferate. Her genes will be carried in most crocodile species in the modern world.

The raptor sisters pay no attention to the croc after she submerges. For them, out of sight is out of mind. The sisters look around again for that special friend in their environment—the friend that can help them with ticks.

It's a lazy afternoon for the pack. They lie near the

iguanodon, casually feeding now and then. The little chicks chase each other in and out of the cavernous rib cage. They've been out of the nest, big enough to explore on their own, for only a couple of days, and they get bolder all the time, expanding the distance they dare to go from their mother. There is so much fresh iguanodon meat now that their sibling competition is temporarily suspended.

Still the scratching and itching disturb Raptor Red's mood.

Her sister squawks, stands, leans forward, and squawks again. It's a funny sound—loud, but not threatening.

Raptor Red stands up too and squawks.

The squawk is a rarely used signal. It means *I'm here—I won't bite—I'm here.*

A soft sound of feathered wings comes from the tops of some tall cycad trees. A bounding troop of sinorns, a Chinese bird species who invaded the Americas along with the raptors, flit down a few dozen feet in front of the raptor pack.

Raptor Red is beside herself with excitement. She scrunches down, laying her head and neck along the meadow floor, trying to look as meek and nonthreatening as she can. But she can't control her tail. Its stiff rear end twitches side to side. The sinorns take off immediately.

*Calm—calm—CALM!* she thinks to herself. She closes her eyes. She focuses inward. Her breathing slows. Her tail stops twitching.

The sinorns return—Raptor Red can hear them. They are very close. One of the birds pokes its snout up Raptor Red's nostril.

*Kah-SNEEEZE!* She can't help herself. She opens her eyes—the birds are gone again.

*Calm . . . Calm. . . .*

She lies motionless for two minutes. Then she feels

what she's wanted all day—tiny bird feet walking up and down her back.

She winces very slightly as a red-hot spark of pain comes from just behind her shoulders. Then another. Then two at once. But after each spike of pain comes a lingering warm feeling—a mixture of throbbing blood flow and relief.

The chicks watch the operation. They've never seen it before. A half-dozen sinorns are methodically surveying Raptor Red's back. Each bird stops every minute or so to reach down, carefully place its beak over a tick, and remove it with a twisting-backward head movement.

The chicks charge the birds, hissing. Raptor Red's sister growls an authoritative rebuke. The chicks shrink back, and the birds return.

For a wonderful hour the adult raptors get groomed and plucked and bitten and deticked. The sinorns even open the edges of the tick-induced wounds, nipping off infected skin. That really hurts, but the raptors endure it. They've been through it before. They know that a few days in the sun will heal the wounds with hardly a trace.

Unfortunately, the chicks are too rambunctious to learn the joys of bird-grooming. When a sinorn alights on a chick's back, the chick tries to bite it. Raptor Red's sister has to interrupt her grooming repeatedly to snarl menacingly at her offspring.

It's too much for a mother to bear. Raptor Red's sister slowly rises, using smooth movements of legs and back so as not to scare the birds. She flicks out one long hand and flattens a chick to the ground.

"Ghurk." The chick gets the message. It lies still. The other chicks stare, speechless. They've never seen their mom so angry before.

Thus the chicks learn, reluctantly, to sit still while being serviced by tick-birds. In Raptor Red's mind, this meadow will always be associated with healing ministrations from the sinorns. "Tick-Bird Meadow" is a good translation of how her memory labels the locale.

———————

"Mmmmm"—Raptor Red and her sister hum inaudibly to themselves, as if to say, *This is the life—now it's very fine.* The afternoon is unusually warm and dry, with no thundershowers. The tick wounds feel much better already. All five raptors are stuffed with fresh meat. Best of all for the two adult females, the chicks' bellies are so distended with oversize portions of iguanodon that they can't walk, so they can't get into any mischief.

The pack stays at Tick-Bird Meadow for a couple of weeks, hunting in the early morning and late afternoon, coming back to be groomed before sundown. Raptor Red senses that, however desirable the spot seems, they'll have to move soon. Too many other predator groups are shifting their hunting ranges. There's great instability and unrest in the geographic boundaries claimed by raptors and by the bigger, ridge-backed meat-eaters.

It's a young, turbulent ecosystem. The invasion of Mongolian dinosaurs, and of species from the other direction—from western Europe—has upset an ecological organization many millennia old. The new arrivals seek to establish themselves, stake out territories, protect their food resources, and raise young. But the breeding groups of old-time native species refuse to give up real estate to the invaders. So populations of native and invader are jostling each other, and predator packs are moving hundreds of miles each season, far more than they would in a normal year.

As the sun sets, coloring the dust clouds kicked up by distant herds, the adult raptors become more alert. The stream valley is so richly stocked with game that many species of predator—large, medium, and small—are being drawn in.

Late one afternoon, Raptor Red can see silhouettes of meat-eating dinosaurs far away on the horizon. Their body forms are outlined with great sharpness and clarity—as if they were paper cutouts hung in a picture window looking out on the sunset. The distant predators walk slowly, then sit down, flexing knees and ankles.

Both Raptor Red and her sister pay very close attention to how the unknown predators sit. Raptors sit upright. They have a big cushiony pad of tough skin below and behind their hips. The cushion lies directly below the huge pubic bone, longest and strongest of the hip elements. Since the cushion is oriented aft and downward, raptor torsos are held nearly erect when the raptors are relaxed in sitting position.

Only raptor species sit this way. All other predators have a built-in pubic cushion that goes straight down from in front of the hips, at a right angle to the backbone. When these nonraptors sit, they lower their torsos into horizontal position.

One by one the five distant predators sit. Each one lowers its compact torso straight down. Each one sits with its shoulders close to the ground.

The predators are too far away for the *Utahraptors* to judge their size directly. But shape is a clue to size.

*Not our kind,* the sisters think.

*Too big—danger.* The sisters can see that the unknown predators have short thick necks and deep heavy muzzles. Those shape contours belong to ridge-backed *Acrocanthosaurus*, giant carnivores that are three tons full grown. Five acros are fifteen tons of unstoppable muscle, tendon, teeth, and jaws.

The giant predators hardly ever travel in groups of four or more. These five are brothers from one brood who have not yet split up to find individual mates. Such bachelor packs can be unpredictable and violent.

The raptor family stays where it is, but both adults rest with eyes half open and nostrils flared. The acros don't stir at all during the night.

"Hssssssss—grhp!" The raptor sisters rouse the chicks before daybreak and nudge them into movement. The wind has shifted, and the irresistible smell of the *Astrodon* calf that the raptors killed the day before has reached the five acros. They are getting up, stretching, making high-pitched calls to advertise their presence to any female acro who might be nearby.

Food and courtship are now conflicting calls for these acros. Two wander away, tracking the scent of a female acro. The three others start toward Tick-Bird Meadow at a fast clip.

The raptor pack leaves the meadow. It's foolish to contest the *Astrodon* carcass with three acros. Besides, there isn't much meat left on its body, and hunting should be good elsewhere in the valley.

---

The raptor sisters move on a couple of miles. Then they start looking for another big kill—something at least a ton. It's much more economical than trying to feed the pack assorted lesser fry, like turtles, crocs, fish. They spot another iguanodon herd—the valley is overrun with them— and creep around to the upwind side.

Raptor Red and her sister are just getting into a superb ambush position, hidden in deep reeds by a spring, when a head pops up abruptly a few yards away and stares at them. It's a raptor head—with a red muzzle.

Another red-muzzled raptor snout pokes up. The sisters realize that they aren't the only pack trying to ambush the iguanodons.

There's no noise. Neither pack wants to spook the iguanodons.

Raptor Red is confused. Her sense of smell tells her that both new raptors are young males—and not close blood kin. She doesn't detect any new females nearby. The two males are nonthreatening. They lower their heads in a quiet head-bob-head-weave. It's a tentative greeting and a prelude to courtship.

Raptor Red wants a new mate. Her biological urge to bond, brood, and raise chicks of her own is becoming more insistent every day. She hasn't forgotten her lost mate. But she feels a calling to get on with her reproductive duties—the highest calling any dinosaur can have.

One of the males advances and begins a more formal courtship dance. He's lithe and graceful and healthy, with smooth motions and not a hint of injury or disease to mar his performance.

Raptor Red watches coyly. She's heavier than he is, and stronger. All Red Snout females are strong enough to repulse most males. Raptor Red is programmed to make the male prove that he's worthy, that his *genes* are worthy for making healthy raptor chicks with her.

The male would score a perfect 10 in difficulty from an Olympic *Utahraptor* judge—he manages to go through the entire courtship ritual without making any loud sounds or movements that the iguanodons could see.

*This one, this male—very, very, smart.* Raptor Red has been courted several times before, but never with such a bravura combination of stealth and exuberance.

She's making up her mind to forget the hunt for today. She can kill tomorrow. . . .

"HssssSSSS." The iguanodon cows stop feeding, turn their heads, and bellow deep alarm sounds. A stampede begins.

"HSSSSS." Raptor Red's sister holds her body high,

making exaggerated strides toward the males, flicking her curved hand-claws in and out.

Raptor Red blinks. Her sister is making a full-fledged threat display. She wants to hurt the two males.

The older chick, who was hiding some distance away, wanders up behind its mother and tries to imitate her hissing malevolence.

The male looks surprised; his pupils dilate at the sight of the chick. He lowers his body as far as he can and starts to back away.

Now Raptor Red is pulled by conflicting instincts. She wants that male. He's the finest male she's ever seen—or at least the finest she can remember. She cannot join in her sister's attack.

But she can't leave her sister's chicks either. Raptor Red watches as the males withdraw. Her sister returns, still visibly agitated.

Raptor Red and her sister resume hunting late in the day and kill a plump iguanodon cow. As they sit down to eat the best parts first, Raptor Red can smell the young male nearby, hiding in a ravine. Later on, his scent gets fainter and fainter.

Her sister comes over to her and lies down. Raptor Red looks at her. She nuzzles Raptor Red and starts to groom her behind her ears, making delicate little bites.

# The Turtle of Trinity

It's midnight, but Raptor Red is wide awake because she's curious. Something is going on in the pond, and she wants to know what it is. She's been staring at a V-shaped series of tiny waves that means a living animal is moving just under the surface.

Plip! Up comes a little black scaly face, pushing its armored eyebrows just above the pond's surface. The moonlight catches the crests of the delicate ripples widening as they pass outward from the disturbance. Pop! The eyes open, and a pair of orange red pupils stare at the shore, where Raptor Red is hunched down, motionless but awake.

Pip! A bubble of air grows quickly at the tip of the black snout, pauses for a second, and bursts.

Raptor Red's mind is on automatic-alert mode. She can't sleep. Her sister is curled up in a temporary nest they made just before dusk.

"Sssnnnrrhht!" Raptor Red flinches a tiny bit as her sister snores loudly, "Plssssshh." The pair of eyes and bubble-blowing nose disappear under the pond water.

Raptor Red is disappointed—she's still curious about that little dark head. She's been watching it for an hour. Raptor Red is a late-night *Utahraptor*. She was born that way. She falls asleep at sundown but wakes up at midnight. It's genetic, a trait she inherited from her father. Her sister is an early riser. She's fully alert hours before dawn, but she falls asleep two hours after dusk and snores all night till she wakes up. Also genetic.

Siblings differ in their wake-sleep schedules, and evolutionary forces can work on this diversity. A diverse range of genetically fixed behaviors in a brood can ensure that at least some of the youngsters will survive to adulthood, no matter what sort of environmental challenges are thrown at them. A late-night gene may help survival when prey abundance shifts and the only vulnerable victims are herbivores who can be stalked after dusk. An early-riser gene could give just the opposite advantage—the ability to hunt before sunrise.

Raptor Red knows nothing about evolutionary theory. But she does know that her sister snores. She glares at her sister's sleeping but noisiferous form. Just as her sister inhales in preparation for another snorting-wheezing-honk, Raptor Red reaches out with her left foot and pushes hard.

Fwwump—ooooph! Her sister rolls onto her side, exhales heavily, stays asleep, and then begins a new cycle of snores, far quieter this time.

Raptor Red goes back to watching for the head in the pond.

Just an inch below the water, the head is listening. A wide oval eardrum has been vibrating with each raptor snore. Each "ssnnrrhht!" has sent high-energy, low frequency sound waves into the water. Some of the sound energy reflects off the water's surface, but some penetrates, generating pulses of waterborne sound. The big eardrum is designed for just such low frequencies. It's a turtle's ear, and it belongs to a *Trinitichelys*, the Turtle of the Trinity River.

This Trinity Turtle is a female, only twelve years old and five pounds in weight. This year is the first year she has mated. Her biological clock went into alarm mode during the night. It's time to try the most dangerous thing her genetically programmed lifestyle demands: It's time to come ashore and lay eggs.

No two minds are more different than the raptor's and the turtle's. The raptor is a bundle of spunky inquisitiveness. She wants to find out about each and every animal in her world. She sniffs strange objects and pokes her snout down holes. She goes out of her way to investigate any strange and new sight. Her mind demands new stimuli, new mysteries to solve.

The turtle lives a life of comfortable monotony that would bore Raptor Red to death. Walking and swimming slowly over the pond bottom, picking up pieces of soft vegetation and an occasional hunk of dead fish. Crawling out onto a half-submerged log and letting the sun warm her turtle belly, assisting in digestion. For every ten degrees Celsius that the turtle guts warm up, the speed of the digestive process doubles. She crawls back into the pond late in the afternoon.

Every day the same routine, every day the exact same hundred square yards of pond bottom. Nothing unexpected, nothing exciting. The turtle's body is undemanding. Her internal metabolic furnace needs only one-twentieth as much food per day as a dinosaur of the same size.

And so she is content to make do with a brain that is tiny and tubular, a brain that lacks the restless curiosity of raptors.

The Trinity Turtle would be scared into her shell and never come out if she had to deal with the range of stimuli Raptor Red experiences every day.

Pip. With a faint sound, the turtle pops her head above the surface again. The alarming sound of raptor snoring has stopped. Raptor Red creeps forward toward the water to get a better look. Her feet make a rustling noise against the dry ferns. Raptor Red freezes, but she doesn't have to. Turtle ears can't pick up soft, high-frequency sounds. The heavy eardrum and the large ear bone attached to it can't transmit such vibrations.

But it is perfectly adequate for the turtle's needs. She doesn't have to stalk soft-stepping prey across the forest floor. She doesn't have to listen carefully for subtle variations in the calls of her mate and her siblings. Turtles live a noiseless life. They don't communicate audibly with relatives, and the Trinity Turtle, like most of her sister species, finds food in water.

Sound is easy to detect underwater. When a crocodile snaps at a fish, the sound waves pass quickly through the aqueous medium and go right through the turtle's body with little impediment. Sound moves through the skin and then the muscle and then the brain tissue itself. Water-loving critters have an easy time hearing low-frequency sounds.

So there's no need for the Trinity Turtle to be outfitted with the delicate ear bone and complex inner ear of a raptor. The only time she will feel a deep-seated anxiety about sound is that one season of the year when she must climb out of her comfortable watery home and seek a suitable sandbank to lay her eggs.

Raptor Red watches the turtle head disappear. A line of ripples shows that the turtle is swimming toward shore. Raptor Red crouches down even further, her calf muscles twitching with excitement. She's not hunting now—she and her sister filled their bellies with iguanodon meat late that afternoon. What excites Raptor Red now is finding out something new.

Inside the turtle brain is the opposite emotion—fear of the unknown. The Trinity Turtle hasn't been out onshore since she herself hatched twelve summers ago. That was the worst day of her life. Being tiny and helpless, cracking open her eggshell, and smelling a thousand unknown things. Being one of fifty struggling turtle-ettes, all scrambling out of their nest, compelled by instinct to climb up through the sand that their mother piled on top of the eggs. Then instinct shifted gears, and the baby turtles were drawn irresistibly downslope to the smell of water.

Only two baby turtles made it to the water. The Trinity Turtle saw a brother three inches away get snatched upward in the toothy jaws of a dactyl. Then two sisters climbed over the Trinity Turtle. A second later, they too were pulled to their deaths. Just as the scent of the pond water was becoming sweet and strong, the Trinity Turtle herself was pulled four feet skyward, her left hindfoot pinioned by a set of sharp teeth. Pain, the first pain she had ever felt, paralyzed her left hindquarters. Then there was a flapping of huge, white wings and a snapping sound. Two dactyls were fighting over this turtle morsel.

She was dropped into the water. The instant she felt the warm summer water engulf her body, a third instinct cut in—to swim *down*. With three legs flailing madly, she made a crash dive at forty-five degrees, hitting a pondweed clump at the bottom. She kept going, burying her bruised, half-hour-old turtle body into the mud.

The baby Trinity Turtle wasted no time grieving over her lost siblings. They meant nothing to her. In the turtle brain there is an almost complete void where the emotional bond between relatives would be in a raptor. The dead sisters and brothers were mere objects in the turtle's environment. Their sudden deaths were useful as a warning that danger was near but had no other significance.

The Trinity Turtle, like nearly all turtle species, understands and appreciates only one individual—herself. She never saw or even smelled her mother, who scooped out a nest, laid the eggs, covered the nest, and crawled back into the water, never to interact in any way with her progeny afterward. A "Lay 'em and leave 'em" parent.

And the Trinity Turtle has never bonded with any brother or sister or any other turtle of her own species or any other species. Her courtship some weeks earlier did take six hours. The competing males had to swim around and around her, trying to impress her with their grace and coordination. She rejected the first five suitors. Mating with the sixth was quick and perfunctory. The male left immediately after the physiological act was completed, and now the Trinity Turtle ignores the male—even when they happen to pass each other in the pond.

To the turtle, the concept of "loneliness" is incomprehensible. She always has been alone, and any other social state is unthinkable.

The Trinity Turtle pushes her whole head and neck out of the water and swivels her face around, searching with eyes and nose. Like most turtles, *Trinitichelys* has only a mediocre sense of smell in the open air, compared to the olfactory powers of a long-snouted dinosaur or crocodile. The turtle snout is short, and the space for the smelling apparatus is squeezed between the front of the beak and the forwardly located eyeballs. This cramped olfactory chamber is perfectly okay for underwater work, where scent is carried by water currents. But out of the water smelling is much more difficult, because air currents carry only a tiny fraction of the scent-laden molecules that water can transport.

Raptor Red can smell the turtle now—she's eaten rancid turtle meat before, scavenged from carcasses washed up on the shore. But this is the first live turtle scent she's experienced. It's a dank, musky, slightly cool, and moist smell. It's exciting, because it's new to her brain.

The turtle drags her heavy shell up onto the shore with slow, jerky steps. Her long, straight claws dig into the earth.

Raptor Red can't bear it any longer. She jumps on the turtle, coming down on the shell with both hands. The algae-coated shell slips between her fingers and goes squirting sideways.

Slapppp, slappp—slapslap. Raptor Red fumbles the slick turtle shell, picks it up, fumbles again.

Raptor Red sits down and tries to figure the turtle out. She attempts to nibble a hole in the shell, but her teeth slip off the sharp edges of the carapace. Then she picks up the whole shell in her mouth, blinks twice, and bites down really hard.

Ting! One of Raptor Red's teeth breaks off at the base of the crown. The turtle is unscathed.

Inside the shell the turtle brain is not panicked. This has happened before. She has been picked up from the water by rambunctious dinosaurs who knock the shell about and gnaw ineffectively and finally give up.

Raptor Red's teeth, which can cut through a two-ton iguanodon hide, are useless against the five-pound turtle. The turtle shell is triple-layered. The outermost armor is a thin but very tough layer of dead skin with the consistency of very hard fingernail. There are no nerves or blood vessels in the outer layer, no delicate tissue to be hurt. The shell constantly regenerates the fingernail layer from the inside as the outer surface gets worn and scratched. The scratches left by Raptor Red's teeth do no permanent harm.

The next shell layer is made up of convex plates of bone on the top and flat plates on the bottom. Top and bottom shell bones meet on the left and right side at the bridge, a zone of especially thick, strong bone behind the armpit and in front of the hole for the hindlegs and tail. The smooth contour of the shell bones doesn't give a predator any thin edges to bite off, and the arched cross section makes the shell nearly impossible to crack.

The innermost armor layer is a brilliant piece of evolutionary engineering and is the main reason that the turtle is safe from Raptor Red's teeth and claws. On the inside surfaces of the bone plates of the upper shell are long, curved girders of bone that reinforce the shell dome and give it exceptional strength and rigidity. These girders are the turtle's ribs. Unlike the ribs of any other backboned creature, turtle rib shafts are fused immovably to the backbone and to the shell plates.

And the backbone of the torso is fused to the underside of the upper shell too, so the entire torso is tremendously strong.

When she ate dead turtles, Raptor Red had no problem pulling the meaty hindlegs and tail out of the shell. But now the legs and tail have disappeared from this living specimen and are hidden inside the rib-braced armor. Raptor Red sniffs cautiously at the holes in the shell where the legs have withdrawn. She nudges the shell with her snout and tries to stick her front teeth into the holes. She picks up the turtle carefully in both hands and utters a growl of frustration. The turtle keeps her legs tucked safely inside.

The *Utahraptor* is completely foiled by yet another unprecedented and unparalleled triumph of turtle anatomy: the shoulder-swivel. The shoulder blade has a pivot joint with the top shell above and the bottom shell below. To swing the entire front leg into the safety of the bone-armored box, all the turtle has to do is rotate her elbow in toward her neck and—voilà! The whole leg disappears within the capacious shell.

No other creature in the entire Early Cretaceous world has a disappearing shoulder.

Raptor Red slowly turns the shell around. A quick "hsssssss" comes from the front end, accompanied by bubbles. Raptor Red can see an eyeball staring back at her. *Trinitichelys* and all other turtles of the Early Cretaceous Age are primitive in one key area—they cannot retract their head all the way into the shell, the way modern-day turtles can.

Raptor Red cocks her head and looks very closely at the turtle face. She lifts the thin, outer finger of her left hand and gently probes the shell half covering the turtle head. She tries to dig into the top of the turtle head, but her claw just slips off. The turtle head is armored with thick bone and a fingernail layer. The Law of Darwinian Compensation is operating here. As long as turtles are in a state where they cannot retract their head entirely into the safety of the shell, the turtle skull wears a thick coat of bone armor and hard skin.

Raptor Red is experiencing the universal frustration of predators who try to crack a turtle. No animal before or since has had such an unbreakable cranial construction.

Right now the Trinity Turtle is just too much of a puzzle for Raptor Red. She sighs. Plop! She drops the turtle and yawns—she's getting sleepy again. She trudges back to the temporary nest, flops down next to her sister, and closes her eyes.

Ten minutes later the Trinity Turtle peeks out from under her shell, sniffs, stares, sniffs again, and resumes her waddling march toward a very special piece of sandy shore. Despite being juggled and nibbled by the raptor, her dedication to her reproductive destiny remains unshaken. The sensors in her small olfactory chamber are dialed to one particular scent—the smell of the very same sandbar where she hatched twelve years ago.

Thirty minutes later her nose tells her brain to stop moving and start digging. Her short, sturdy hindpaws begin to shovel sand with alternating strokes, first left, then right. When the hole is as deep as her shell is tall, she stops and deposits eleven spherical eggs.

If Raptor Red were still awake and understood the process, she'd feel a pang of jealousy. The turtle's instinct-driven, single-minded reproductive drive is simple compared with the social complexity of Raptor Red's present life. The Trinity Turtle doesn't have to balance the competing demands of sisters and mate. The turtle has no responsibilities other than to her own eggs, and even that duty is fully discharged as soon as she covers the nest with a layer of sand.

And so on this particular Early Cretaceous night, one turtle mother completes the life cycle of her species and returns to the comfortable monotony of her watery world. One female raptor must go to sleep with the vague hope that the entangling alliances of raptor society will someday give her another chance to reproduce.

# Flood and Panzers!

Raptor Red wakes up in the middle of the night as she often does. Her pack-mates are sleeping on an abandoned croc-nest, heaped high with dried vegetation cemented with mud. It's a comfortable lair, dry, with a view over the valley so the adults can keep track of the herbivore herds and the comings and goings of Yellow Snouts and giant acro predators.

The pack has used the croc-nest as a base for a month after they were forced to leave Tick-Bird Meadow when the *Acrocanthosaurus* took control of the astrodon carcass.

Raptor Red stares to the west. A mixed herd of iguanodons and astros is making a terrific racket, bellowing, snorting, screaming. Iguanodons often join their social units to a pod of astros. Iguanodons have excellent eye-sight, but their short necks and low shoulders make it hard for them to survey their surroundings and detect predators at a distance. Astros can see for miles when they raise their long necks twenty-five feet above ground level.

The astro sentries have been making it hard for the raptor pack to sneak up on the iguanodons in the last few days. And the huge, nervous masses of iguanodons, ready to charge or stampede at the slightest provocation, have been making it hard for the raptors to isolate single astros.

Raptor Red and her sister have still managed to keep the chicks fed. But it's been hard work. Back at Tick-Bird Meadow, nearly every one of their attacks had ended with a kill. Now only one out of five attacks succeeds. And there've been close calls. Raptor Red's sister was cornered by thirty or forty angry cow iguanodons, advancing shoulder to shoulder. The iguanodons, their courage multiplied by their numbers, made a group decision to switch from flight to murderous defense. The sight of one of their sisters lying dead, ripped open by raptor claws, pushed their iguanodon minds to a fury of revenge.

Then Raptor Red's sister made a serious misjudgment: She screamed at the cow herd and stood her ground next to the kill. Raptor Red had already retreated. She is the more cautious of the pair, the one who always evaluates and reevaluates the balance of risk and reward. But her sister can be like a whirling dervish, convinced of her in-destructibility, lashing her claws, snapping her teeth, at-tacking when she should withdraw.

This time her frenzied belligerence almost made her chicks orphans. The iguanodon herd split up and made two wide crescents that almost surrounded the raptor mother. She backed up into a gully, but the upstream end was steep and slippery.

Thirty iguanodon cows started advancing up the gully,

swinging their deadly thumb-spikes. Another fifty or sixty were closing in from the left and right.

Raptor Red saw that in a second or two her sister would be flattened by a hundred angry hindpaws and jabbed by the spikes on a hundred iguanodon hands.

Raptor Red made a loud mock-attack from behind. For a moment the iguanodons' unified spirit was distracted. Those nearest the raptor mother stopped and looked around. Raptor Red's sister scrambled up the gully wall and escaped by climbing into a stack of fallen branches of a conifer tree.

That was yesterday morning. In the afternoon the raptor sisters found a cow who had been crippled in a fall and was abandoned by the rest of the herd. Easy kill.

Now Raptor Red monitors the movement of the herbivore herd in the night. The moon is nearly full and casts a cold, ivory light on the scene. Now and then the cool light plays across a hundred iguanodon backs.

Flickers of angry orange light appear on the western horizon far away. Cobalt-blue clouds are illuminated from underneath. A dull rumble reaches Raptor Red's ears.

Suddenly, the western sky is brightly illuminated by a jagged white streak. Raptor Red tenses herself, knowing that a loud noise will come in five seconds or so.

Crackkk! Raptor Red shudders involuntarily at the noise.

The iguanodon-astro herd is coming close, passing a quarter-mile to the north. That's alarming. The herd is downwind—they should be able to smell the raptor lair. Raptor Red worries that the cows are coming to avenge the death of their colleague. But that's rarely happened before. Iguanodons don't hold grudges for long. When raptors make a kill, either the cows attack immediately, or they go away and seem to forget all about their recently deceased kin.

Raptor Red gets ready for action, for quick evacuation of her kin group. But the noisy herbivores just keep going eastward, paying not the slightest attention.

Raptor Red stares up at the moon.

Then she stares down at the moon. The moon's reflection on the ground is almost as bright as the moon itself. But the ground reflection shimmers and quakes, and ripples seem to pass through it.

Raptor Red becomes alert. This isn't right. The moon shouldn't reflect off dry mud. It reflects that way only in *water*.

Then she feels a cold current on her toes!

She jerks herself up. The rippled moon reflection is rising up to the level of the croc-nest. Pieces of foliage float by, fast.

She backs up to the top of the mound, bumping into her sister, who jumps up and falls over her chicks, who squeak in alarm, scurry over themselves, and promptly roll off the mound and right into the water.

Plop, plop, plop!

Raptor Red would laugh if evolution had given her a way to generate that sound. The chicks were particularly naughty yesterday, getting in the way of the adults in a very serious situation. Raptor Red wanted to swat them hard.

Her sister gets very excited and jumps in after the chicks, deluging them in splashes as she hops from one foot to another. Raptor Red calmly wades in, making hardly a ripple. Her sister is the better swimmer, but Raptor Red is better at wading and feeling her way through water in the dark.

A chick clambers up Raptor Red's thigh and hangs on to her neck like a jockey. Another chick climbs the base of her tail and crawls, inchworm style, up to the first chick.

Raptor Red now has trouble balancing. The two chicks

insist on shifting their weight first to one side, then the other. She sees the third chick, upside down, caught in a waterlogged cycad frond.

Raptor Red picks the chick up in her mouth.

Meanwhile, her sister is in panic mode, beating the water with her hands, trying to gather her chicks. She always was the high-strung one in her brood, given to fits of hysterical activity. Yet she raised three chicks to adult size last year and is doing quite well this year.

A huge turtle, a yard across, floats by.

Raptor Red is now worried. The water is coming faster and getting higher and she can't go back to the summit of the croc-nest—it'll be submerged in a few minutes. She has never experienced a life-or-death test in water. She doesn't know what to do. She has no learned experience to help.

If she were able to fly up and over the storm flood and view the hills miles to the west, the way a white-winged dactyl is now doing, she would have been even more afraid. The dactyl has seen rain falling in the foothills for an entire day. He has seen rain clouds, heavy and gray, sitting on the western mountains for five days. The white dactyl has seen something like this before, on three occasions during his long life. He's aloft in the darkness now because he knows the floods are coming.

From three hundred feet above, he sees streams swollen beyond capacity. A billion tons of unrestrained water are escaping the confines of riverbanks.

Trees are being knocked down like twigs. Mud and sand, in volumes measured in cubic kilometers, are choking the waters.

Raptor Red's family is experiencing a geological catastrophe, a disaster, a thousand-year flood.

When the climate cycle reaches a certain point of coincidence, when moist air from the Pacific mixes with moist air from the southern seas, and when temperatures are just right over the Nevada mountains, the thousand-year rains come. And Utah is flooded with muddy waters ten, twenty, and thirty feet thick. Mud blankets yards deep are left everywhere, burying living and dead dinosaurs. Crocodiles, fish, turtles, and tiny fur-bearing mammals too, are caught up in the mud torrents.

It's a bigger flood than even the long-lived dactyl has seen. Floods of this magnitude occur so infrequently that there's no memory stored in the raptor genetic code. Once a thousand years is simply too rare an event. Raptor Red has an instinctive inventory of responses to the usual types of storms, to the cloudbursts her species experiences every year. But she cannot be prepared for this night.

Many raptors will die. Hundreds of iguanodons will drown, their bloated carcasses washing downstream and going aground on sandbars in Colorado. Mother Crocodile will survive, carried far to the east by the flood. After the flood is over, she will re-immigrate, swimming slowly back upstream. She will build another nest close to where her old one was buried in mud.

Raptor Red would die if she were alone. She cannot come up with a tactic of survival by herself. But her sister can.

Raptor Red's sister has different behavioral genes—all dinosaur siblings differ a little bit this way, except for rare identical twins. Raptor Red's sister is too high-strung, too quick to violence, too eager to attack in the face of hopeless odds, too slow to recognize when she should move her brood away from danger. Raptor Red is smarter, calmer, and a much better tactician in the hunt.

But Raptor Red doesn't know how to swim in a strong current or how to climb trees in pitch-darkness. Her sister does.

Raptor Red deliberately follows her sister now, walking through the dark water. The enormous load of sand and silt carried by the flood increases the kinetic energy of the current. It's like walking through liquid cement being shot out at high velocity.

Raptor Red slips and falls halfway, her left knee going down into the moving muck. The chicks scream. Her sister comes back and leans against Raptor Red. Two chicks jump ship, transferring to their mother's body. Raptor Red gets up.

Her sister leads them deeper into the water. Raptor Red feels her feet losing contact with the terrain. She thrashes her tail, trying to swim back to higher ground. But her sister keeps swimming with the current, not trying to fight her way across the trajectories of maximum hydraulic energy.

Raptor Red starts to swim too. She would swim slowly in calm water, but now, swimming parallel to the current, her velocity is added to the floodwater's. Trees zip by. A bull astro, looking dull and confused, stands like a stone bridge in the current, the flood splashing high on the upstream side of his legs. He'll live through the night by simple virtue of his forty-thousand-pound inertia.

Raptor Red has not been dependent upon another member of her species since she was a nest-bound chick, unable to go out on her own. On this terrible night she decides to follow her sister, even though it makes no sense. Raptor Red is impressed by her sister's steady, unruffled response—either she is mad or she knows how to escape.

The two raptor sisters swim for three hours. It's actually not difficult. They keep just enough speed beyond the current to navigate easily. Other raptors will exhaust themselves fighting the current. They'll give up and float helplessly. And they'll be drowned when they get entangled in fallen foliage or swept up in whirlpools.

A tall, dark massive grove of centuries-old conifer trees looms up on the right. Raptor Red's sister turns toward them. Raptor Red follows close behind.

They bump into the fallen trunks of smaller trees, and Raptor Red feels her knees get bruised and bumped and bruised again. She grabs at a low-hanging branch, digging her foreclaws deep into the bark. This brings relief—the current is gentle. Raptor Red could hang on for hours.

But her sister goes on, swimming in between the biggest, oldest trunks. Reluctantly, Raptor Red lets go and follows. In a few minutes that branch will be under water.

At last her sister stops at the base of a huge tree. Its trunk slants at a forty-degree angle; its top is jammed into the crowns of six other big trees. It has half fallen down, but it doesn't look like it will fall further that night.

Raptor Red's sister reaches up with both hands, grabbing the bark. Then she flexes her hips down with a quick, powerful jerk. Her two hindlegs grab the trunk underwater. She moves her right leg up and grabs the bark opposite her right hand. Then she repeats the operation with the left hindleg. Then she shifts her right hand up—then the right hindleg.

Slowly, very deliberately, with great strength and slow coordination, she climbs the sloping trunk. Ten feet, twenty feet. She stops when she reaches the crown, where a maze of branches extend at right angles to the trunk. There are already some flood refugees wedged up there. A half-grown Yellow Snout raptor glares balefully at her. Raptor Red's sister extends her head, opens her mouth, and utters a very low snarl.

The Yellow Snout falls backward but catches himself in the crown of another tree.

Raptor Red has watched her sister's climb in amazement. She had no idea that *Utahraptor* bodies were capable of climbing. Last year she chased some *Deinonychus*, the smaller raptor species, up trees and saw them ascend beyond her reach. She hadn't attempted to follow.

Raptor Red is not too proud to learn by example. If her sister can climb that high with chicks hanging on, so can she.

Raptor Red grabs the bark with her foreclaws. The bark is surprisingly hard, and her claws slip off. She grabs again, piercing the bark with the sharp claw tips. She uses her instinctive style of claw-work, the style she uses when she attacks a thick-hided astro. Her finger-tendons flex at maximum power. The claw tips dig deeper. They hold.

She places the sole of her right hindfoot against the tree trunk, flexing her rear toe so the claw grabs into the bark. Her killing claw too now becomes a strong climbing apparatus. Digging the killing claw into the tree is a lot like slashing through the skin of a big iguanodon—except in climbing the motion is much slower and more carefully controlled.

Instinct and intelligence work together to make Raptor Red a tree-climber. Climbing is not really new for her. She's climbed up the hulking carcasses of astros on several occasions. She's climbed up the backs and necks of live cow iguanodons a dozen times. Climbing this tree really isn't more difficult. The tree doesn't try to shake her off, the way a struggling prey-victim might.

Raptor Red thinks through every step. She modifies her instinctive attack movements so that they keep her securely on the tree, going upward. *Utahraptors* are too big to be regular climbers. Nature imposes strict rules of engineering. The bigger the animal, the tougher it is to move vertically.

A *Utahraptor*, weighing five hundred pounds or more

as an adult, isn't born with the confidence to climb. But it can be learned. Raptor Red is learning this night.

Raptor Red reaches her sister. The raptor pack huddles closely, hanging on to each other and to the tree. When their claws cut the young branches, their nostrils sting with the smell of poisonous sap. Raptor Red feels the tree swaying and shuddering as fallen logs wash against the base of the trunk. The water is still rising. The moon is blocked by heavy clouds, and the rains have spread from the western hills to directly overhead.

Raptor Red is cold.

———————

The sun finally breaks through after thirty-six hours of rain. The Yellow Snout raptor's grip was loosened by the chilling breeze. He fell and was drowned. Raptor Red heard other creatures—she couldn't identify the species—fall too. Most were small. Some were pushed off their branches by newcomers who were stronger and meaner. Two or three were large and made loud splashes when they hit the water. There were screams and hisses too, marking fights for the safest perches.

Raptor Red and her sister move their bodies to get the benefit of the sun's warmth. The chicks are fine—all through the day and a half of rain, they kept themselves stuck under the adults. The soft, thin belly skin of Raptor Red and her sister kept the chicks warm.

The tree crown comes alive with animals stretching their joints. Fingers and toes that had been tightly clenched for so many hours are painfully, slowly extended and flexed and extended. Species who are mortal enemies on the ground are side by side now. But the predators are too chilled, too shaken to resume killing.

Raptor Red sees something moving below that appears to be half-turtle, half-crocodile, half-iguanodon. She's never seen anything like it. It's about forty pounds, its back covered with armor plate, its sides studded with bony spikes. Its long tail ends in a small club of bone. Even its upper eyelids are armored.

Raptor Red reaches down to sniff—her curiosity makes her forget the rainy ordeal.

She can just touch the strange armored animal with her left foot. She extends her toes and gives it a shove.

*Wham-thwack-thwack-thwacky-thwack!*

She pulls her foot up just before the beast flails its spike-edged tail convulsively. Branches break, and the armored beast falls ten feet onto a soft, soggy mound of conifer needles.

*Whacky-thwack!* Another convulsion. The beast falls again, onto a tangle of flotsam and jetsam.

It's a baby *Gastonia*, an armored dinosaur. Raptor Red has never seen one before.

The sun gets very hot. Raptor Red can see dry ground not far away—it will be an easy swim once she has warmed up a bit.

Other dinosaurs are sunning themselves too, in preparation for their descent. In a few hours the flood-truce will be over. Predators and herbivores who now share branches in peace will be back down on the ground, trying to kill and avoid being killed.

Raptor Red looks around at the many pairs of eyes staring out from the conifer crown. One pair of eyes is staring right back. It bobs up and down. Raptor Red can see a long snout in front of the eyes, and on the snout is a bright crimson streak.

It's the male who tried to court her near Tick-Bird Meadow. Now he goes into a modified courtship dance, hanging on to the tree with his hindfeet, moving his shoulders and neck gracefully.

# Whackity-Whacks

*Whack-whack-clank-crack.*

*Ouch!* the big *Acrocanthosaurus* thinks as his tooth crown breaks off, leaving the nerve exposed. He drops the little armored dinosaur he was trying to swallow.

*Whackity-whackity-WHACK.*

*Ouch.* He reacts again to a sharp pain on his shin where the armored dino's spikes hit.

*WHACK-WHACK-WHACK.* The little dino is like a big ultraprickly pinecone, made of bone and muscle, powered by a spastic motor. The acro backs up again, his ankle smarting from a dozen hits from the armored protuberances.

*Whump-whack-whump.* The baby *Gastonia* twitches nose to tail again, sending clods of mud over the acro.

*No good—not worth the trouble,* the acro thinks to himself. He doesn't like food morsels that make him bleed inside and out. He's swallowed crocodiles whole before. Their bony ridges were a bit painful as they slid down his gullet. But this little armor-clad demon is much worse.

His broken tooth throbs—it was a fully developed tooth, not ready to be shed. There's no discomfort when a tooth crown drops out on schedule. The root gets resorbed, the nerves and blood vessels dry up, and the new tooth growing in under the old crown simply pushes the remnant out of the jaw.

But the gaston has whacked the acro's teeth hard from inside the acro's mouth as the big predator was about to gulp it down. Several healthy crowns, still connected to nerves, are now cracked.

The acro backs up again. Then he runs forward and tries to kick the gaston. The little dino hunkers down so close to the ground that the acro misses. The acro steps hard on the gaston's body, flattening it into the mud.

Blurp. The gaston blows watery mud out of his nostrils.

The acro comes to a conclusion: *Pinecone dinosaurs— not food.*

The acro certainly doesn't need this nasty tidbit. A hundred tons of carrion lie piled up along the river sandbars after the flood—thousands of dinosaur bodies, limp and battered, caught in groves of trees and thickets of cycads. It's a scavenger's smorgasbord.

After the frustrated meat-eater wanders away, the baby gaston stands up and sniffs the breeze. The gaston's not real bright compared to a raptor. Like most dino-herbivores, the gaston has only a medium-size brain, about the size of a crocodile of the same body bulk. That's far less mental mass than a *Deinonychus* or a *Utahraptor* has.

And being an herbivore doesn't supply the mental challenges that an active predator gets every day. A gaston doesn't have to hunt very far for food—it uses its broad, low muzzle to crop off wide mouthfuls of conifer seedlings and cycads, food that doesn't fight back or run away.

The baby gaston knows only a few things, but he knows them very well: Eating the right plants. Avoiding poisonous plants. (He was born with a poison-alarm system, programmed into his olfactory sense.) Avoiding falling off cliffs. (Most land vertebrate species are born with a fear of steep slopes.)

And go *whackity-whack* when he's bothered by something.

Since every vulnerable corner of his body is protected by strong bony plates of armor with sharp ridges or spikes sticking out, *whackity-whack* is a pretty useful response to most threatening situations. The gaston has a short but strong neck, with wide muscles for swinging the armored head side to side. The long torso is so broad and low that predators have a hard time flipping the gaston over on its back. And the long tail has the strongest sideways-flexing muscles, compared to body weight, of any dinosaur.

*Whackity-whack* has been the simple and successful defensive game plan of the *Gastonia* species and their ancestors for thirty million years, since the first member of the Ankylosaurian order evolved, far back in the Jurassic Period.

The baby gaston hasn't a clue how he ended up in the tree. He remembers that he was huddled with his family, facing downwind to keep the rain out of their eyes, on a tall levee—a raised mound of mud that bordered a river. All of a sudden the levee broke. A brutally strong wall of water smashed through the breach, hurling jagged chunks of soil and muck across the floodplain, bowling over the adult gastons and washing away the little ones.

The baby gaston shut his eyes and went *whackity-whack* at the floodwater. He kept his armored eyelids shut for nearly two days afterward. He remembers being bumped in three dimensions, going up, going down, and then far up; then movement stopped. The sun came out, and he was just beginning to dry out when someone kicked him, and he fell into the water again.

He found himself beached on a low spit of sand. Had he kept his eyes open, he would have seen that he had, in fact, performed a spectacular trick worthy of the finest circus.

He had gotten caught in the branches of a ripped-up cycad tree. Cycad trunks are low-density compared to most other trees, and the cycad with the gaston aboard had bobbed like a balsa raft. It washed downstream for two miles, then jammed itself against a grove of old conifers. A particularly fast burst of floodwater pushed the cycad around and around and finally slid the lightweight cycad wood up the sloping trunks of three partially fallen conifers. The gaston had fallen off the cycad and landed on the lower branches of an old conifer.

Thanks to Raptor Red's curiosity, the gaston had been pushed out of the tree. But the currents were abating, and he was carried only a short distance before being left aground.

Now that he's sure the acrocanthosaur is gone, the baby gaston starts pumping his chubby legs as fast as he can—toward the source of a scent that shows where his family is.

Gastons have fared well in the flood. Their wide bodies float right side up even in rough water, unlike the poor iguanodons, who often get tumbled sideways. And the armor plate protected the delicate gastonian viscera from all the collisions with rocks and fallen logs.

The baby gaston sees a high-stepping predator of about four hundred pounds coming right at him. He hunkers down again, waiting. A young male red-snouted *Utahraptor* is approaching, curious. This carnivore is far more careful than the acro had been. The raptor tentatively reaches out with one forepaw, stretching one finger.

One little tap and—*whack-whack.*

*No—no good to eat,* the raptor thinks, *but—good to play with.*

The male raptor tiptoes around to the other side and reaches out. *Tap-tap—whackity-whack!*

The male raptor has had a fine day so far—there's free meat everywhere. No worries about food for the next week or so. He's the most inquisitive of all the brothers and sisters who hatched out five years ago. He gets away with it because he's also the quickest. He can jump sideways or backward or straight up and land facing the opposite direction.

He likes to poke strange animals—to see what will happen. Now he creeps around the baby gaston till he's dead astern. The raptor swings his own tail in anticipation. He notices his own tail movement. An idea!

The raptor turns around and swings his tail at the gaston. Just missed!

He creeps backward a half-step, and swings his tail again. The raptor tail tip barely brushes the end of the gaston's tail.

*Whackity-WHACK.* Sand flies sideways as the gaston performs a particularly vigorous full-body swoosh.

The male raptor moves to the front, behind a tussock of fern fronds. He crouches. Then he charges, stopping abruptly a yard from the gaston's head.

No *whackity-whack* this time.

The raptor sighs. He crouches, then leaps over the gaston.

Still no *whackity-whack*. The male raptor is getting bored with his toy.

He backs off, takes a running start, and jumps over the gaston while dragging one toe just low enough to touch its back.

*Whackity-whack.*

A deep coughing roar announces the arrival of seven adult gastons. The baby coughs a reply. The male raptor studies the gastons as they advance. *Short legs—very slow* is his analysis. He's learned that the higher the body and the longer the shins and ankles, the faster the dinosaur. He can outrun nearly all his dinosaurian neighbors except for the ostrich dinos, small-headed omnivores with exceedingly elongated lower legs.

He knows he can run rings around the gastons. He trots up to meet them. They stop, lower their heads in a threat, and swing their tails.

*Too big whackity-whacks here—dangerous.* The raptor's brain evaluates the one-ton size of the adult gastons. If those adult bodies whack him, it won't be fun anymore. So if he can't eat them and can't play with them, he'll just go away.

The raptor terminates the game of Taunt the Gaston. He moves up the sand dune and turns west into a wide valley. Here are posted thousands of messages from other dinosaurs. Challenges from young male *Utahraptor*. Sexual invitations from deinonych widowers who lost their mates in the flood. Panic signals from *Astrodon* young, separated from their parents and uncles and aunts. Pompous declarations from acros who boast of their indisputable position as Kings of the Cretaceous.

There are even the small-voiced messages from multis, plant-eating furballs who live in colonies: *I've just dug a*

*new burrow here, and all the shrubs within a ten-yard radius
are mine.*

The young male *Utahraptor*'s mind is swamped with all
the messages criss-crossing in claim and counterclaim. It's
a cacophony of aromas, like a dozen rap songs sung at
once in the language of scent. He tries to read every one.
It's a Cretaceous highway of information, all written in
shit.

Dung is the queen of media in the Cretaceous. With his
voluminous olfactory chambers, the male *Utahraptor* can
distinguish ten thousand different individuals of his own
species from their dung-aroma. He can tell whether a
young female is alone and available or firmly bonded in
monogamous union. He can tell how long the message has
been exposed to the sun and rain.

Appearances may be deceiving, and like all raptors the
male insists on a dung-document to prove the identity and
status of strangers. It will always be this way with long-
snouted predators. His distant cousins, the great tyrannosaurs of the later Cretaceous, will have huge snout
chambers for their sense of smell. So will the bears and
wolves and hyenas much farther in the geological future.
Of all the land animals who hunt big game, only one will
come along who cannot read the dung-sign—*Homo sapiens*.

After reading his way through a half-mile of the shit
bulletin board, the male raptor comes to a small, brand-
new pile of dung, one clearly deposited after the flood, on
a high crest of sand. He sniffs. He stares. He paws at the
ground to refresh the scent.

It's raptor shit. He sniffs again—it's *Utahraptor* shit, not
the Yellow Snout species but his own red-snouted kind,
one who has been eating fresh astro meat with a little
iguanodon liver.

Very interesting. He sniffs very slowly, very loudly.

There are some undifferentiated signals—raptors whose fecal signature doesn't say whether they are male or female. And the strongest signal comes from—adult females—and he recognizes one particular individual.

Very, *very* interesting.

It's very confusing to a young male, but very exciting too. He turns around, three complete circles, sniffing, and delicately overlays the pile with a message of his own.

*I was here after you—I—a young, healthy, unattached male.*

The male begins to follow the trail of that one particular female. He searches with his nose, trying to untangle a dozen overlapping raptor scent-trails. He's after just one particular family group. He finds them a day later.

---

Raptor Red and her sister are feeling fine. The sun and the limitless banquet of flood-killed corpses everywhere are a predator's dream come true. The night of terror in the water and up the tree has been pushed back to the far reaches of memory. For Raptor Red the experience will come in handy several times later in her life, but right now the joy of the present occupies all her consciousness.

The only irritation today is the huge flocks of carrion-loving dactyls and birds. Not just the big aggressive *Ornithocheirus* but more timid *Ornithodesmus* too, very agile fliers with short, sharp-edged teeth arranged in a broad semicircle around the front of the beak.

The raptor pack are lying next to a chewed-up *Astrodon* calf. Raptor Red gets up to shoo away a pair of cheeky *Ornithodesmus*. They whistle and squawk and jump around. Raptor Red hisses and makes fake attacks. It's hard to be convincing when her belly is so full and she's feeling so warm and comfy.

The *Ornithodesmus* reek of rancid seafood. They've

been feeding on grounded "panzer-fish," trout-size species covered with thick, shiny scales. The sight of so many dinosaur hulks tempted the dactyls to try to steal some meat. These dactyls are smart and flexible—they'll try a new food source just to see what it's like.

*Why bother—I'm stuffed—don't care,* Raptor Red thinks to herself. Every time she chases the dactyls away from the neck of the astro, they flutter over to the tail. If she were lean, with an empty stomach, she'd be mean and nasty and would try to bite their pretty white heads off.

But *Ornithodesmus* is too unaggressive to be a danger to the chicks. With a mental shrug that could be translated *What the hell,* Raptor Red gives up and walks away. The delighted dactyls bounce on top of the astro and yank away at strings of meat hanging from the edges of broken bones. They have little success—they're not strong enough to rip the tendons and ligaments holding the meat to bone—but they seem to enjoy the novel exercise.

# Reluctant Sister-in-Law

He came with a dried-up turtle in his mouth. He walks with exaggerated steps, bringing his knees high, silently, like a dinosaurian mime.

Raptor Red has been watching him for several minutes now. The young male has already completed the first act of the dance. Now he's beginning the much more difficult second act. She hasn't awakened her sister, who is snoring, lying on her side because her gut is too stuffed to lie on her stomach.

The male raptor lowers his head almost to the ground and swings it left and right. This part of the courtship dance is the toughest. The slow-motion head and neck gestures are done with the hands pulled back against the chest. Balancing is difficult. Proper execution of the dance requires that the deadly hand claws be out of sight—there can be no suggestion of a threat.

Raptor Red marvels at the smooth execution of the dance. Intuitively she knows that only a male in the peak of health can perform this way. She begins to flex and extend her own knees and ankles just a little bit, while she remains sitting, following with her eyes the step routine the male is performing.

She hasn't the slightest interest in the dried turtle as a food item. It's a symbolic gift. Even if she were hungry, she wouldn't look at the turtle as lunch. Long, long ago, a thousand generations or more, raptor males gave fresh meat, recently killed, as a gift to reluctant females. It was a courtship bribe—and a promise of parental duties that would be fulfilled.

*Take this meat—see, I can help feed you and our unborn chicks* was the message.

Now Raptor Red is watching a gift-dance of stylized formality, the program rewritten and rewritten again by that most innovative of choreographers, natural selection.

Raptor Red knows what she likes in a male dancer—slender, muscular limbs, and supple S-curves in neck movement—but she doesn't know why. She was born with a vague idea of male beauty, an idea that was refined by watching her mother and father. She doesn't know that these strict standards will help guarantee a mate who will be faster than she and more maneuverable—key assets when lovers hunt together as a team.

Raptor Red doesn't know the history of her own species. Only one kind of animal will ever evolve the capacity to discover its own past—that will be *Homo sapiens*, a hundred and twenty million years hence.

But Raptor Red does know that she wants a male at

least as good as the one she lost. Better. Her standards are much higher than average for her species.

Now she is very, very impressed.

The male reaches far forward and, without the slightest muscular tremor, stretches his neck a few inches above the ground, extends his snout, opens his jaws, and drops the turtle a yard from Raptor Red's feet.

He withdraws by walking slowly backward, facing Raptor Red as a medieval servant faces some all-powerful empress, his eyes focused on the ground.

At the last moment he stumbles on a half-buried astro rib. But he recovers—it's an almost-invisible error in his program.

Raptor Red cocks her head, as if she were disturbed. It's the response she's supposed to give, to make the male more nervous. But in reality she doesn't mind at all.

*Quite splendid—overall,* she is thinking in unspoken judgment. If she had a concept of numbers, she'd give him a 9.6 out of 10.0 for the execution of the dance, and a 10.0 for the difficulty of the routine he chose.

There is a long pause. The male looks up from the corner of his eye but doesn't move. Raptor Red feigns disinterest. She looks up at some big dactyls—they're *Criorhynchus*, big fellows with vertical crests on their snout tips. She yawns. She hisses at the dactyls.

Now she looks at the turtle. It's been dead for a month, at least. There's hardly any digestible meat left.

The male shifts his weight on his legs. His calf muscles are cramping.

Raptor Red picks up the turtle and flips it in the air high above her muzzle. To the male, the turtle seems suspended, turning in slow motion in the air. He's just about decided that Raptor Red will let it drop.

Gulp! The turtle disappears down her gullet. The brief

taste she got was quite terrible, and she'll throw the turtle back up in five minutes.

That won't matter. The male stands up, tall, and lets his hands fall straight down. He walks over to Raptor Red and sits down next to her and begins to groom her neck lightly.

*Hısssss . . . HSSSsss.* Raptor Red's sister wakes up and stares angrily at the male. She tries to get up, baring her teeth. The chicks get alarmed and retreat to the top of a tussock. But Raptor Red's sister's belly is just too full. She doesn't have the energy to generate a full-scale threat. And Raptor Red doesn't even turn around to acknowledge her sister's displeasure.

Laboriously, Raptor Red's sister drags her bloated body over to where the chicks are and lies down in front of them.

She sighs—as if to say, *All right, if you insist, I won't bite him—but keep him away from me and my chicks.*

# Manure, Love, and Flowers

The male *Utahraptor* stands dead still in the shade of a cycad's palmlike leaves. Usually he has the fearlessness of a young adult. He's pumped full of hormones, and he has confidence in his muscles, his athleticism, his senses. He's not afraid to attack strange plant-eaters three times his size. He has little reluctance to challenge a mature male *Utahraptor* a hundred pounds greater in bulk.

But now he's afraid of the color red. The young male is unnerved by the mass of red-purple objects hanging from bushes and low trees a few hundred yards away. Here is more red in one place than he's ever seen before. The six-foot-high wall of crimson stretches for a quarter-mile, and when the wind blows, the red objects undulate in a threatening manner.

The young male's brain cannot cope. He can't deal with this scarlet overdose—there's no programmed instinct to make the proper choices when faced with so much color.

Red is the most evocative hue in evolution among land animals. Red is the color that elicits the strongest emotions in birds, in lizards, in frogs—and in *Utahraptor*. Red triggers courtship and mate-bonding. But red is also the color of blood, the cue to fear death.

The male raptor is used to handling red in small amounts. Red is the color he wears himself on the sides of his long muzzle. Red is the color he's programmed to seek in a mate. The first time he saw Raptor Red, he responded strongly because she wore an especially bright oval patch of red on her snout.

Red is an eternal come-on. Long before the Cretaceous, red has transfixed the attention of animals with color vision. It shows up clearly against the green of foliage or the brown of soil. It's a universal language that will be understood by parrots and apes and human beings long after the Cretaceous.

Reds and purples penetrate the environment and advertise their wearer as either a lover or a fighter; they are a loud message for females to come near and for other males to stay away.

Evolution is a smart cosmetician. The male raptor has a two-stage recognition system: First, he's attracted to any raptor who wears the correct hue. Second, he scrutinizes the face for the correct pattern.

He saw this mass of color five miles off, and his subconscious made him investigate. Up till this moment, the male raptor has grown excited every time he's seen a moving spot of red. But hundreds of yards of scarlet and crimson is far too much stimulation. It overloads his circuits.

And that's what he sees now in the woody shrubs growing in dense confusion at the base of the conifer wood: thousands of gaudy purplish-crimson blobs swaying in the wind. They are flowers. Primitive flowers with wide, simple petals arranged like a modern magnolia's. The male raptor has never seen flowers before, and it's a scary sight.

Plus, there is all this buzzing. The closer he gets to the wall of red, the louder the sound becomes—a million insect wings humming.

*Utahraptor* and all the other dinosaurs in its ecosystem have evolved in a world that's overwhelmingly green and brown. All the trees have been conifers or palm-leafed cycads or tree ferns—plants that are flowerless. All the undergrowth has been ferns, ground pine, horsetails, and conifer seedlings—strictly green and brown in every case. Raptors are used to seeing brown cones hanging from conifers, and the dark spots on fern fronds that contain the reproductive spores. Brown and green, green and brown—that's been the unbroken rule for every day the male raptor has lived. That's the world he's comfortable with.

Big gaudy flowers are a New Thing, and predators are very suspicious of New Things.

The male raptor grew up in a dull green flowerless environment, and the reason is simple: Flowering plants are evolutionary newcomers in his world. There were no flowers of any sort in the Jurassic Period, when the ancestors of raptors were being shaped by Darwinian forces. And when *Utahraptor* itself evolved, very early in the Cretaceous, the flora was still devoid of reproductive color.

As the male raptor was growing up, the most important revolution in land plant life was occurring. Here and there, hidden in isolated patches of disturbed forest, where drought and floods and grazing dinosaurs put great pressure on the woody plants, a totally new life-form appeared.

It was a small tree that did not trust the wind to spread its pollen. Instead, it evolved a colorized welcome mat to attract bugs to visit—a mat constructed of modified leaves that became petals.

Purple and ultraviolet hues are visual bug-magnets. Once drawn to the petals, bugs are persuaded to linger, feeding on nutritious surplus pollen or at nectar pots built into the center of the flower. Then off the bugs will go to visit another floral attraction, each bug exporting pollen from the first flower.

The flower is a stupendously clever adaptive device. Not only does it give more efficient fertilization inside the female plant organ, the flower guarantees that pollen will be carried from one plant to another with far less waste than is possible among nonflowering plants.

Now, during the Early Cretaceous, Nature is adding other adaptive novelties—greater efficiency in growth of woody tissue—and so flowering plants are poised to make a momentous ecological leap. These plants will become the fastest-growing component of forests and woodlands in the middle and later days of the Cretaceous Period. By the time of *Tyrannosaurus rex*, forty million years after *Utahraptor*, every habitat will be brightened up by a profusion of flowers—red, orange, yellow, metallic blue.

Dinosaur eyes and dinosaur brains will become used to seeing bright colors in the undergrowth. But right now, at this moment in *Utahraptor* history, the unexpected appearance of purple flowers causes even more consternation among dinosaur societies than a spaceship from another galaxy, full of little green men, would cause in downtown Los Angeles in the modern era.

The young male becomes aware that he is not alone. The red flowers have acted like dino-magnets, drawing in *Utahraptor* packs from all over. The big raptor species is usually rare. Its small clans are scattered widely, and except during the mating season, the families avoid each other. But the red-flowered shrubs are situated on a hill and can be seen by the keen-eyed predators thousands of yards away.

The young male notices two bachelor *Utahraptor* carefully tiptoeing on the other side of the bushes. They advance with knees and ankles flexed, bodies held low to the ground, necks lowered.

A gust of wind ripples the flowers unexpectedly, tossing a dozen petals into the air. The two bachelors turn and flee in full-speed retreat.

Farther away the young male sees a large *Utahraptor* pack—six females, one adult male, and chicks. They sway back and forth, rising as high as they can on their toes, staring and sniffing loudly.

The young male jerks his snout up involuntarily. His nostrils flare as he draws in air in explosive bursts. It's the flowers. They smell. They smell very strong—they smell . . . *delicious!*

They smell like overripe meat and liver mixed with fresh iguanodon dung.

He marches with deliberate steps, pausing to cock his head and examine the bushes. Closer, closer. The red color swamps his visual centers. But the aroma of rotting viscera and ripe herbivore feces is compelling.

He examines a patch of flower-heavy shrubs. There are three flower species growing together—one deep purple-red, one pale lavender, one white. All have petals arranged in a loose spiral around an odoriferous center. It's the white one that smells like rotting meat. The purple-red flowers smell more like liver and old skin. The lavender ones are dung-scented.

Bffffffffft. A beetle blunders into his nostril, makes an annoying ruckus, and exits.

Bffffffffft-bffffft. More beetles buzz around the shrubs,

drawn in by the meaty aroma. The male raptor knows this type of bug. They're in the carrion beetle family, the sort of bugs who visit raptor kills to feed and deposit their eggs. Overripe stinky carcasses soon swarm with a wriggling mass of beetle larvae—voracious, hard-shelled maggots that gnaw off every residual scrap of flesh and leave the skeleton gleaming white.

Other bugs are walking all over the pinkish flowers, big beetle species with metallic green shells and wide antennae. The male raptor knows these too—he's found them many times on manure piles left by plant-eating dinos. There are small black wasps and blue beetles as well.

Now the male raptor is even more confused. Buzzing carrion beetles should mean food—a carcass nearby. Dung beetles signal the presence of live herbivorous dinosaurs—prey waiting to be killed. But here among the flowers he can't find any real iguanodon flesh, either on a dead carcass or on a living animal. And no real dung.

He nips at the white flowers. "Bleachhhhh!" The flowers are bitter. He spits them out, disgusted.

He's learned a new lesson and files it away in his memory bank: Meat-smelling plants = fraud. He won't be fooled again. But the bugs will be. The carrion beetles, wasps, and dung bugs have been drafted into the first wave of insect-flower coevolution, species tricked by flower scents. In a few million years, carrion flies too will be fooled into helping pollination. Later still will come the pollinators par excellence—bees and moths and butterflies.

But these later pollinators will be Darwinian sophisticates—they'll require continuous coevolutionary bribery to meet the expanding needs of more and more flower species. The flowering plants will have to offer brighter petals, more complicated pollen chambers, and sweeter nectar in great quantity.

Raptor Red has been watching the flowers too, following every movement of the young male. She's anxious. She doesn't like the mass of unknown red substance. She's not intrigued with the carrion aroma. Something else has taken over her mind, an emotion stronger than confusion and inquisitiveness—jealousy.

Raptor Red lifts her head very high, half closes her eyes, and makes short, loud sniffy noises. She sucks in air around the very front of her snout. It's an instinctive action that most backboned animals use—seen today among horses in a barnyard. It's a way of evaluating potential mates and potential sexual rivals.

The air drawn into Raptor Red's mouth doesn't go the usual route; aft to the center of smell, which is housed in a chamber just in front of her eyes. Instead, the air is diverted into a small, special channel far forward in the roof of her mouth. This channel leads to a special sensory region, the organ of Jacobson, reserved for pheromones, those potent perfumes of evolution.

Just a few pheromone molecules tell Raptor Red that she's in danger of losing the young male. The breeze coming from the direction of the flowers carries the distinctive pheromones of three different female *Utahraptor*, and all three are in a state of sexual aggressiveness.

Raptor Red strides forward, directly toward the young male. The smell of manure + carrion from the flowers is almost suffocating, but her brain filters out the scent molecules. Her whole sensory being is focused on two groups of female raptors who are approaching her young male from the far side of the thicket.

She looks back at her sister, who's pacing back and forth, flailing her long arms, and snarling and hissing at the flowers, at the unknown female raptors, and at the young male.

Raptor Red is relieved that her sister isn't following her. The young male is squatting down, his nose buried in a deep profusion of pink petals. His brain refuses to accept the notion that there's no iguanodon dung down there.

He pops his head up, and sees that he's surrounded by *Utahraptor* femininity. A strange female, much larger and older than he, is making head-bobbing movements of greeting. Another strange female, younger, taller, thinner, is making mock-charges, spreading her arms outward as she lowers her head. That's a more intense courtship greeting, and it scares the male.

He backs away.

"Sssssss—rrrrrRK!" The older female smacks the younger one with her tail and bites. For a second there's a violent barrage of strikes and counterstrikes, as arms and feet, tails and necks slash back and forth.

The younger female retreats, crying loudly. Clumps of skin, ripped off her back, drift down onto the flowers. The older female turns toward the young male and repeats a courtship dance three times, getting closer and closer to the male.

He forgets about the manure-scented flowers. He's scared of the big female. He hasn't been fought over before. He's engaged in courtship dances—six times last year he tried out his mating choreography, and six times he was rejected by assorted females. Each time it was a one-on-one situation. He performed, and a single female reacted.

This year he tried once, with Raptor Red. She gave him equivocal responses, her enthusiasm damped by her sister's presence. *Utahraptor* courtships between first-time breeders can last for months, since it takes a long time to cement male and female together in a pair-bond. And first-time couples that finally do bond may not actually reproduce in the first season.

Raptor Red isn't the ideal mate, if her situation were evaluated by some dispassionate computer. The sister is an obvious liability. Still, the young male is captivated by her. Something about Raptor Red makes him want to hang around, to try to make the pair-bond firm. Raptor Red has been gentle in all her responses to his advances, and he finds that attractive.

"SKKKKKAWK!"

The big strange female is growing agitated. The presence of so many *Utahraptors* in one spot is heating up emotions. The sight and scent of the flowers have caused an unnatural concentration of unattached females. The young male finds himself in the unwanted status of Most Desirable Male. It's a self-amplifying situation. As soon as one female pays attention to him, the other females shift their efforts toward courting him.

It's a universal phenomenon—if you appear desirable, more members of the opposite sex will desire you. The appearance of popularity automatically raises your popularity. It's not a bad evolutionary system—if you see a potential mate being pursued by members of the opposite sex, it pays to check it out. There's a better-than-even chance the potential mate has some superior quality that will lead to a brood of high-survival kids.

"SKKKAWWK!" An even larger female *Utahraptor* now interrupts the scene, cutting in on the older female who's been displaying to the young male. This newly arrived female is stupendous—six hundred pounds bigger than he is—and is totally buffed, with huge muscles in her shoulders, thighs, and calves.

He tries to look away, to avoid having to give a response to the dance. She wheels around, coming at him sideways.

"Skrrawk . . . skrrawk . . . skrrawk."

She's insistent. She repeats the beginning moves of the courtship routine, demanding that he reply.

He steps sideways. There's another strange female,

more slender than the dinosaur Valkyrie in front of him. She has an exceptionally bright red snout-patch. He nods to her.

She nods back and commences a low-key dance.

"Sssssssssss." The big female lurches, half dancing, half threatening, her mouth wide open. She turns toward the young female, then back to the male, then back to the young female.

The young female looks away, avoiding eye contact. She turns and slides sideways, putting distance between herself and the Valkyrie.

The young male feels his Jacobson organ fill up with dueling pheromones. A dozen female *Utahraptors* have opened up their throat-glands, narrow slits on the underside of their lower jaws. Each gland releases a potent cocktail of sexually provocative molecules.

The giant female advances fast, in a series of runs. He can't avoid looking at her massive muzzle.

THHHHHHNK!

He's bumped very hard. This female is very insistent—and pissed off that he refuses to play his part in the ritual. The raptor dance is a duet. One partner makes a move, and the other must respond, inducing the first partner to continue. Either partner can break off the ceremony, but usually the breakup comes after the two partners have danced for many minutes, checking each other out, evaluating size, vigor, health, and athletic prowess.

Thnk! He gets another forceful nudge from the monstrous female. Her behavior is becoming uncontrolled—stoked by unnatural levels of competitiveness.

He still refuses to join the duet.

Snp.

He flinches. He can see a tiny red spot at the base of his shoulder. She's bitten him. Love and hate are adjacent emotions in the mating season.

FWWWNNK!

A flying object sends the huge female sprawling twelve feet. She slides on her back into the flowers, looks up and emits shrieks of rage, beating the branches with fury. An avalanche of pink flowers cascades down from the tree and gradually hides her from view.

The young male draws himself up to full height and stares at the object that collided with the giant female.

It's Raptor Red.

The young male tries to make himself look as small as possible. He lowers his body and lays his head down among the purple-pink flowers. He knows he's about to be fought over by two female *Utahraptors*. He's seen this happen to other males—and it's not an event he's ever looked forward to.

The giant female lying on the ground puffs out her chest and hisses. She contracts her finger-flexing muscles so that Raptor Red can see the tendons, thick as pine saplings, bulging at the wrist. The female Goliath looks awkward and clumsy sprawled out on her backside, so Raptor Red advances, making her own hissing threats.

But with one quick push-off from her thighs, the female rolls over, throws her torso four feet into the air, and lands on her feet. It's a marvelously graceful motion. Raptor Red takes a short step backward. The giant female bobs her head in a slow, exaggerated movement, as if to acknowledge the unspoken admiration for the move. And then she turns to the young male and makes a low, hoarse cooing noise.

Raptor Red half closes her eyelids and jumps forward, howling a threat-call that makes the young male cringe. But the giant female doesn't move an inch. Instead, she chomps her jaws together noisily, showing the gleaming-white row of recurved teeth. The young male can't help noticing that those teeth are of exceptional dimensions for a *Utahraptor.*

He sees the giant female's eyes locked with Raptor Red's, and he takes the opportunity to move out of the way a few yards to the right. The giant shifts her gaze for a half second, gives him an eyelid threat that means *Now don't YOU move!* and returns her stare to Raptor Red.

Raptor Red fought some female-female battles when she courted her first consort, years ago. It was all puffery and shadow-boxing, the combatants making fake charges and indulging in grandiose gestures with head and arms. Raptor Red discovered she was very proficient at this sort of Darwinian histrionics.

The giant female won't play this game. She makes no theatrical movements. She just sways back and forth on her hindlegs, the motion that raptors use just before they lunge forward to kill.

Raptor Red watches the giant's ankles. One, two, three swaying cycles. There's an almost imperceptible pause, and the ankle tendon tenses. Raptor Red throws herself to the left.

Whmmmmp! The giant's hindclaws land on the spot where Raptor Red had stood.

SssssssSSS. The long arms swing outward and a claw tip rips a thin, shallow wound down Raptor Red's calf.

Raptor Red retreats another three yards. She stares at the giant's chest—it rises and falls slowly, evenly. The female giant isn't breathing hard, and that makes her much scarier.

Raptor Red's thoughts evaluate the dreadful situation. *That one isn't normal. . . . She's not a courtship-competitor. . . . She's a murderess. . . .*

Raptor Red makes a high-pitched distress call. She listens for her sister's response. There is none. She repeats the call. Sisters are supposed to help each other in tough situations like this one. Normal *Utahraptor* genes are coded for dual-courtship, when two sisters join together to win a desirable mate.

Raptor Red tries the sister-assistance call once more, but she already knows that no help will come. She knows that her sister-bond isn't a normal one.

The female giant takes a few long, smooth strides in the direction of the young male. Raptor Red notes that the giant isn't merely huge—she's also quite limber and possesses great balance.

Raptor Red isn't ready to give up—not yet. She gives ground slowly, keeping enough space between her and the giant so she can dodge the next attack. The giant tenses. Raptor Red jumps. But she's been fooled—the giant doesn't lunge.

Raptor Red feels a twinge of panic. She begins to worry not just about losing this courtship fight, but losing her life.

The giant's eyes are bright yellowish orange and show no emotion other than a steady confidence. Raptor Red stops monitoring the ankles and watches the giant's eyelids.

The two females make a slow half-circle, the giant advancing to her left, Raptor Red retreating to her right. And then Raptor Red sees a slight flutter in the giant's eyes, a contraction of the pupil. The big female holds her breath for a moment, exhales noisily, and moves her weight back on her right foot and tail.

Raptor Red feels the hot breath of another dinosaur behind her left shoulder. She doesn't have to turn around—she knows from the musky scent that it's her consort. He starts to hiss, louder and louder.

The giant hesitates, then very slowly backs up. Raptor Red is now shoulder-to-shoulder with her consort, and they raise and lower their heads together, smacking their jaws open and shut. He snaps his muzzle forward and bites at the air a few feet from the giant's nose.

The female Goliath knows she's beaten. These two *Utahraptors* work as one double-headed adversary, and their demeanor shows that they will attack in another step or two.

The big female sighs, her head lowers, and her body language becomes submissive. She's very sad. All day males have rejected her. All day her unusual size has caused anxiety in potential mates. She's the victim of discrimination built into the courtship instinct, the inbred distrust of anyone who is too different from the norm.

With her body held low, the unhappy giant walks away, not looking back.

Raptor Red bumps her forehead against her consort's, and they make cooing noises. The male grooms the nape of her neck with his small front teeth, smells the wound on her leg, and licks it gently.

# Tank Destroyer

*What is she doing?* The young male *Utahraptor* turns his head one way, then the other, trying to understand what Raptor Red's sister is up to.

Raptor Red can't figure it out either. Her sister is grunting and growling with her head stuck down a hole in the ground. Now she pulls her head out, sticks her thumb in, and pulls. Nothing happens, so she pulls her thumb out and sticks her big left hindclaw inside the burrow.

"OOPH!" Her claw cuts through the soil, and her body falls over backward. She squints, growls, and repeats the procedure.

*She's trying to dig out furballs,* the young male concludes. *That's foolish.*

Raptors are poor diggers. Their sharp, curved claws don't make good shovels. But Raptor Red's sister has decided this morning that her chicks must have food, that furballs are food, that furballs are down in their burrows, and that she'll get them out.

"GrrrrRRRRRRRRR—OOOP!" She tries to cut away another burrow wall but falls sideways.

Ck-ck-ck-ck-ck. The furry four-pound multi clicks his gnawing teeth in defiance from three feet down. Raptor Red's sister loses what little composure she has left. She whacks at the burrow opening with both forepaws and bites the rocks embedded in the dirt, breaking three tooth crowns.

Ck-ck-ck-ck.

The young male raptor senses that sanity will return to the pack only if they find meat. He looks around, sniffing and listening. Far away there's a low, haunting sound.

WHOOOOOooo—CLUNK!

WHOOOOOooooo—CLUNK!

Raptor Red picks up the sound too—she doesn't recognize it. Her sister doesn't pay any attention—she's too busy trying to untangle her thumbs from roots growing around a multi burrow.

"Whooooooooooo—clunk!"

But the young male thinks he knows what the sound means. It's a noise he heard three years ago, when he was still with his own family. A sound that may mean a pack of *Utahraptors* can do something otherwise impossible—kill the spike-armored herbivore.

The young male gets up and starts down the hill. Raptor Red looks at him, gets up, looks at her sister, and sits down. Her sister isn't budging. In fact, she's stuck, with both arms and her left foot entangled in the base of a small tree growing over a big burrow.

Raptor Red calls to her sister. Her sister grunts, pulls

herself free, and turns away, refusing eye contact, a gesture that says, *I won't go hunting with that male friend of yours.*

Raptor Red gets up again and nudges her sister's neck gently. There is no reaction.

Whmmmp!

Raptor Red kicks her sister's ribs hard. Her sibling's eyes fly open, and she raises her head in a jerk.

With a deep sigh, Raptor Red's sister stretches her thighs and ankles, raises her body off the ferns in slow motion, and stands up. The family needs food.

The two sisters trot downslope, and the chicks follow.

WHOOOOOO—CLUNKKK!

Raptor Red pauses. The noise is much louder now, and she can hear an undercurrent of struggle-sounds—heavy feet pushing in the mud, giant unknown creatures huffing and puffing and snorting.

A canebrake of tall horsetail plants blocks her view.

WhhhhhOOO—THUNK-CLUNK-OOOOF!

CRASH!

A wide, ugly object smashes through the horsetails. The thing wriggles back and forth in a huge arc, breaking off the brittle horsetail stems.

Raptor Red backs up.

WHACK-WHACK-CRASH!

The object grows larger—it's a horrible headless monster with a long tapered neck. Sharp-edged chunks of bone armor stick out in every direction.

CRUNNNCH!

The monster's four-toed paws squash the horsetails flat. Raptor Red backs up even further. She weaves her head back and forth, trying to figure out this armor-plated apparition.

At the end of the neck, where the head should be, the

monster carries a small, solid ball of bone devoid of eyes, ears, and nose.

Whunk-CLUNK! Something strong and heavy rams the headless monster and pushes it another ten feet through the horsetail thicket.

Raptor Red sees a strange, slitlike mouth open up at the base of the creature's neck. The mouth emits a dense cloud of gas.

Snff-snff—SNFF!

Raptor Red's snout takes in a sample of the gas. It's methane, mixed with more malodorous scents.

Her brain rings with recognition: *That's belly gas—that's gas from some herbivore's gut!*

She's been watching the monster from the wrong end. The bone ball is at the end of the tail.

WOOOOOOOO. She sees the real head emerge as the armor-plated beast continues to back up. The deep, resonating hoot comes from the echo chambers in the snout, just in front of an unbelievably wide forehead. Overhanging the large, bright red eyeball is a thick triangle of armor.

It's a *Gastonia* species, far wider and heavier than the ones Raptor Red has met before.

WOOOOO—WOOOO—WHUNK!

The wide-bellied beast's hooting is cut short by a heavy blow to its forehead. Another gaston is ramming from the opposite direction.

WooWHUNK! The first gaston rams back, meeting its adversary forehead to forehead.

Then the two combatants pause, their chests heaving with exhaustion. One of the gastons tries to hoot, but its energy level has fallen too low.

Raptor Red moves quietly around the two grunting beasts. Her young male is already in the thicket, standing motionless. The *Utahraptor*-dappled camouflage works well here. The two predators are nearly invisible.

WWWWWWOOOP!

CRASH!

The thicket opens. Plant debris is flung everywhere. A third bull gaston bursts out of the horsetails and stands bellowing in front of the other two. There's a pause as the three bulls look one another over. The newcomer snorts like a steam locomotive and charges. He rams one of the other bulls with his forehead, hitting his opponent's eyebrow spike and twisting its head around.

Raptor Red and her young male consort hunker down behind a pile of thick horsetail stems and watch the action.

The young male has led Raptor Red to a gaston lek, a parcel of land where every year the big armored bulls whack each other on the forehead while the females watch and evaluate the battle. It's dangerous to be around the lek when *Gastonia* pheromones are in the air, and *Gastonia* tempers are short-fused.

Raptor Red knows what all Early Cretaceous meat-eaters know: Armor-plated gastons are nearly immune to all forms of attack. She once watched her parents try and fail to kill small gastons. She's tried herself, with miserable results. The problem isn't the sheer bulk of the gastons—even the biggest are only two tons—smaller than a big iguanodon, much smaller than an astro.

The problem is the highly active, martial-arts style of gaston defense. Their heads, necks, torsos, and tails are covered with a flexible coat of armor, bone plates from an inch to a foot long, all interconnected within a tightly woven layer of the toughest ligaments.

Even if it stood stone still, an adult gaston would be very hard for a *Utahraptor* to kill. The only unprotected spots are the underside of the belly. But gastons don't stand still. When attacked, they lower their spiked heads and lurch forward, swinging their necks back and forth. The row of armor starts above the eye and continues aft along the side of the neck and above the shoulder. One favorite gaston tactic is to twist the forequarters to one side, trapping an unwary predator's leg in a half circle of protruding hornlike points.

Even more dangerous is the gaston's rear defense. The base of the tail is of exceptional width, and it's all muscle. One quick contractile spasm can pull the entire tail around full circle, driving the tail spikes into the thigh or chest of a carnivore.

*Gastonia* and its close kin gravitate to water holes and moist meadows, so nearly every adult *Utahraptor* has had at least one run-in with these Early Cretaceous tanks. The results of the confrontations are nearly all the same: *Utahraptors* with crushed toes, lacerated calf muscles, bruised ribs, and dislocated shoulders.

However, this young male raptor has a plan. He comes from a family line of *Utahraptor* that has found a solution to the gaston problem. Generations ago, his ancestors discovered purely by chance the one tactic that will work against an adult bull. Then his grandparents learned it by watching his great-grandparents. His parents learned it by watching his grandparents.

Carnivores—smart carnivores—are like that. They're flexible. They're observant. So different carnivore family lines tend to acquire a unique set of family heirlooms— bits and pieces of wisdom handed down by the young mimicking the adults.

The young male leads Raptor Red through the edge of the canebrake. She's very uneasy. Snorting, puffing, hooting bull gastons are all around, ramming each other with vigor.

The two raptors reach the far side of the canebrake, where a sluggish stream dissipates itself into a series of shallow pools. There's no ramming of bulls here. There's no loud hooting. This is the loser's locker room where players are sent after they're thrown out of the game. Bull gastons, bruised and battered, trudge over here to get away from the winners, to drink at the pools of water, and to roll in the mud to medicate their wounds.

Gastons are not smart dinosaurs. Their adult brains are only slightly larger than a crocodile's of the same body bulk. That's big by cold-blooded standards but puny compared to a raptor's. When gastons are in their herds of up to fifty strong, the massed might of so many armored bodies is better than high intelligence. But when a bull gaston is alone and injured and exhausted, he's at his most vulnerable.

Raptor Red sees another *Utahraptor* snout emerge, tentatively, through the six-foot horsetails. It's her sister. She looks nervous too.

Raptor Red doesn't know what the next step is. She looks over to the young male. She'll trust his judgment. This is the first time she has followed the lead of a male since she lost her mate under the dead *Astrodon*, many days ago.

Her sister doesn't trust anybody. But she decides to go along with the other two, simply because her chicks are hungry again and the pack hasn't detected any easy prey today. A *Utahraptor* mother with chicks in tow can't expect to bring home the needed meat by herself.

The young male moves to the farthest pool and slinks down into the thicket. The two sisters follow closely.

They watch a sorry parade of defeated bulls. Some are youngsters, gaston males who've tried their luck at the lek for the first time—these chaps are beaten but unbroken. They've withdrawn from combat because they sense that they're not yet heavy enough to meet older bulls on equal terms.

The middle-aged bulls are more sullen. Many have been fathers in seasons past but were displaced by bulls larger or stronger or meaner. These fellows are still dangerous—they've got pent-up aggression they'll unleash on any animal that happens by.

Crash! A big bull suddenly turns on a younger male gaston and whacks it on the torso. It's a stupid move. The young bull is armored here with bone spikes, and one of the points jabs the older animal in the eye socket.

The wounded bull turns around awkwardly and ambles off, hooting. The younger bull backs away, scared.

The raptors just wait.

Raptor Red becomes alert. A very wide bull is approaching. He's walking slowly, with even steps. Raptor Red senses that this bull is special. He's not severely injured. He's not limping. But something is missing.

His light has gone out.

His eyes have a dull, constant stare. He looks but doesn't focus on anything. He doesn't react to the other defeated bulls.

Inside his small gaston brain, this male has given up. Too many spring ramming-contests. Too many seasons with his body pumped up with hormones. This is the third year he's left the mating grounds without a female consort, and his biological clock has wound down—he's genetically superfluous. The genes that run his behavior don't provide specific orders for an elderly loser. Why bother? Even if he tries his best, his chances of fathering offspring next year are too low.

The young male raptor moves cautiously through the thicket, following the tired bull. Raptor Red and her sister follow.

The bull plods through a pool of muddy water and lies down. The warm water feels good. He rolls halfway onto his left side, then to his right, letting the mud ooze into countless bruises.

The male raptor starts to twitch in anticipation.

The bull drags his body into the deeper part of the wallow. He rolls onto his left side and closes his eyes, his body two-thirds submerged. His brain is lulled into a stupor by the warm, soothing bath.

The male raptor moves swiftly, quietly. He strikes with his hindfeet at the exposed gaston underside. Raptor Red strikes immediately after.

The bull howls. His legs flex helplessly. But the raptor attack pushes him onto his back. Raptor Red's sister jumps onto his belly and rips him open. The older chick joins her mother, attacking with adult-style ferocity.

The bull gaston's mind succumbs to the attack before his body does. He's aware of his own death, but in the final moments he is free of pain and fear.

---

The raptor pack feeds on the bull for three hours, ignored by the other gastons, who feel no loss at his death. Raptor Red's sister eats with noisy satisfaction—this is the first time she's had *Gastonia* bull, and she finds its texture and taste quite satisfying. She bumps and nuzzles Raptor Red in gestures of victory and appreciation. She nuzzles her oldest chick too, in celebration of her taking on the mature role of killer.

Raptor Red's sister is in a rare good mood. But she still won't look at the young male and she won't acknowledge his head-bobbing. He tries to bump her snout with his, but she answers with a curled-lip snarl, and he backs away and sits by himself. Raptor Red looks back and forth, from her sister to her male consort. Then she gives him an especially long, affectionate muzzle-nuzzle.

When night falls, the well-fed chicks find their usual

sleeping places, side by side next to their mother. Raptor Red pushes open a space between a chick and her sister with her right foot and lowers herself down. She closes her eyes.

Something isn't right, and she snaps her eyelids open. The male is still standing up, looking around awkwardly, sniffing in the direction of the raptor sisters. He shuffles off to a pile of dry brush and starts to scrape a temporary nest together with his hindclaws. Raptor Red notices that he is very unskillful at this activity.

Raptor Red sits up. It's warm and comforting, being wedged among her blood relatives. Still, she has a churning feeling in her head and it gets worse as she watches the male's pitiful attempts to construct his nest.

She extends her knees and ankle joints, rising above her snoring kin, and steps out of the sleeping group. The hole she leaves among the somnolent bodies is immediately filled by a chick leaning to its left and her sister leaning to her right.

Raptor Red walks over to the male and knocks him in the flank with her snout. Then she gathers fallen branches with vigorous sweepings of her hands and feet. There aren't enough, so she reaches up with her jaws and breaks down some fresh branches from the trees.

When the nest is big enough for two, she sits. The male stares for a minute, walks slowly over to her and lowers his body with great care, leaving a foot of space between their torsos.

Raptor Red sighs and leans toward him. As she drifts off to sleep, she can feel him just barely begin to apply his own body pressure back toward her.

# Famine and
# the Wing Shadow

It's the time of summer drought. Streams fail, and the
ponds dry up into dead layers of sun-hardened mud. The
herds of plant-eaters flee the lowlands, and the predators
who remain must squabble over a dwindling supply of
meat. And it's the time when famine pulls apart the social
bonds of *Utahraptor* packs. The carnivore parents become
lax in watching where their youngsters wander off to.

The alpha male deinonych can't believe his good for-
tune. There, within easy striking distance, is a *Utahraptor*
chick, wandering alone, without an adult in sight. The deinonych holds his 130-pound body as low as he can and
chirps a *hurry up!* message to his two brothers.

*We can kill that chick—before its parents know we're here,* he thinks. He's hungry. But he'd try to kill the chick even if he were well fed. Predator species have spite hardwired into their behavior. Killing the competition before it's grown up is always a good ecological strategy for meat-eaters.

The little *Utahraptor* chick has wandered off from its pack for the first time in its life. There's no food back at the temporary nest the adults have built, and the baby raptor is sniffing at holes where the multis hide, the roly-poly furballs shaped like woodchucks.

"Chck-chck-chck . . . chck." The chick runs to a hole where a plump multi is making its alarm call.

Fwwoop! The multi disappears down its burrow as if it were sucked by a vacuum.

*"Chck-chck-chck-chck-chck-CHCK!"* Another multi twenty feet away makes a loud protestation at the chick's presence. The foolish little *Utahraptor* turns and runs at him.

Just as the chick reaches his burrow, the multi ducks underground, and a third furball starts clicking his lungs out ten yards in the other direction.

*Stupid chick—this will be easy,* the deinonych leader thinks as he watches the little raptor get dizzy running back and forth across the multi colony.

The alpha deinonych crawls along a dry arroyo till he's at the edge of the colony. With every zigzag maneuver, the chick gets closer and closer to the hidden predators. The furballs are so busy playing the decoy game with the chick that they don't notice the deinonychs.

But up at three hundred feet, a very alert set of eyes has been watching. A huge white dactyl has been making silent spirals down from a thousand-foot altitude. He banks steeply to his left and makes a low-angle pass at the multi colony.

Dust clouds erupt in the overgrazed soil between the multi burrows. The dactyl's immense white wings stir up a tornado of dried multi droppings and plant bits, and the swirling maelstrom of dirt and dung blinds the dei-nonychs. The *Utahraptor* chick falls over, gets up, runs back toward its nest, trips in a multi hole, gets up again, and is gone from view before the dust settles and the dei-nonychs can see what has happened.

To the deinonychs and the *Utahraptor*, the situation is life or death. To the dactyl, it's a game.

The dactyl climbs to five hundred feet to survey the scene he's created. He likes intervening in the lives of predators—it amuses him. He's spent all his waking hours amusing himself, ever since that day in the spring when he decided he would not take a mate.

The great white dactyl is a very special case. He's sixty years old, healthy, fit, his senses keen. He's observed many generations of raptors in their struggles to raise families. He's helped raise dozens of broods of his own species, with the help of five mates, all now dead.

Dactyls live longer than dinosaurs—a general advan-tage of life on the wing. If it survives the dangers of youth, a young adult dactyl can look forward to thirty or forty years, average lifespan. This particular dactyl is an old-timer even by pterodactyl standards. And he has decided this year that he has had enough. He intends never to breed again. He's a biological oddity—a widower who is content.

The hidden hand of natural selection is nearly every-where. Every time a dinosaur makes a choice that affects its reproductive success, the beast is playing the evolution game. Every time a bird helps her sister or her daughter or her granddaughter raise a brood, the act is recorded in the book of genetic success. Every time a turtle seeks a mate, the deed affects the standing of the turtle's genes in the Darwinian playoff.

But the old dactyl has bowed out of the Great Game.

He's ended his own contribution to his gene pool entirely. He doesn't breed himself, and he doesn't help his kin to breed. In fact, he avoids all others of his species. He's outlived his Darwinian usefulness, and he's enjoying it immensely.

Joy is built in by evolution to keep animals doing what's good for their genes. The great white dactyl flies because it gives him pleasure. Since he has given up the responsibilities of reproduction, he's free to make up the rules of life as he goes along. He likes soaring to heights where he can spy on the earthbound dinosaurs below. He likes flaunting his aerial expertise by zooming at the predators who rule the underbrush.

Pound for pound, his brain is even larger for his size than the raptors', and big brains demand to be exercised. So the white dactyl invents games. He dives at giant plant-eating dinosaurs, just to see them panic and mill around nervously, the adults trying to shield their calves. He zips close to the water when the crocs are sunning themselves. He likes to see the long sequence of splashes erupt as one crocodile after another launches itself into the algae-green water.

And the old dactyl likes eating. He likes sharks, lungfish, pond turtles, baby crocodiles, and the eggs of other dactyl species. The drought has cut off his seafood and poultry, but he's in no danger of gastronomic deprivation. He has learned how to get *Utahraptors* to serve him aged red meat.

———

Raptor Red's sister didn't notice that one of the little chicks had wandered away from the pack. When the chick comes squawking back, she gives it a perfunctory greeting that does little to reassure the hungry, frightened youngster.

The young male watches the interaction between mother and chick, and he gets more and more worried. Raptor Red's pack seems to be coming apart: The social bonds are getting weaker, and he's afraid the group will disintegrate if the drought lasts much longer.

The raptor family has camped along one of the few rivers that is still flowing during this severe midsummer dry season. Adult raptors can go without food for a week, but they must have water every day—water to keep their nerves and muscles working, and water to cool their bodies. The small chicks suffer the most. Their fast-growing bodies make enormous demands for food, and they whine and nudge Raptor Red and her sister, begging at the adults' muzzles for food to be regurgitated. But the adults have no food.

Raptor Red looks at the chicks, then at her sister. Without making a sound or a gesture, the two adult females have come to a dreadful agreement: Soon they must abandon the two youngest chicks. Raptor Red's sister has defended her offspring with deadly vigilance for five months, but now she's ready to leave them to die.

It has to be this way. Adult predators must sacrifice their chicks so that the mothers can survive to next season, when they might breed again. The cruel calculus of evolution permits no sentimentality. "Save the children first!" is a motivation that would kill off the entire genetic line, mother and children both. It would be gene-foolish for Raptor Red's sister to risk her life now—she might have twenty more reproductive seasons, so any one set of chicks is expendable.

All through the ages, most predator young die during the famine season—raptor chicks die in the Early Cretaceous, just as allosaur chicks died in the preceding Jurassic, and just as lion cubs will starve to death, abandoned in the summer on the Serengeti.

The *Utahraptor* chicks don't realize that this could be their last day. But they do have an instinctive urgency; their genes have turned on their last-ditch defense, a pitiful display of begging designed to appeal to their adult protectors.

Raptor Red's stomach tightens into a knot. She feels very empty and looks away from the chicks. The young male walks slowly over and bumps her snout. She doesn't respond. The famine will drive them apart soon.

When the herbivore herds provide abundant victims, it's best for the pack to stay together, so that two or three raptors can bring down big, dangerous prey. But when big herbivores disappear, the raptors must revert to a more primitive mode of life, searching for biological garbage, the small prey and chewed-up leftovers of the ecosystem. That mode of life is best carried out by single predators operating alone.

Raptor Red has been there before, and so has her male consort. They know their bond is tentative. They are consorts now, not yet pledged to lifelong partnership. In Raptor Red's mind her loyalties go like this: Give up the chicks first; then if necessary, give up her consort. Only if the famine gets truly terrible will she consider leaving her sister.

In times of famine it's best to sleep during midday, so Raptor Red finds a comfortable spot, partly shaded by a dead cycad tree. The dreamtime offers a refreshing escape from hunger.

———

Raptor Red jerks her head, suddenly awake. She's been daydreaming about food. She's seen lovely iguanodon haunches, pink and fresh, floating by. Then there were images of plump torsos, neatly stripped of their armored skin, dancing slowly with each other.

She chomps her teeth twice. Now she can feel the meat against her gums. Hmmmm . . . meat, wonderful meat, soft and warm. She closes her eyes tight, and a chorus line of trees pull up their roots and saunter around, their trunks metamorphosing into iguanodon drumsticks.

Chmp—chmp—chmp. Her jaws make involuntary chewing motions.

She opens one eye. Great piles of cumulus clouds move slowly. She closes the eye. The clouds turn pale pink, then red, then red-brown. They're airy mounds of liver now, succulent and warm. She squeezes her eyes shut. She feels her body become lighter. She's airlifted upward. She soars among the liver-clouds. She lowers her muzzle and dives into the top of the biggest one.

Chmp—chmp—chmp—chmp. She can feel the soft dino-innards against her gums.

Her empty stomach moans, and something twists inside. The liver-clouds turn pale. Their texture and taste evaporate. Raptor Red's eyes half open. She sees the clear sky. Her conscious brain takes over—insisting that the parade of dino-steaks exists only in that other reality, dreamtime. But she doesn't want to leave the feast, and she tries to reenter the dream. She closes her eyes, and the liver-clouds reappear, but farther away.

Raptor Red's dream is cut short by a wide object passing over her head. Something was flying just a few yards above, something very large.

The instinctive fear of pterodactyls kicked in the millisecond the wing-wake touched Raptor Red's head. Even with her eyes closed, the slight cooling effect of the disturbed air is enough to trigger the dactyl-fear response. When she was a chick, this instantaneous response saved her life more than once.

She ducks and leans to her left. She sees a grand expanse of white, the underside of a set of wings many yards wide. The winged creature makes no sound whatever. In a few seconds the dactyl is a hundred yards away, spiraling upward on thermal currents generated by the morning sun, recycled into the air through the heat given off by the warmth of the soil.

Raptor Red sits up straight and watches the dactyl. The recognition centers in her brain register the wingtip markings—three green bands. She instantly relaxes a bit. She raises her muzzle and sniffs deeply. A faint olfactory trail lingers in the air. It's a familiar scent. She knows this particular winged beast. He's been her distant companion for as long as she can remember. He's never been a threat to her or her family.

The big dactyl rises rapidly to a thousand feet and pauses. Then he utters a quick burst of chirps. Raptor Red's male consort and her sister are awake now too, staring intently at the aerobatics.

The dactyl zooms down in a dive, crossing over the raptor pack at fifty feet, then climbing another hundred to zip over the treeline to the south.

The raptor sisters raise their bodies up, extending knees and ankles and lean forward in anticipation. They know what to expect. The young male follows their lead.

The dactyl disappears behind the trees. Raptor Red blinks and stares and blinks.

Without a sound the white wings with green bars reappear in a near-vertical climb, five hundred yards away. Six raptor eyes are fixed on the movement.

Raptor Red knows this aerial display might mean fresh food soon. Real food—not dreamtime drumsticks.

She remembers well how she met the white dactyl, years ago. It was when she was taken out on her first hunt. The *Utahraptor* family had gathered around an armor-plated dinosaur, one of three whose drowned bodies the adult raptors had found on a riverbank. Raptor Red and

her sisters had been led by their mother to the one-ton
carcasses, fragrant with sundried blood and fresh viscera
spilled on the pale yellow sand.

Her mother had prepared the chicks' meal. Great
gashes were ripped into the torsos of the prey, gashes big
enough for Raptor Red to stick her head in up to her
shoulders. It was an exciting, adult experience. Up till
then, Raptor Red and her sister had fed on regurgitated
meat slabs, brought back to the nest in the throat pouches
of their mother or father.

Raptor Red's eyes had widened when she saw where
the meat slabs came from. She was vibrating with excitement when she got to rip her own meat portions from the
still-warm carcass. Then the dactyls came. They swooped
low, and her parents snarled. For the rest of the day, she
watched her mother and father chase off the dactyl scavengers. But they never left—the vulturine pterodactyls
had hung around, clattering their yard-long jaws in exasperation.

On the third day the raptor family had eaten their fill.
The adults didn't care about the airborne scavengers anymore. A flock of black-winged dactyls, *Ornithodesmus*,
swarmed over the carcasses and began to tear off meat
strips—when a tremendous white object flew at great
speed into the mass of wings and bodies. Black-winged
dactyls scattered like feathers from an exploded seabird.

Raptor Red was fascinated by that white dactyl. It in-
spired fear in all other flying creatures, but it never tried to
attack the raptor chicks or come close to the adults. Time
and time again she would see the same white flying giant
appear at kill sites after the raptors had satisfied their appetites. Again and again Raptor Red and her sisters
watched the lone white giant disperse all the other scavengers.

Raptor Red gradually accepted the white dactyl as a

benign element in her world, an elegant aerial camp-follower who never pushed his participation in the feast.

Raptor Red's parents didn't worry about their chicks when the white dactyl was around. He functioned like an aloof baby-sitter or sheep dog. He kept the other flying predators away, and often chased the smaller land predators too. Raptor Red learned that raptors could, on occasion, profit from watching the white dactyl. When the great white beast flew in ostentatious circles a quarter-mile away, the raptor pack would investigate. Often they'd find a big dead dinosaur half-hidden in the undergrowth. The raptors would feed. The dactyl, whose snout was too weak to break through the skin of an intact carcass, would wait patiently until he was allowed to glean scraps from the dissected body.

On this day in the middle of the August drought, the appearance of the white dactyl is most welcome. The *Utahraptor* sisters get up and lead the chicks at a trot toward the sand flat beyond the treeline. Raptor Red's male consort sits in confusion. He's uneasy with all dactyls—but he decides to trust Raptor Red's judgment and rushes to catch up.

The white dactyl is very fond of the giant raptors in Raptor Red's family. They seem to have a more immediate effect on their surroundings than any other species. And they respect his position as Dactyl Emeritus of the ecosystem, a position that entitles him to scraps from every kill the big raptors make. He's spotted a mummified *Astrodon* body, and he wants his raptor friends to help share this multi-ton hoard of meat and entrails. He can't break through the mummified hide himself, but he knows that Raptor Red and her sister can.

The white dactyl definitely does *not* like *Utahraptors'* smaller relative, the deinonychs. Those raptors travel in large unruly packs, and they're rude to dactyls. They've tried to ambush him when he's fed from their kills. So he buzzes them when they least expect it.

He never leads deinonychs to carcasses, the way he's doing now for Raptor Red's pack.

The raptor sisters break through the dense thicket of saplings and rush out over the hot sand. They pause, sniffing the stale air. *There it is!* their olfactory systems scream inside their brains. They run to the spot where a huge carcass lies buried under sand and driftwood.

*Utahraptor* claws pull through the suntanned hide.

Ribs are broken by raptor hindlegs pulling on claws hooked through the astro's chest.

Raptor Red and her sister push their scale-covered snouts through the gaps ripped into the body cavity—and find gastronomical heaven. Hunks of liver and lung, nicely seasoned by early decomposition, slide down the sisters' throats. It's a splendid feeling.

Raptor Red's mood changes as her digestive enzymes turn on all through her stomach and intestines. The imminent prospect of loneliness evaporates. She grabs a big piece of astro innards and bounds over to the young male, bobbing her head.

*For me?* he asks with a submissive lowering of his head.

*YES!* Raptor Red answers by shoving the food right up to his upper lip.

The big dactyl waits till the adult *Utahraptors* are finished, then pokes his long snout deep into the carcass and gleans select morsels.

The chicks tiptoe up to the carcass, still afraid of the dactyl. They nip at shreds of meat hanging from leg joints. Soon the sensation of filled bellies makes them bolder. One of the young chicks makes mock-charges at the big old dactyl, who's perched on a low branch. Holding its head low and growling in a falsetto voice, the chick runs forward, then jams its toes into the sand, screeching to a stop with its head raised and mouth open.

The old-timer in the tree doesn't move. He lets the chick get closer and closer. Each mock-attack makes the chick braver—and more self-deluded. At its sixth charge the *Utahraptor*-ette stomps its feet directly below the branch where the dactyl sits like a statue.

There's no sound, no movement from the big flier. His wings remain tightly folded against his body, making his body mass appear small.

The chick is puzzled. It rises as high as it can go, sniffing loudly. Its snout tip touches the branch where the dactyl sits. It moves the snout to the underside of the dactyl toes. The chick nudges the dactyl's feet.

The white wings snap open in one quick movement. The great wing-finger, equivalent to our human ring finger, sweeps upward at the wrist, unfurling the immense white wing surface. In an instant the dactyl's size seems to increase a hundredfold.

The chick is enveloped by the dactyl's shadow.

Clunk!

The chick tries to accelerate backward but falls over instead. It flails its arms and legs, trying to get up, turn around, and run away all at once.

The dactyl stands, wings outstretched, motionless.

The chick tumbles over itself and rolls up to Raptor Red. It gets up, mouth wide open in horror, and leans hard against Raptor Red's side. She glances sideways at the chick and gives it a rude shove.

The chick hurls itself toward its mother, squealing.

Raptor Red's sister looks over at her chick, at the dactyl, then back at the chick, then resumes chewing on some gray-brown meat from the inner thigh of the dinosaur carcass.

# Bubbles

The white dactyl decides he'll make some bubbles.

He's watched the raptor pack for half a day. He's eaten as much as he can without hindering his ability to take off from the ground. Now he's bored again.

The breeze is blowing hard over the sand flat. The white dactyl hops off the tree and feels the hot sand under his hands and feet. He walks batwise, with knees turned outward and his elbows strongly bent. He looks awkward and uncomfortable, but the ultrastrong chest muscles that power his flight give his arms the strength to hop quickly over the ground.

The white dactyl is a very cautious walker. He will go for a stroll only when there's a strong, constant breeze, enough wind energy to lift his body if he unfurls his wings. He never walks far in still air. That would be suicidal—too many land predators would be tempted to run him down.

His three walking foreclaws dig into the sand at every step, cutting deep incisions each time. Right next to the clawprints comes the narrow hindpaw, with its four small, straight claws.

The trackway he leaves behind on the sand flat looks wide and inelegant compared with Raptor Red's footprints. The white dactyl is a distant cousin of the raptor's—both could trace their ancestry to fast-stepping land predators. But dactyl limbs have become ill-suited to land locomotion. The three sharp, narrow, hooklike foreclaws on each hand are perfect for hanging on to trees and cliffs but inefficient for walking. The dactyl chest muscles are gigantic flight engines that power the wings but cannot give a fast terrestrial gait.

The dactyl's strongest extremity is his giant finger, increased in length and bulk a thousandfold over the usual dinosaurian condition. This is the flight finger, thicker and stronger than the dactyl's thigh, the flexible strut that holds up the entire wing leading edge.

The white dactyl does have a sense of how different he is from all his distant dinosaurian kin. He puts all life into two categories: can-fly; can't-fly. He knows that if it's clever, any can-fly can avoid injury and death from can't-flys.

FWP! He jumps across a narrow streambed onto a tall river-channel sandbar. He swivels his thin, flexible neck around to check out the raptor pack. Three chicks are asleep in the warm afternoon sun. Three adults are nearly motionless too. No sign of nervousness.

The low-angle sun highlights the long line of dactyl footprints leading from the kill site to the river. The white dactyl cocks his head and stares. He's used to seeing dinosaur footprints from the air, laid out map-fashion. He can identify a dozen dino-species from two hundred feet up from their characteristic stride pattern and foot geometry. But he hasn't seen his own tracks so close and clearly marked before. He knows how to identify dactyl tracks from the air—by their widely spaced imprints and the un-usual three-fingered hands—and he enjoys a moment of self-realization as he surveys the record of his own foot-steps.

It's interesting, and the sight relieves his boredom for a moment.

He finds a spot where the wind is screened by a high sand-dune crest. He peers into a pool of murky water. There's a brownish object wriggling in slow motion in the bottom muck.

His beak stabs down, and he swallows a juvenile lung-fish, a foot and a half long.

But he's not really here to fish.

Zip—blb—blb—blb.

Big brown bubbles rise lazily to the surface as he ex-hales with his entire face under water.

Pip—pip—pip—

The bubbles pop as he neatly pricks each one in turn with his beak tip.

He invented this game a month ago, when he ac-cidently coughed underwater while trying to catch a tur-tle. He was intrigued by the big bubbles that hung around the water surface. And since his basic approach to Nature is "When in doubt, poke it!" he had the exhilarating expe-rience of exploding bubbles bursting around his snout.

Blb—blb—grrg. An especially corpulent bubble, the largest he has blown, rises and sits like a crystalline dome, motionless on the surface.

He looks with admiration at his handiwork. A water-strider bug zigzags crazily around the bubble, bumping into it repeatedly. A dry fern fragment drifts in on the wind and falls down onto the bubble's roof, sticking there. Now a flotilla of smaller bubbles joins their flagship, some adhering to the big bubble, some merging with it.

The white dactyl is startled to see the sky reflected in a spherical distortion, the bubble acting like a fish-eye lens. He cocks his head and stares very closely.

He sees clouds in the bubble, and a dactyl flock very far away—and a raptor face very close.

His whole body jerks up into an emergency take-off. His left wingtip hits water. His feet spread sand everywhere. With panicked clumsiness he ascends the sandbar and catches the breeze. He's aloft and downwind in a few seconds.

Raptor Red doesn't even look at the dactyl disappearing along the riverbank. She's absorbed with the thousands of bubbles, large and small, left by his sudden take-off.

Exploration is mental play, and big-brained carnivores are the most playful in any ecosystem. Raptor Red was enjoying the sense of well-fed well-being on the sand flat when she saw the dactyl doing something strange out on the river. She has no fear of this dactyl—and no desire to eat it either. So curiosity took over.

She's been watching the bubble game for several minutes. She shares with the dactyl a predator's love of slap-and-grab games. Anything that's small and that moves suddenly is a target for grabbing. When she was a chick, she learned snout-eye coordination by slapping at leaves that danced across the ground in the wind. As a young adult she sharpened her reflexes by trying two-handed grabs at the multis, the plump furballs who live in colonial burrows like Cretaceous prairie dogs.

She's never tried to slap a bubble.

She sticks her muzzle into the water and pulls it out. Too slow. The bubbles are tiny and unsatisfying.

SPLSH! She whacks her muzzle into the pool. Too fast. Ripples everywhere, and foam, but no big fat bubbles.

She sputters and coughs. She can't figure it out. She's bothered—most of her life she's been able to learn new predator tricks by mimicry. She's watched her parents, her sisters, even raptors of other species.

This time she gives up. The capacity to learn is a combination of inborn intelligence and long experience. The white dactyl is too clever and too long-lived and too wise. Raptor Red will never know all that he knows. She looks up, scanning the sky. The white dactyl is already far away.

And he is in a foul mood. He dislikes being forced to take off suddenly. He dislikes having a dinosaur creep up close behind him—even a dinosaur he considers friendly. He dislikes not being in complete control.

He ascends to a thousand feet, making grumbly noises to himself. He checks out the *Utahraptor* sisters and their chicks. He sees a *Deinonychus* pack, a big one. Twenty of the medium-size raptors are camped downwind ten miles from Raptor Red.

The white dactyl knows what will make his bad mood disappear. He rises slowly upwind and makes a wide turn to get the sun directly behind him. Then he closes his wings and dives.

He builds up speed fast. He adjusts his dive angle with slight movements of the membrane between thigh and tail. At 200 feet he opens his wings and flattens the dive.

He comes over the treeline at 150 miles per hour in nearly level flight. The deinonychs have no warning. The alpha male is standing up, scratching himself behind the ear, enjoying the warmth of the sun on his back.

FWOOOOOOOOP!

The deinonych ducks at the last millisecond and loses his balance, falling into a group of subadult males, who scatter. The white dactyl scores with his beak tip, leaving a small but painful wound on the alpha male's hip.

As he ascends again in the afternoon air, the white dactyl can see the entire *Deinonychus* pack milling around in great agitation.

The old pterodactyl feels much better now.

# Always Go for the One That Limps

*Too fast, too fast, too fast* . . . Raptor Red is hidden in a brown tangle of ferns, dead still. Only her bright eye betrays her presence, watching a flock of ostrich dinos run by.

*Much too fast.* She blinks, a long deliberate blink she uses to clean dust off her eyeball, the sort of blink an eagle will use while it waits for the ideal moment to dive down on an antelope fawn. Her nictitating membrane, a clear, moist sheet of tissue that travels sideways across her eye, passes over her eyeball like a high-tech windshield washer.

Raptor Red knows she must operate at peak performance in all senses, all locomotor organs, all powers of reason. She and her sister and the young male face a tough challenge today: feeding themselves and satisfying the voracious appetites of three fast-growing chicks, all on a diet of ostrich dinosaurs, the smartest, fastest, most difficult prey a raptor dares to attack.

But Raptor Red has great confidence in the efficiency of her newly enlarged pack. The addition of the young male has doubled the kill ratio. The older chick helps too when she can. When operating as a foursome, the *Utahraptor* pack succeeds in half of their attacks.

*Too fast—too fast.* Raptor Red watches the ostrich dinos prance by. She can see the young male raptor at work. He is spooking the flock, moving around the far side, exposing his head and shoulders for a few seconds so the ostrich dinos will get agitated and move over toward the spot where Raptor Red and her sister are hiding.

*Much too fast.* A big ostrich dino hen, three hundred pounds at least, shifts into passing gear. Her body floats in the air. Her unbelievably long shins and ankles strike down and backward in short strokes, throwing up a yellow puff of dust each time the compact toenails dig into the dried turf.

She's going more than fifty miles per hour—effortlessly. No dinosaur in the Early Cretaceous is faster. Her intelligent eyes do quick surveys right and left and behind her, her graceful swanlike neck turning constantly. This hen too is confident—confident in her powers of escape, in her supreme velocity that guarantees no dinosaur can catch her once she has reached her full speed.

The hen's sense of invulnerability comes not just from the feeling of raw power in her leg muscles. She's clever and a quick learner. She's seven years old, a mother twice, a survivor of twenty-five previous ambushes by raptors and six by the hulking acrocanthosaurs.

The hen is almost smug. She knows that there are raptors to the left and raptors to the right, and she knows that she has enough of a head start. The only thing that could bring her down right now would be if she put her foot into a burrow made by the furballs, who live in immense underground colonies. At this speed jamming a foot in a burrow would break her ankle, and she'd be dead in a few seconds.

The hen doesn't worry about the burrows. They're there. But at such a high speed she can't see them. She doesn't worry about things beyond her control.

The hen's left foot just barely touches the outer rim of a multi burrow. Inside, the family of furry mammals huddle together, wincing at the thunder of feet above. The hen stumbles once.

Raptor Red sees the misstep. She cocks her head in that direction. But the ostrich dino hen recovers without losing much speed. In three more strides she's back at maximum velocity.

Raptor Red moves her head quickly, in jerks, trying to take in all the action. The ostrich dino flock is breaking up, fragmenting into six or seven units. A light-brown blur passes—three ostrich dino chicks, half grown, almost as fast as their mother.

*Even the chicks—too fast.* Raptor Red's automatic prey-evaluation computer cranks out the discouraging results.

*THERE!* Raptor Red's eyes lock onto a male ostrich dino, far behind the mother-chick subgroup. Her visual mode changes immediately from wide-scan search to monofocus. Her keen sight has picked out that male—he's limping.

Her sister has locked on the same male. Their predator visual system is superb at picking up the slightest irregularity in the rhythm of running. The slight asymmetry of right-left leg strokes. The almost imperceptible clumsiness on one foot that shows a joint injured or diseased.

Raptor Red starts running, hunched down. She can see her sister running low down ahead. The entire ostrich dino flock veers away and picks up speed. All the ostrich dinos are pulling away from the raptor sisters.

All except one.

The raptor male leaps over the bushes, lands in a full crouch, and takes off. For a few seconds he gains on a group of hens in the middle of the flock. His short, bulgy calf muscles give him quicker acceleration than the ostrich dinos. He gets within ten feet of a young hen. But she's reaching her maximum speed now and pulls away from him.

The whole flock turns away and crosses obliquely in front of the raptor sisters.

Raptor Red's ears are full of a hundred *thud-thuds* a second, the rapid-fire beating of ostrich dino hindpaws on the earth. The dust cloud now grows to fifty feet high. Raptor Red can't see them clearly anymore, even though they are very close. Individual ostrich dinos appear as dark or light phantasms—sometimes one catches the light filtering through the dust, sometimes another is in deep shadow.

Whooooph. A big hen cuts right in front of Raptor Red's nose. She pays no attention.

Whooooph-whooooph. Two ostrich dino chicks zip by, right astern. Raptor Red feels their wake in the air behind her. But she keeps running ahead.

A big shadowy mass just misses her and flies a foot over her shoulders. It's an ostrich dino cock, leaping in terror.

For a second Raptor Red sees her sister and the older raptor chick in the dust, coming the opposite way. Raptor Red stands upright, still running. A long-neck with a nearly toothless head emerges from the dust, then disappears. Raptor Red can see a pair of slender arms with three straight claws, poking wildly.

She ducks down and just avoids being stung by the ostrich dino hands. Raptor Red catches a glimpse of the huge eyes of the ostrich dino, turning in every direction, looking for escape. The head vanishes again into the dust.

KLUMP! Something falls, hard, a few feet away.

Raptor Red slows, stops.

There is her sister, sitting on top of the male ostrich dino who was limping. He's already dead, his chest cut open by slashes of her left hindclaw.

The male raptor comes up, panting. He's run harder and longer than the rest of the pack. And it's very hot now. The dust has plugged up one nostril, and he sits down to clean the dirt out with his hindfoot.

Raptor Red's sister glares at him. He tries to pretend he doesn't see. She begins to huff and puff and pull the carcass away, toward the treeline where the two smaller chicks are waiting. They were with their mother at the beginning of the hunt an hour ago, but the heat got to be too much for them. Their mother and aunt let them get away with this lazy behavior for now.

---

As the two little chicks play with the long ankle bones of the ostrich dino—all that remains of the beast after an hour of chewing and scratching—the young male inches closer and closer to one of the youngsters. Raptor Red is watching.

The young male is only a foot away from the chick's tail tip. Raptor Red stares at the young male's lips. She won't be alarmed until she sees the upper lip curled back, uncovering the glistening ivory of the teeth.

"SQWAKKKKKKKKKK!" Raptor Red's sister comes flying through the group. Chicks scatter to both sides, like a six-seven-ten split being converted by a pro bowler. The young male rolls completely over into the defensive-submissive posture: both pairs of clawed feet, two aft, two forward, protecting his vulnerable belly, his back slightly arched against the ground.

"SssssssssHSSSSS." Raptor Red's sister gets between the chicks and the male. She paws the air with strokes of her left hind killing claw. She's serious—and he knows it. She's ninety-nine percent of the way to a kill-or-be-killed confrontation.

Raptor Red pretends that she is calm, unaware of the bloody-minded emotions being displayed. She saunters over to her sister, her back to the male, and makes groom-ing noises with her jaws a few inches from her sister's head.

For a full five seconds, the male and Raptor Red's sister just stare unblinking at each other. Raptor Red nuzzles her sister's neck. Her sister recoils and bares her teeth. Raptor Red nuzzles her neck again.

Her sister turns her head and looks at Raptor Red, eyes full of hate. But the pupils contract, and her sister turns away.

The male rolls over and slinks across the ground in the other direction.

Raptor Red is only acting calm. Inside she's agitated, torn up. She wants to be a fully mated couple with her chosen male. She has a tremendous hormonal surge. But her bond with her sister goes far back. And when the male bares his teeth at the chicks, Raptor Red feels like attack-ing him. Forces are at war inside her head, and she can't figure them out.

She looks at the male, then at her sister and the chicks. She realizes that she doesn't want to leave her sister or her chicks—that bond is strong. It's the heavy hand of kin selection, the investment a sister is willing to make in her sibling's health and happiness and in the health of her chicks. It's a form of genetic selfishness. By helping your sister and her children, you're helping your own genes survive.

Of course, genes can't plan a strategy. Genes can't think, can't feel, can't mourn the loss of a loved one. Genes can't bite, can't bleed, can't feel pain. Genes are tiny pixels of inheritance, devoid of feeling. They're short segments of chemicals, each carrying commands for building small parts of a body or small portions of programmed behavior.

Raptor Red does think and feel and weigh the conflicting demands of her young consort and her sister. She does indeed carry genes that have survived ten million raptor generations by inducing *Utahraptor* females to favor their relatives. But she's no gene-dictated automaton. The genetic bond of sisterhood works through complex emotions and a conscious sense of the right thing to do.

Raptor Red has a deep pervasive belief that what matters is getting her young relatives into the next generation of breeders. That's more important than her own individual happiness or the happiness of her mate. Genes have given her this morality, genes that gave her ancestors a bit of an edge in reproduction generation after generation. And at this moment these very same genes are producing a terrible emotional conflict.

Raptor Red is close to loving her male consort. But she knows the young male might kill her sister's chicks. And if he tries to, Raptor Red will kill him.

The crime of infanticide is built into the *Utahraptor* family system, as it is throughout nature. Male genes demand it. What's a male to do if his consort already has young from a previous mating? Those chicks don't carry his genes. The cruel arithmetic is this: The male will help his own genes most by killing the young that aren't his, so he and his mate can get started raising a new brood.

Long before the time of *Utahraptor*, infanticide was commonplace among dinosaurs and tiny mammals and frogs. And long after *Utahraptor* it will guide the actions of male lions, male alligators, and male apes.

Raptor Red belongs to a species that is making a momentous transition in family life from a male-dominated pack structure to an incipient matriarchy. The adult females have become larger and stronger than the males. They can accept or reject suitors. They tend to mate for life. The ancestral raptors had a different social system. The males were larger. They fought each other to control all the breeding females in a pack. And they'd drive away or kill the chicks from different fathers, unless the mother left the pack with her chicks and struck out on her own.

That's how Raptor Red's species got its start. A group of sisters left a big pack and descended into a dry valley where their evolutionary path diverged. The mothers obtained greater power, and they're no longer at the mercy of the alpha males.

Raptor Red and her sister still carry genes of distrust, genes that were fixed ages before, when strange males were always dangerous to chicks. And these distrustful genes are still valuable, because males can still lapse into the vicious old ways. Raptor Red has seen it. She has seen *Utahraptor* chicks pulled to pieces when a strange male bonds with a mother whose mate has died.

And Raptor Red sees the slight upcurl of the lip in her young male when the chicks bump against him. She sees him stalk the chicks when he thinks Raptor Red and her sister aren't looking.

Yes, her chosen mate, this young male who can be so courtly and attractive and graceful, still carries the genes to be a child murderer.

The young male doesn't know why he has such violent impulses toward the chicks. But he does know it upsets Raptor Red, and he doesn't want to do that. His intelligence and his devotion to Raptor Red can override ancient impulses.

The adult raptors remain in a state of extreme tension for the rest of the day. Every time the male gets up and walks around, Raptor Red's sister and her oldest chick stand with mouths open, menacing him. The younger chicks cower behind their mother, while the young male backs up and averts his eyes. Finally, as night falls and the pack must make a temporary nest, Raptor Red tries to bump snouts with her sister, who growls.

Raptor Red grunts to the chicks and walks over to her consort. She gives him a play bite on the neck, as she has done many times.

He thinks it's a very hard play bite.

———

*Ridge-backs are everywhere—dangerous.* Raptor Red's mind is in high alarm mode. She's on guard duty in the morning, sitting on the edge of a one-hundred-foot cliff, looking down onto the plains, where three big gaggles of acrocanthosaurs are milling around, crunching the chewed-up carcasses left by the raptor pack.

The acro populations have boomed because of immigration from drought-stricken areas to the east. Raptors don't like to tangle with acros in large groups. So the *Utahraptor* packs have been shifting their hunting territory nearly every day to the north and west as the acro invasion gets worse and worse.

An acro is wandering up an arroyo where the spring rains have cut a deep gash in the red earth. It's a male, mature this season. He's been driven out of his family group—a fate that happens to all male acros at this time of their life. Now he has to find a piece of biological real estate to claim as his own.

It's an anxious time for any dinosaur. This one isn't full of bravado. He doesn't know yet that his species is the biggest and strongest predator in all of North America. All he knows is that a week ago he was safe and comfy in his family, sharing kills. Today he's on his own, and he feels awfully unprepared.

He's used to making short expeditions on his own, to investigate exotic scent trails. But up till now, whenever something frightened him, he could retreat back to mother.

He stops to lick the inside of his gums with his narrow triangular tongue. He can't put much pressure on his mouth lining because the tongue is very muscular and can't move much side to side. There's still a sore place where a prickly animal had gone *whackity-whack* inside his mouth earlier in the season.

He doesn't like having to get all his food by himself. But when he tried to go back to his mother's group, she shooed him away.

*Snff . . . snff . . . snff . . . SNFFFFFF! Easy food— maybe—raptor smell!* His mood improves. His family group has made a living by stealing kills from raptors. Acros don't feel like felons—they consider it as noble to steal a carcass as to make the kill themselves. More noble, because usually they waste less energy stealing.

The young acro has learned to associate the raptor-pack smell with easy-to-steal prey. Usually raptors don't fight back—unless the acros threaten the raptor chicks. Then all hell can break loose.

SNNNFFFFF. The acro presses his snout against the base of an old gnarled tree with a split crown. This is peculiar. The raptor scent seems to go *up* the tree. The acro hasn't run into this situation before.

The acro stares straight at the tree. He's not programmed to look up, because prey usually isn't found high above the head of an acrocanthosaur. He's programmed to look down and look around.

Some dried leaves and a branch fall on the acro's forehead. He shuts his wide upper eyelids. The top of his head is covered with thick, horny skin, reinforced below by layers of dense bone. Things falling on his head rarely do damage.

Whunk! A big dead branch hits him right between the eyes. He flinches.

This is a new sensation—being bombed by heavy objects from above. He doesn't like it.

The raptor scent becomes overpowering, and it's coming from right overhead. The acro does something he's never tried before. He rolls his head to the right and looks up with his left eye.

*The raptor!* his mind screams. The raptor is in the tree.

The acro backs up and measures the distance. He reaches as far as his neck and head will go.

*Nope—too high,* he thinks.

He snuffles around the tree and bumps it accidentally with the low horns that stick up in front of his eyebrows.

The dead, rotted wood shudders.

*Wow—I didn't know I could do that . . . make a tree wobble.* The acro is discovering his own physical strength.

He bumps the tree harder, and it wobbles harder. The raptor chick twenty-five feet up hisses and screams.

*Cool—I can rattle the raptor* would be a loose translation of the acro's thoughts.

The acro butts the tree hard. The raptor chick makes a panic noise.

The acro circles around, rolls his head, stops, lowers his snout, flexes his knees and ankles, and runs straight at the tree.

The tree trunk cracks away from its roots. The wood splinters straight down from the crown. Thick sections tumble on top of the acro's head and shoulders. He closes his eyes tight, hears scrabbling noises and a thunk.

The acro opens his eyes. Lying upside down on the ground, looking right back at him five feet away, is a half-grown raptor chick, bruised, dazed, and scared.

# Two-Tiered Drama

At this moment, on that Early Cretaceous day, a double-level drama is being played out. On top of the stage made by the ground surface, raptors and acros play the leading roles of large and superlarge predators. Below the stage, underground, another storyline is being played out, by a supporting cast of tiny creatures who shun the daylight.

If you are the size of a mouse, a frog is a grotesque monster from a fairy tale. The *Aegialodon* is only a one-ounce insectivorous Cretaceous furball, a twitchy lump of hard muscle, long snout, beady black eyes, exquisitely sensitive whiskers, and spreading five clawed feet fore and aft. A frog face has appeared in the aegi's burrow. The frog's mouth is almost wide enough to swallow the aegi.

A frog or a large beetle is a dangerous animal to the aegi. But a raptor is simply too big to be noticed. To the aegi, the acrocanthosaur and the raptors pounding the earth above his burrow are Forces of Nature, like earthquakes. He's been feeling his burrow walls shake for a half hour. Then a bunch of leaves got jammed into his burrow opening. And inside the ball of leaves was a burrowing frog who had just been kicked by an acrocanthosaur foot, moving the amphibian sideways across the ground and into the aegi's domain.

The frog, with his tiny frog brain, cannot grasp what's happened. All he knows to do is seek cover from the mammoth animal-mountains clomping around and threatening to squash his little froggy body flat.

The frog squeezes into the aegi's hole headfirst. The aegi feels the unpleasant sensation of moist, bumpy frog skin pressed against his own face and ears. The aegi backs down his hole into the living chamber, a space two body-lengths wide, lined with soft, dry fur shed by the aegi. The frog is already there. It's backed its squat body into a corner and tufts of aegi fur are sticking to the wet amphibian skin.

It's totally dark inside. The aegi, with a good sense of smell and the finest high-frequency hearing of any Cretaceous critter, keeps track of what's going on topside. It's strangely quiet.

There are some situations your genes don't prepare you for. The acrocanthosaur above finds himself in this predicament now. He stands amid the pieces of shattered tree trunk, not knowing whether to bite, charge, run away, or just keep standing there.

The fallen raptor chick makes a sound that mimics a big tire going flat slowly. The acro is tempted to reach down, bite, and shake. That's what he always does to small prey items that make noise or wriggle. The chick is only 160 pounds—one-twentieth his own weight.

But raptors are dangerous. He noticed while growing up that his mother always got tense around them. And next to the chick is a hunk of ostrich dino carcass that the chick had dragged up the tree. It's thirty pounds of fresh meat. Maybe he should just reach down, steal the meat, and run away. That would be safest.

To complicate matters further, a full-grown raptor is now screaming at him from several hundred yards upwind. One raptor isn't enough to be a serious danger to an adult acro. A single raptor usually keeps its distance from a single acro, and vice versa. But this *Utahraptor* is coming at him, waving her arms, lashing her tail, and acting as if she were a veritable kamikaze dino, bent on crashing into him.

The chick's body starts to come alive. Its hand claws are flexing and extending, and its hindfoot is vibrating.

*Two raptors, too many—bite this one and run.* The acro slowly makes up his mind. He can grab the little *Utahraptor*, shake the life out of it, and still have enough time to retreat out into the open ground, away from the adult raptor, where he can defend himself if necessary.

The acro uncoils his neck from the tight S-curve he normally carries it in. He opens his jaws, three feet from snout tip to ear. The chick starts to roll over, but its right side is still too stunned to stand up.

Below, the aegi furball hears a high-pitched sound, very loud, almost painful to his mammal ears. Then he hears a terrible collision noise, the ground rumbles and quakes, and his burrow collapses. Soil and roots momentarily pin the frog and the aegi down onto the floor of the living chamber.

The acro never saw the other adult raptor coming. Just before he can snap his jaws shut on the chick, the acro's aim is spoiled by a mind-boggling noise from behind. He ducks instinctively.

The male raptor hits the back of the acro's neck with his foreclaws. The clawtips rake diagonally down and backward, just missing the acro's eyes.

The skin is tough here. The acro shakes his wide neck and torso violently, flinging the male raptor off onto the pile of broken wood. The acro leaps with both feet, missing the raptor but destroying the domicile of the aegi.

*Get me OUT OF HERE!* the acro's brain yells at all his motor nerves. His reflex-loops start firing at random. He whips his tail around, not aiming at anything in particular, hitting the male raptor by pure luck.

The acro starts accelerating in the wrong direction. The adult female raptor is almost on top of him. He pivots awkwardly on one foot and does a U-turn, lowering his armored forehead.

The acro just grazes the male raptor again and knocks him down. He leaps over the fallen tree, once more shaking the underground shelter of the aegi.

*Run, run, run, run,* the acro thinks. His heart-lung machinery shifts smoothly into overdrive. Every breath he draws through his nostrils goes directly to huge air cells in his neck and torso and skull. Every contraction of his rib cage sends air already in the cells up and forward into the compact lungs housed in the ceiling of his body cavity.

The air is forced at high speed into thin tubules that pass tiny capillaries full of blood pumped from the heart's pulmonary artery. Energy-giving oxygen is transferred from air tubes to bloodstream, at an efficiency twice what mammal lungs can do.

The acro covers a half-mile before he slows down. He's glad to be alive.

*Those raptors—VERY DANGEROUS, and smart.* He's

convinced that he just barely escaped a deadly three-way ambush. He'll never again get close to any raptor.

The raptor chick struggles to its feet. It was sure it was about to be eaten. Its mother rushes by to snarl at the retreating acro. She stops and returns to her chick, nudging it hard. The chick falls over, but it's suffered no vital damage.

The male raptor, on the other hand, is hurting—three cracked ribs from the blow of the acro's forehead. It's painful to breathe.

Raptor Red's sister sits down next to her oldest chick. For the first time since she met the male, she doesn't want to bite him. And right this minute she could.

Raptor Red shows up a few minutes later. She heard the commotion from beyond a sand dune, where she was helping the other two chicks dismember this morning's kill. Her genetically programmed behavior isn't ready for the scene that greets her.

Her mate is lying hurt on the ground. Her sister is sitting next to him, at a loss as to what to think or do. The chick, rapidly recovering, is sniffing down a hole, trying to catch whatever was making such a fuss underground. And piles of panic-shit from an acrocanthosaur are spread all about.

The male raptor is depressed. He's thinking something like this to himself: *What a dope! Why did I do that? Ouch— what a dope—why did I do that—ouch!—the chick isn't related—and Raptor Red didn't even see it—ouch!*

He sees Raptor Red coming toward him. His pupils contract and dilate, looking like the lens of an autofocus camera. It's a reaction of extreme excitement—and joy.

*"When in doubt in a social situation, groom"* is Raptor Red's unspoken motto. She sits between mate and sister, alternatively nuzzling each.

# The Cutting Edge
# of Bug Boppers

The aegi's nightmares always come when it's daylight
above ground and he's deep asleep below. Sometimes the
Horrors are huge and amorphous, giant vague shapes that
threaten to crush him flat. His body shakes with convul-
sions. His feet make running movements. His jaws open
and close in quick defensive bites. Tiny squeaky noises
come from his mouth.

In his dreams he can never outrun the Giant Horrors.
They envelop his world like a dense suffocating cloud.
Just as he feels his body being crushed, the nightmare
ends. He sighs, still asleep.

Sometimes the Horrors are smaller and more personal.
He sees himself hunting through a lush forest. Ferns

tower above his head. The air is moist and rank with the heavy scent of mushrooms. He hears his quarry, plump and vulnerable, scuttling between clumps of ground pine. He gives chase. He sees his prey close up and gets ready to lock his jaws onto its armor-plated rump.

Then the Long-Armed Horror strikes from above. He feels the air rush beside his body as the clawed fingers grab at his fur. He tries to jump up, but he can't. Then the dream stops.

The worst is the Horror That Follows You. In this dream he's asleep in his home, his body touching the four walls, floor, and ceiling. He dreams that he's happy and secure. But then his nose detects an awful smell. The soles of his feet are being licked by a fast-flickering tongue that is cold. He realizes too late that there is no way to run, no escape. The cold body coils against him.

That dream usually ends when he wakes up.

All the dreams are in black and white. And in all of them the *feel* and *smell* of the Horror is much worse than the sight.

But there are good dreams too. His favorite is the Endless Crunchy Worm With Feet. It goes like this: He's hungry. He's been searching for food all night. He hears a faint patter of hundreds of feet moving in rhythmic waves over dry leaves. He pounces. His molars hit a hard, curved carapace, tough armor that keeps his teeth from the luscious goodies inside.

He contracts his jaw muscles in his sleep. He feels the prey's carapace bending. *Pop*—his molars go through. He feels the yummy body juices flowing into his mouth. He eats and eats and eats and never gets to the end of the prey.

It's a wonderful dream. It's a dream only an insectivorous little mammal can have. It's a dream of catching a millipede.

Mammalian furballs dream. So do birds and big-brained dinosaurs like raptors. But a rich dreamtime requires much extra brain capacity where memory can mix with fantasy. Turtles and lizards and snakes sleep the dreamless sleep of the small-brained. So dreaming is an advanced evolutionary exercise, a way the brain can go on an extended journey into that other reality.

Mammals are dreamers par excellence. When the aegi ventures far into the dreamtime, his eyes flick back and forth inside their closed lids. His face muscles wrinkle up, and his lips contract into a tiny snarl. He runs to escape the Horrors—his minute five-fingered forepaws executing rapid but ineffectual cycles of locomotion as he lies on his side.

The aegi even squeaks in terror—or in satisfaction when he catches the dreamtime millipede.

The aegi dreams best in the late afternoon, before he wakes up for his nocturnal foraging expeditions. Shortly after sundown the earthquake-animals—that's how the aegi labels the big-footed dinosaurs—curl up and go to sleep. Their heavy tread no longer threatens to crush his burrow. The night sounds begin. Insect wings hum. Creatures too timid to venture out on the meadows and forest floor in sunlight make delicate footfalls on the carpet of dried bracken at night.

In daylight the giant meat-eaters—raptors and acros—are the lords of their universe. But dinosaur eyes don't do well in the dark. The hawk-style optics of raptors can detect a rainbow of colors in strong light—even beyond the spectrum seen by human eyes today. But in the dim light of dusk their visual acuity decays. They lose objects in the shadows. Outlines of potential prey and potential enemies become obscure.

It's a penalty most dinosaurs pay for the visual richness they enjoy in sunlight. Evolution cannot maximize the efficiency of the same eyeball for both bright and dim light. The aegi has paid the opposite penalty from the dinosaurs. His eyes can't stand strong light and can't discriminate most colors. But in low-light situations, his visual system works superbly, resolving images invisible to dinosaurs.

When the first rush of cool night air funnels down to his burrow, the aegi pokes his snout out. He has to clear the shattered soil from the crushed burrow walls, pushing away the collapsed earth that plugged the entrance when the raptors fought with the acro. His long, sharp snout wiggles left and right, up and down—an anatomical trick no dinosaur can perform. The aegi has face muscles in his snout, muscles organized into a half-dozen groups that can move his lips and nose. By furball standards, dinosaurs have thin-skinned snouts nearly devoid of muscular tissue.

In fact, dinosaur heads would seem stone-faced and expressionless if the aegi ever stopped to examine them. Raptors can't wiggle their noses, furrow their brows, or scowl at food that tastes bad. Acros can't curl their upper lip high into a full snarl. No dinosaur can put its lips together in front and suck liquids into its mouth.

When dinosaurs want to communicate, they must use a lot of exaggerated body motions—head-bobs, torso-squats, tail-swooshes—because the range of their facial expressions is so limited. Mammals, as they will evolve in the later Cretaceous and beyond, will have far greater subtlety in body language. Dogs and monkeys and finally humans will acquire ever-greater powers of transmitting emotions through the face.

The aegi flexes his snout tip down into the earth churned up by the earthquake-animals. One group of snout muscles is attached to a cartilage cap embedded in his nose, giving the aegi the ability to use his snout like a flexible shovel.

The aegi's scent-detector locates a beetle larva. The reflex arc that connects nose to brain to jaws fires in a milli-second. The aegi's sharp-cusped front teeth skewer the larva, who writhes like a worm on a hook.

With a click, the aegi deftly shifts the wriggling grub aft, onto his molar teeth. His molar cusps work like lilliputian guillotines, notched blades that are self-sharpening. His upper and lower molars click together with each chewing motion and slice off whatever unfortunate part of the prey is caught in the notch.

The multiple slice-and-dice action is terrifically destructive to bug-size victims. There are five guillotine-cusps in each molar, and there are eighteen molars in aegi's skull.

If the aegi understood dental anatomy, he'd be immensely proud of his own set of choppers. Every jaw stroke neatly deconstructs a grub into dozens of easy-to-swallow pieces.

The beetle larva is killed, chopped, and ingested in less than a half-second.

No dinosaur can do that. No bird will be able to, either.

*Aegialodon* is equipped with a set of dental tools as high tech in design as the most expensive French Cuisinart.

Another sniffle, and another grub is detected. Another quick burst of molar action. Another puree of beetle slides down the aegi's throat.

He's feeling good.

*Whoaaaa . . . BACK!* The aegi leaps up. His body responds to a galvanic message from his whiskers. Something's out there in the dark, something alive and sinister.

The aegi's whiskers fan forward, powered by yet another set of snout muscles. Each whisker is a hypersensitive radar beam, extending out a full body length. At the base of the whisker, where it's embedded in the snout muscle, a huge tactile nerve runs backward to the brain. The slightest disturbance of the whisker tip induces massive nervous discharge.

The aegi can control the zone of tactile-scan by flexing the whisker muscles. He advances cautiously. His whiskers move in quick jerks, outward, forward, outward again.

*There it IS!* The left whiskers regain contact with the suspicious living mass ahead. The aegi doesn't like the smell. He backpedals.

His eyes can make out the shape, silhouetted against the faint light filtering through the underbrush. He shudders.

*SCORPION!*

The shape is unmistakable: The low-slung body. The pair of pincers in front. And worst of all, the tail-stinger held back over the head.

The aegi hates scorpions as much as any one-ounce furball can hate anything. The scariest night in his entire life, all four months of it, was when he was stung by a scorpion. It took six hours for him to recover—and in the meantime he almost starved to death.

The scorpion makes a swipe with one pincer. The aegi is fast, jumping three inches straight up.

The scorpion can sense the aegi's body heat. The aegi's supersharp hearing can track the scorpion's footsteps. The scorpion has tactile hairs too, and chemical receptors that operate for sensing smells.

But the aegi has three advantages. His whiskers have a much longer reach. His eyes are much better at forming an image. And his brain is thirty times larger.

The scorpion advances, nipping right and left. The aegi jumps backward and sideways. The scorpion follows. The aegi leaps up onto a piece of gravel, then across a branch, then down onto another piece of gravel. His whiskers keep contact with the scorpion.

But the scorpion has lost the precise location of the aegi, whose whiskers brush over the scorpion's body too fast for the arachnid to follow. The scorpion's tail quivers and shoots out.

The aegi jumps at the tail base, biting hard just below the poison barb.

Click-click.

The scorpion feels its tail tip fall away. It grabs at the aegi with its pincers.

The aegi's hair is standing out at right angles to his body. The scorpion pincers grab and pull but only succeed in ripping out two tufts of *Aegialodon* pelt.

Click-click. The maestro of molars shears off one pincer. The scorpion turns to flee.

Click-click-clicky-clicky-click. The scorpion's brain senses the loss of the other pincer and all the legs on one side.

CLICK-SNAP. The aegi bites down hard with his long front teeth. One tall cusp penetrates the shell of the scorpion and cuts the main nerve going to the body.

There's a pause. The surviving scorpion legs wiggle.

Clicky-click! They're off.

The aegi doesn't pause to gloat. He proceeds, in workmanlike manner, to dismantle the scorpion body, reduce it to tiny cubes of shell and meat, and eat all the nonpoisonous parts.

The aegi feels good. He's halfway to filling up his metabolic gas tank. He has to eat roughly the equivalent of his own body weight every twenty-four hours, or he'll drop off into torpor, a state of hibernation that can occur anytime during the year, whenever food supplies cannot meet the huge demands of his tiny body.

*Whoaaa—sleeping earthquake-animal!* The aegi's whiskers feel the immense wall of flesh that is a sleeping raptor. His nose tells him that there are others nearby. But he's learned that at night, if he's careful, he can hunt bugs around earthquake-animals, because they hardly move at all, and they never try to catch him.

*Bug alert!* His whiskers touch an unknown insect crawling near the raptor. There's another, and another. A whole swarm.

*Poisonous? Stingers? Pincers?* The aegi automatically evaluates the unknown insects. They smell like fat, slow-flying bugs with long thin snouts, of a sort he has eaten before. But these are a little different, a particular species he's not met.

*To eat or not to eat?* The aegi pauses.

*Eat!*

Clicky-clicky-click! One bug after another is treated to the *Aegialodon* food processor.

*Stuffed—stop.* Aegi's bulging belly tells his brain it's quitting time.

He's killed every bug in the swarm anyway.

----

The *Aegialodon* returns to his burrow early. He snuffle-shovels earth around the entrance back into its proper state. He digs quickly with his forepaws, throwing earth backward between his legs.

The frog exits in a hurry, knocking the aegi over. The aegi then goes back to work and has his living chamber in first-rate shape in only a few minutes. He curls up and enjoys the feeling of bug parts being digested, emitting a nice warm glow from his tummy. His eyes start moving rapidly beneath his furry lids. His body convulses. His molars clack. He's enjoying this dream immensely—it's a replay of how he defeated the Terrible Stinging Bug With Pincers.

As dawn approaches, millions of furballs are bedding down. The hairy armies of the night are retreating to holes in trees, holes in the earth, holes beneath rocks, holes in rotted logs. A hundred mammal species are seeking refuge in this part of Utah. Beetles and bugs and scorpions and millipedes—thousands of species—disappear from view too.

The Dinosauria are waking up. Astrodon herds start munching leaves. Acrocanthosaurs stretch and scratch their muzzles with their hindpaws. Under a clump of cycads, a *Utahraptor* family is awakening. They'll never know that during the night a single *Aegialodon* has saved one of their number from a hideous death.

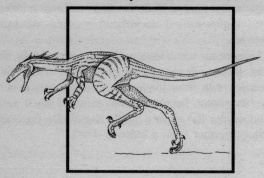

# Furball Liberator

Raptor Red doesn't like to bed down on moist earth. None of her species does. They evolved in a dry climate, and their skin is designed to deal with exposure to sun and wind so severe that it would blister other dinosaurs' hides. Prolonged contact with moisture, on the other hand, can lead to a fungus infection and other, deadlier ills.

Raptor Red stands up and faces the early morning sun's rays. She's hot-blooded, bird-style, but even hot-bloods take advantage of solar warmth, especially after a damp, cool night. The young male struggles to his feet to join her. His ribs ache terribly, reminders of his run-in with the acro, but his legs are okay.

One of the chicks starts sniffing around, as young carnivores of many species do, looking for something to play with. He inhales some chewed-up bug parts that have a peppery taste. The chick sneezes loudly, waking up every other dinosaur for a half-mile radius. An acro family down the valley answers with a dull roar.

The whole raptor pack suns itself on the fallen tree for an hour, then trudges off to the west. They leave behind the remains of a swarm of assassin bugs, killed that night by the *Aegialodon*.

Raptor Red is vaguely aware that the slain legions of bugs give the air near the ground a strange scent. But she doesn't think about it. Her acute vision focuses on the long, tubular bug-muzzles that lie like severed hypodermic needles everywhere. She doesn't realize it, but those tiny arthropodous syringes can kill raptors by injecting them with biotoxins.

Raptor Red has been bitten by syringe-snouted bugs before. They usually sneak in at night or during rest time, when the raptor pack is lying in the shade. They come for blood. The bugs prick the dinosaurs' hide, suck for a half hour, and drop off.

Raptor Red tries to avoid the bugs—they leave itchy sores that can lead to infections. But her innate fear of bugs has another, far more profound motivation: Dinosaurs who ignore bugs have died out from infections. Syringe-snouts are vectors of plague.

The Cretaceous bugs the aegi killed carried a deadly virus that is fatal to raptors. The disease and the bugs evolved in Europe, and the bugs hitchhiked on astros when those vegetarian giants passed over a land bridge that connected Europe to Greenland and Greenland to eastern Canada. Once in the New World, the bugs and their microbial fellow travelers ran amok, spreading everywhere, because there was no native predator who could handle them.

Fortunately for Raptor Red, her part of the American ecosystem has a natural control agent—a species of *Aegialodon* who specializes in eating just this general type of bug.

By sheer bad luck, Raptor Red and her pack bedded down just where there was an infestation of Cretaceous assassin bugs, every one carrying plague. However, good luck balanced bad. The *Aegialodon* and his brothers and sisters had colonized this piece of ground recently too. In one night the furry bug boppers slaughtered thousands of assassin bugs. In another few years, the plague-carrying insects will be reduced to a few refugee pockets scattered here and there in Utah.

Sometimes it works out this way. More often it doesn't. The invading pest spreads, unchecked. Horrible epidemics result, and the native fauna is devastated. That's why *Utahraptor* females reject any male who appears to be bug-infested.

Raptor Red and her pack were lucky—very lucky.

---

The big ostrich dino hen is cocking her head from one side to the other. She lowers her neck so her ears are close to the ground.

Her ears are the best of all the Early Cretaceous Dinosauria—better than Raptor Red's. They have to be. The ostrich dino ear must detect the faintest scrambling noise of underground prey.

The ostrich dino hen puts her outer eardrum an inch from the soil. The eardrum vibrates, amplifying the sub-surface sound, sending vibrations through the thin ear bone, which amplifies some more. Instantly the inner eardrum receives the amplified signals and sets up waves through the fluid in the inner ear.

This is a battle of ear versus ear. Below ground, furball ears are straining to follow the movements of their huge enemies topside.

It's an even match. Both furball and ostrich dino have a long, coiled inner ear canal where fluid waves move tiny hairs that trigger electrical impulses to the brain. The longer the coil, the wider the range of frequencies the brain can hear. Both furball and ostrich dino hear high frequencies well.

The aegi is awake. The soft tread of the ostrich hen was enough to rouse the furball from his morning slumber. The other aegis are awake too. They don't like ostrich dinos—to the aegis, the big hen is the Terror From Above.

The ostrich dino hen pokes her head up to do an antipredator scan. Far to the south are some acros. Not close enough to be a danger. Far to the west is a dust cloud marking where a family group of predators is marching away.

She sniffs—there's just the faintest scent of giant raptors. She shudders involuntarily.

But the raptors are too far away to waste time worrying. She puts her head down again, cocks her ears, and listens.

A very light rustling noise comes from six inches below. She squats on her long ankle pads and braces her torso with her tail.

She jabs her three-fingered forepaws down into the dirt.

Her long, straight claws go down vertically, probing the earth. These claws don't have the wicked meat-hook curve a raptor claw has. Instead, the ostrich dino's hand is a garden tool, a combination three-pronged spade and rake.

Her three claws are almost the same length, a unique hand pattern for dinosaurs. Usually the thumb is far shorter than the other two fingers—raptor hands are built that way. The three equal claws give the ostrich dino hen better probing efficiency, because all three points reach down to about the same level.

*Squeak.* A tiny voice betrays its owner. It's a mistake—if the furball hadn't squeaked when the claw brushed past its shoulder, the little mammal would have lived.

The hen stares from one side. Then the other.

Her eyelids blink the dust away.

THNKTHNK! Both hands go down. Six straight claws penetrate on either side of where the squeak came from.

Down in its burrow the aegi feels the floor of his living chamber crumble and rise up. The burrow walls collapse, letting in bright sunlight. The sun fills the burrow in a painful explosion of white beams. The furball's eye can't take such a frontal attack of solar radiation.

He closes his eyes, turns around, and tries to dig deeper. Too late—six claws lift him bodily. He tries to wriggle through the space between two claw tips. But the hen brings her palms together and the claws make a dreadfully effective cage, trapping the furball inside.

The ostrich dino hen examines her prize. The furball squints and can just barely see the outline of the hen's bulging forehead.

Gulp! The hen tosses the furball into her mouth and gobbles him down.

On to the next burrow the hen goes. Another furball is detected, excavated, analyzed, and gobbled.

And another.

Deep in his renovated burrow the scorpion-killer aegi sits. He feels the tremors coming closer. The burrow next to his—his brother's—suffers a rumbling attack. He hears a squeak. The scorpion-killer knows that the Terror From Above has scored another victim.

Sunlight stabs at his eyes. He's lifted. The Terror From Above pushes its giant mouth next to him. He sees the giant jaws open.

The aegi's teeth strike blindly and gnash twenty tiny holes in the dino hen's cheek. Then the aegi locks his jaws onto a flap of ostrich dino lip, hanging on.

The ostrich dino hen grunts in disgust. She doesn't like her brunch to bite back. She shakes her head.

The scorpion-killer feels himself being propelled a hundred body lengths. He falls. He scrambles toward the scent of his burrow. He reaches the edge of the hole, now churned up by the hen's claws.

The hen drives all six claws down hard. They come upholding a wriggling piece of prey. She's more careful this time. She doesn't put her nose right up to her claw trap.

She flips the little body into the air.

Gulp!

"Yeaccch!"

It's a frog. There's nothing wrong with frogs for brunch, but she was expecting the taste of furball. Oh well, one gulp is as good as another.

Still, she pauses a minute, thinking, *I grabbed a furball—tossed it—it became a frog. Never saw that happen before.*

If she were interested in metaphysics, she might invent the first dinosaur religion then and there. Instead she moves on, hunting, digging, and gulping.

*Aegialodon* the scorpion-killer stays absolutely still. He's survived, and he'll live to a ripe old age—eleven months. By that time his aegi genes will be in swarms of children and grandchildren.

Over a hundred million years later, the flow of aegi

genes will produce wonderful creations—giraffes, elephants, rhinos, whales, bats, monkeys, chimps, Democratic senators, Republican majority leaders. Charles Darwin himself. All can be traced back to the supreme bug bopper, the *Aegialodon*.

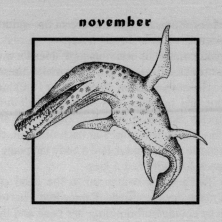

# Cretaceous
# Water Lanterns

Raptor Red doesn't know why the little chick is dead. Its body lies peacefully in the sand, as if it were napping, not far from the pack's new seaside nest. Raptor Red thinks it is a pretty chick. She always liked it best of her sister's three children.

Raptor Red very gently touches her upper lip against the chick's chest. There's no blood, no visible wound. But the body is cool and stiff. The chick lost an internal battle two hours ago, overcome by a runaway respiratory infection.

Raptor Red has seen death a thousand times. She's watched dinosaur viscera ripped out of still-living bodies.

And yet, this *Utahraptor* chick is one of the saddest sights she has seen.

Her male consort is nervous—he doesn't want to be blamed for the death—and he tries to make himself inconspicuous. He sees Raptor Red's sister walking slowly toward him, and he hides between two small dunes.

The chick's mother approaches Raptor Red and stops, looks at the adults, and stares at each of them, then sees the chick in the sand. Raptor Red's body language tells her that the pack has suffered a loss.

Raptor Red's sister comes up to the dead chick and begins to make crying sounds. Raptor Red tries to console her sister by cooing and nuzzling her neck and by leaning against her chest. But the bereaved mother starts to howl and shake, her eyes wild and wide. First her neck, then her shoulders and thighs tremble. The other young chick scrambles away in fear—she's never seen her mother like this. The oldest chick joins Raptor Red in preening her mother.

It does no good. Raptor Red's sister collapses on her ankles, pawing at the chick, turning the little corpse over and over until its hide is covered with wet sand grains. Raptor Red is afraid to leave her sister alone but afraid to stay next to her too. Her sister's weird moaning gets louder, and she swings her arms in spastic arcs.

Raptor Red pushes her sister's body with her own. She presses her head against her sister's neck, trying to stop the shaking. It's all she knows how to do. It's the *Utahraptor* way of comforting a loved one.

Raptor Red feels her sister's body go limp and start to fall away from her—and then it stops and stays still. Something is holding her sister up from the other side. Raptor Red looks over her sister's shoulder to see what it is.

It's her male consort.

He's pushing gently and making cooing noises.

Raptor Red and her consort spend two hours holding her sister. Gradually the moaning grows quieter, the shaking stops, and Raptor Red's sister closes her eyes and goes to sleep. Raptor Red's consort drags over some branches to make a temporary nest right there. The entire pack huddles together when sunset comes. It's a difficult night. Raptor Red has to groom her sister every time she wakes up.

---

The morning comes, and Raptor Red feels drained. Her sister is finally sound asleep, snoring noisily. The young male looks at Raptor Red—she's sitting up with a dull, lifeless expression. He nudges her. Then he decides that he must get her a present.

Off to the beach he goes, sniffing and digging at curious objects half buried in the sand and mud. He needs something to cheer Raptor Red up. He needs play-food.

Over the last months he's watched her enjoy herself many times, poking and nipping and clawing at strange food objects, creatures of bizarre shape and pungent taste. Fish heads, dried lizards, bloated furballs, fresh-water clams that no raptor can pry out of their shells. He's learned that Raptor Red likes food that challenges her mind.

What he wants to find is some animal so weird that he himself would never think of eating it.

Smells of rotten and half-rotten sea-critters come up from the sand, but none seems quite right. Some are too gooey and sloppy. Some have hard-edged body parts that cut his lip when he tries to pick them up.

An eight-inch-long object, pointed at both ends, has promise. It smells fishy in a general sort of way, but it's not like anything he's eaten. And it has a very strange outer shell with hairs and pointed things sticking out. He

taps the body with his hindfoot. To his immense surprise
the pointed body runs sideways between his legs and under a rock.

*Sideways running—weird,* he thinks. Carefully he lifts
up the rock, and the pointy thing runs sideways the other
way.

Fhhhhwhop! He jumps on the sideways-creature,
smushing it down into the mud. Bubbles come up. He
fishes down to grab the thing—but the thing grabs him.

His index finger suffers a sudden sharp pain, and as he
pulls his hand up, the crab holds on with one of its big,
heavy pincher-claws. *This is perfect,* he thinks.

He runs back to where the family is sitting. Raptor
Red's sister is still snoring. The chicks are just waking up.
He bobs his head at Raptor Red. She doesn't look up. He
drops the crab between her legs, and it scuttles straight up
her chest.

"Eeeeep!" Raptor Red makes a little cry and stands up.
Suddenly she's out of her mood and into figuring out this
new thing.

She chases the crab up the beach, and her consort
chases it down. They push it down into the mud, and they
dig it back up. He holds it against a rock, and she tries to
pry into the crab's shell with her thumb and her teeth.

At last she succeeds in popping the bottom shell off.
Her male consort refuses to taste it, but Raptor Red immediately chews off pieces.

She likes it a lot.

The rest of the day is spent crab-catching and crab-
eating. They catch them together, and Raptor Red eats
every one.

Raptor Red and her consort spend the day with the
chicks. It's not a bad life at all, being a pack of beachcomb-
ers. The sea offers many gifts. The oldest chick finds the
fresh carcass of a half-ton sea-reptile, a streamlined body

with two pairs of backswept flippers. The head was already gone—bitten off in some unseen mortal combat below the waves.

Raptor Red tastes the meat. It's like crocodile, with a bit of the aftertaste of turtle. It's not salty at all and just a little overripe. It will feed the pack for days.

As the sun sets, Raptor Red and her young male sit together along the beach, watching the breakers pound the Cretaceous pebbles into sand. Her sister is asleep again. The chicks have bellies full of scavenged seafood.

Raptor Red's consort takes a walk down the coast—he doesn't want to go to sleep just yet. Raptor Red follows. They find more free food: dead sea-crocodile, dead tarpon-fish, and dead saw-shark. The saw-shark is a bit strange—pungent and salty. Still, Raptor Red gives it a try even though she's not hungry.

Raptor Red's consort feels accepted now. He considers himself a full pack member. Over the last two months, as the pack made its way slowly to the sea, the bond between him and Raptor Red has become very strong.

The pack began its passage westward when conditions became intolerable in the open floodplains of Utah. It was the exploding populations of acrocanthosaurs that pushed the raptors farther and farther toward the great western sea. At first Raptor Red's sister growled and snapped at him every day. Then little by little, she became more toler-ant.

Yesterday, when he leaned against Raptor Red's sister, was the first time he had ever touched her without being bitten. He knows he'll never really like Raptor Red's sister, but he has learned to tolerate her and to work around her personality quirks and to avoid her when her bad moods set in. And he knows that Raptor Red appreciates his ef-forts.

The supply of sea-creature carcasses looks inexhaustible, and so to the young male, the prospect of being a dinosaurian beach-bum seems splendid. He can raise a family here.

Raptor Red feels good despite her sadness at the loss of the chick. Her sister has stopped trying to kill her consort. That's the firm foundation for a permanent, stable family life.

Their present situation is not without complications. They are not the only pack of raptors who has found the Pacific shore a safe haven from acros. The evening air is full of fresh scent.

Raptor Red catches sight of a pair of dinosaurs silhouetted against the setting sun. *Utahraptors,* strangers. The male sniffs and takes a few steps toward them. Raptor Red catches their scent-signal. They're females, unattached.

The young male stands for a long time, then comes back and sits at Raptor Red's side, growling. The strangers lower their heads and withdraw. They do pause to dung-mark a sand dune. Raptor Red watches them until they are completely out of sight, and she and her consort settle down to listen to the ocean and watch.

————————

Raptor Red stands up straight. She sees something totally new and perplexing. Phosphorescent green-yellow light is dancing just below the surface of the waters. Another burst of light comes from the left, and another from the right.

She and her consort walk slowly toward the surf. They jump back when the warm water washes over their feet. There are more flashes—a wide zone of flickering light dances across the water.

The raptor pair doesn't swim out to satisfy their curiosity. The breaking waves scare them. And Raptor Red sees huge, dark shapes cruising just below the water's surface—menacing shapes with eight-foot-long heads.

One of the lights starts to glow from a tidepool, and the raptors investigate. The male peers at the illumination that flickers across the rocky rim of the pool.

Raptor Red snaps her jaws at the light. She expects to feel the struggles of some unknown prey, wriggling to free itself from her teeth. Instead, she feels her lips coated with icky slime, like congealed fat.

She pulls her head back, coughs, and shakes her head. Bits of glowing green protoplasm fly away from her head and land on her consort's feet. He rubs mud over his toes. Globs of goo cling to her gums.

She suddenly loses her temper at the lights. She hisses and coughs and wags her head up and down in a threat display. The jellyfish can't see her.

Inside the tidepool a transparent phantom with long tentacles glows yellow-green. A dozen of the tentacles have been bitten off. Two dozen remain. The creature doesn't think—it has no real brain, no center of rational analysis. Its nerve net responds to the shock of being attacked by sending messages to the swimming muscles. Its gelatinous body bumps against the rock walls of the pool.

A triple wave, made strong by the melding of multiple crests, sends a surge of water up the beach and over the tidepool. Raptor Red jumps straight up. A three-foot-thick wedge of salt water nearly knocks her off her feet. The glowing gelatin body is lifted up and carried back to the open ocean as the wave recedes.

Raptor Red and her consort watch the light sail out to sea. The jellyfish—a stingless species, part of the ctenophore clan—floats passively away, spared the slow death by desiccation that will end the lights of a hundred of its relatives who remain trapped on the beach.

A huge head rises smoothly above the surf ten yards

away. A gigantic eye, unblinking, focuses on Raptor Red and her male. They backpedal up the beach. She's afraid but overcome with curiosity.

SsssssHHHWOOOOSH! An explosive cloud of foam covers Raptor Red. Salt spray stings her eyes. She's aware of an immense presence waving its head just a few feet from hers. She smells fetid breath—the stench of a thousand fish and squid fermenting.

Raptor Red stumbles backward and sideways. The sea becomes calm. She blinks her nictitating membrane across her eye. She brushes away wet sand from the corner of her eyelid.

Her eyes focus. Lying on the beach is twenty tons of sea-monster.

It's a kronosaur.

The head, three yards long, swings left and right over a wide arc, throwing hundreds of pounds of sand into the early evening air. But the fearsome beast cannot advance an inch farther up the beach. It has gone as far beyond the water's edge as its four-flippered body shape will allow.

Raptor Red senses immediately that the behemoth from the sea is now no danger. While her consort snarls protectively, she examines this strange invader from another ecosystem carefully. It's as big as an *Astrodon* but has a profoundly different body style.

The kronosaur emits a deep exhalation and then belches. A triple wave crashes over its back. The forty-foot-long body wriggles in a clumsy wide turn, like a multi-ton worm. The kronosaur bends its head back toward the sea. It cannot breathe out of water. It has lungs, but the crushing weight of gravity pulls its body bulk down onto the pulmonary chamber, squeezing the lung apparatus. The kronosaur's flippers are not attached firmly to the backbone, so they cannot prop the body up against the sand.

A paroxysm of wriggles and head movements finally pull the kronosaur into the water.

Raptor Red watches and thinks.

When she is feeling well fed and content and well loved, her mental powers are allowed to indulge themselves. She can experiment.

She walks parallel to the shoreline, watching the waves carefully, focusing her eyes *below* the surface. She keeps her distance from the average line where the waves break.

There! She sees another huge shape cruising parallel to the shore. She watches—and a giant head breaks surface.

She stands on tiptoes, trying to look as tall as possible. She waits . . . waits . . . waits. . . .

*Here it comes!* she shouts to herself. She flexes her knees and ankles. An immense dark torpedo comes right at her, plowing through the breakers.

Just as the head and front flippers begin to slide up the beach, Raptor Red turns and jumps four strides diagonally, upslope and to her right.

Whhhmmmpp! The big kronosaur stops exactly on the spot where Raptor Red was standing a few seconds earlier.

Fsssshhhh! Foam and steam exit in two jets from the kronosaur's nostrils, just in front of the eyes. The great sea-reptile pauses, then retreats awkwardly back to the water.

The male raptor is amazed.

Again Raptor Red plays her newly discovered game, Bait the Sea-Monster. She walks just close enough to the water to elicit an attack. But as soon as she sees the monstrous head breaking through the interface between water and beach, she retreats.

The male raptor understands the game, and he joins Raptor Red in teasing the king of the surf. Seven times they trick the kronos. These big beasts are slow to learn.

The kronos' tactic of ambushing land animals close to the shoreline usually works, especially in the twilight. Many an iguanodon has been snatched to a saltwater tomb. Even twenty-ton astrodons have been dragged screaming into the foaming water.

But the kronos have never met quick-witted raptors before. At last, Raptor Red and her consort get bored and wander off to find something new to engage their interest.

As the last rays of the sun sink over the western horizon, there is a changing of the guard in the near-shore ocean realm. Great fourteen-foot fishes with shiny silver scales, like tarpon, retreat to quiet, deep water. Sea-reptiles with sharklike tails and flippers in place of legs seek kelp beds to spend the night. And a white-winged pterodactyl closes up his aerial fishing expeditions, carrying his final catch of fish toward his hungry offspring in the rookeries in the sandy shore.

The kronosaurs lie silent, resting.

It's time for the armor-plated mollusks to ascend from the depths. It's the time of tentacles.

# Tentacles

If Raptor Red and her male consort could dive into the Early Cretaceous sea at dusk, they'd see the armored shellfish coming up. Shells with tight spiral coils, like giant land snails, are swimming along the sloping ocean bottom, armor-protected mollusks that scan their surroundings with intelligent eyes, each with a wide iris and a small, dark center.

When a fast-swimming fish-lizard tries to grab one of the panzer-squids, its eye closes, and a heavy hood of protective tissue comes down over the mollusk's head, sealing off the opening in the shell.

When the disturbance disappears, the hood opens again and the beast's jet propulsion resumes. A muscular cylinder protrudes from the shell opening. A high-pressure stream of water is directed downward, and the armored spiral body shoots upward.

These are ammonites and nautiloids, the most intelligent and mobile of all the armored Mollusca. Even faster are the Cretaceous squid, who zip by at twenty knots, their cigar-shaped bodies made lighter by the near total lack of shell armor.

Raptor Red and her consort watch this extraordinary shellfish circus through the moonlit water. Every once in a while an ammonite or squid breaks the surface and becomes marooned in a tidepool, where the raptors can gawk at these exotic beings. The two raptors paw the empty shells of ammonites washed up on the beach—there are dozens of varieties.

Some of the shells are so smooth, Raptor Red can't hold on to them with her claws. But most ammonite shells are sculpted into ridges and furrows, knobs and bumps. She pokes and scrapes each shell with her hand claws and then with her lips and teeth. It's fun.

And sometimes tasty. When she nibbles at the opening in one big ammonite shell, she's rewarded by a live, plump crab with one big claw and a naked, soft-skin body.

Crnch—gulp. *Very fine meat. And soft-shelled too!*

Raptor Red isn't the only crab-loving predator active tonight. She sees movement down in the quiet, clear pool. A beautiful ammonite with a deep and narrow coiled shell pauses a few feet below the surface. His sensory tentacles zip out of their protective sheaths. He's intrigued by a thick-shelled crustacean, plowing up mud. The ammonite jets closer. He zips out another dozen tentacles. The supple, muscular arms swarm over the crustacean. The lobsterlike crustacean feels its grip on the sand bottom loosen as the tiny grappling hooks on each tentacle lock onto the crustacean's horny hide.

The crustacean is pulled up to the center of the ammonite's tentacles. A heavy, parrotlike beak protrudes.

Cwack! The central nervous system of the crustacean erupts in a flurry of electrical signals. Then its neuronal switchboard goes dead.

Raptor Red hears the ammonite jaws crunching the big crustacean, and she pulls her head back. *That must be a dangerous mouth!* is her conclusion.

The ammonite squirts water fore and aft, moving his muscular jet-hose quickly to the front and the rear, counteracting the water currents sweeping over the pool. Each piece of prey is dragged into his mouth by the raspy ammonite tongue, its surface armed with backward-directed barbs.

The ocean night has endless delights. The male raptor sees a swarm of big coiled ammonites, three feet across, rise through the water column, a swift-swimming shadow pursuing them at thirty-knot speed. There's a flash of a slender snout, and one ammonite is plucked from among his fellows.

Strong conical teeth crunch across the ammonite where the body is attached to the inner shell surface. The long snout shakes the shell, and out falls the soft, still living mollusk body, forcibly freed from its armor.

Sssssssgulp. The plump molluscan morsel is swallowed by a snout carried on a streamlined, shark-shaped body.

It's a wide-fin fish lizard, *Platypterygius*.

The wide fin swooshes its tall, tuna-shaped tail. Upper and lower prongs of the tail are narrow, tapered, back-curved blades that push against the water in quick strokes. The sharklike top fin cuts through the air-water interface.

The wide fin breaches the surface. It gulps air in the corner of its mouth and submerges a half-second later.

*Fast—very fast.* The male raptor is good at judging

speed—that's why he's such an efficient hunter on land. *Fast—faster than me.* He watches the wide fin swim just under the surface.

The wide fin turns and attacks a huge school of bullet squid—belemnites—ten thousand strong. Hundreds fly out of the water, their cigar-shaped bodies skipping across the surface.

Raptor Red ducks her head as she's bombarded by bullet squid landing onshore. Most have eight tentacles that thrash about, trying to get their owner back into the water. Some, the males, have an extra tentacle set. All have an armored core of thick shell in the rear of their bodies.

Raptor Red picks up a live bullet squid and bites down, hoping for a repeat of her experience with crab meat. But instead she breaks a tooth and spits the belemnite out. *Much too crunchy* is her gastronomic verdict. She tries another, holding it down with one hind foot as she bites it underwater.

Suddenly a blob of squid ink squirts out and covers her snout. She has to wiggle her snout in the water to get the ink off. She makes a mental note: cross squid from the list of edible seafood.

The wide fin is still hunting just offshore, his gigantic eyeball searching the water for another group of bullet squid. Moonlight playing down into the water column reveals a second school. That's enough! The wide fin comes in at twenty knots.

The fish lizard's eyes focus on faint reflections from the squids' rear steering fins. At this high speed the targets will be in jaw range in a few seconds.

The squid disappear, replaced by blobs of inky black hanging in the water column. The wide fin shakes his head vigorously, snapping blindly. No good—he misses The squid are too wary tonight for his style of attack-from-the-rear.

Raptor Red and her consort know that the prey-predator game is being played down there, and it excites them to watch.

Below the school of squid a dark body mass is moving slowly, smoothly. It's an elasmosaur, a long-necked sea reptile, swimming too far below for the squid to see. But the upwardly facing eyes of the elasmosaur can see the squid—they're silhouetted against the moonlight.

The dark body of the elasmosaur speeds up just a little, and its long, snakelike neck coils into tight S-shaped flexures. Four tapered flippers give the elasmosaur a smooth maneuverability.

Three squid are plucked from the school by darting strikes of the elasmosaur head. Then two more disappear, struck from below and behind. The elasmosaur thrusts its neck from the squids' blind quarter, the direction where their visual detection systems work least well.

Finally another squid is impaled on the forward-slanting elasmosaur teeth.

Just then, the elasmosaur is forced to bank left in an emergency evasive turn. It's bumped something large. No worry—the elasmosaur can see the unmistakably lumpy form of a sea-turtle, plowing through the water with its two foreflippers. There's a bright explosion of green light—the turtle has bitten a jellyfish.

The elasmosaur banks again, this time to avoid a pair of Meer-Krokodil, an oceangoing crocodilian with the shape of a long-bodied shark.

The raptor pair climbs a rock ledge to get a better view, but they can see little of the three-dimensional aquatic ballet. They hear a flopping sound coming from a pool below the rock. Raptor Red pokes her hand in to investigate, but something wet and awful wraps itself around her fingers. Hundreds of tiny hooks adhere to her skin. When she scratches with her other hand, a pretty coiled shell falls, and dozens of sinuous tentacles writhe around. Raptor Red kicks the shell with her hindfoot and watches the ammonite right itself in the water six feet offshore. A Meer-Krokodil with armor plate embedded in its back snatches the ammonite and swims quickly away into the depths.

Raptor Red thinks about the sea. *Slimy things—grabby things—too-crunchy things—big, fast, scary things.* It's all too much. She leans hard against her consort, and he leans back. She's glad she's a land animal.

The sensory input is too confusing. Raptor Red likes poking at unknown animals, discovering things that move and sound and smell different. But this watery world is too full of strangeness.

She sits down. Her consort sniffs the air for a few minutes, then joins her. He leans toward her and she leans toward him.

## december

# Death from the Sea

The old white-winged dactyl awakens early, to take advantage of the exceptionally fine masses of air rising over the beach. Sitting at the edge of his nest, he opens and closes his twenty-foot wings slowly, stretching the thick wing-finger tendons at the four joints, getting the winter night out of his muscle fibers. This is his preflight warmup.

The entire wing is held by just a single great finger, number four counting from the thumb outward. He adheres to a strict program of exercises to limber up the living machinery that will keep that finger operating in peak condition once he is aloft.

He tests the air and turns his body upwind. He props his torso up at an angle, holding on to the nest with the three small hooklike claws on each wrist, and folds his wing tight against his body. He flexes his knees and elbows and wrist, lowering his body. Then he jumps, hurling himself off the edge of the cliff.

His body plummets down fifteen feet, gathering momentum. Just as he seems doomed to crash into the surf, his flight-finger muscles contract at the elbow and shoulder, putting tension on the thick finger tendon. The muscle force instantly is passed outward as the tendon flips open the four finger joints and locks the wing in extended position. Air flows over the top wing surface, creating lift.

The dactyl hears a whoosh of air generating the force that pulls the wing up. His body tilts. He's airborne.

Automatically he twists one wing finger up and one down and banks into a spiral-climbing turn. It takes a full minute to make a complete circle, and another, and another, and another.

The circles get wider as he ascends. He enjoys the feeling of effortless upward flight. At fifteen hundred feet the light of the rising sun hits his wings and floods his body tissue with warmth. This is the moment he likes best. His circulatory system responds, opening capillaries close to the skin so the solar energy can be absorbed.

The dactyl banks steeply, and the wind sends him scooting at high speed parallel to the shore. It's exhilarating.

At ground level it's still dark—the rising sun is yet below the horizon. The dactyl's acute eyesight lets him see shapes and movement on the dimly lit beach. He likes to check out the situation on the ground at this time of day.

He can see two *Utahraptor* packs. One is made up of his old friends, Raptor Red and her sister, and Raptor Red's male consort, plus one large and one small chick. The other pack has three young adults and is camped a half-mile away. The white dactyl swoops lower to inspect Raptor Red's pack. They are up and awake and milling around. Their movement patterns are awkward and violent and uncoordinated. That's not how a well-organized raptor pack should look.

The dactyl sees movement within the deep shadows behind the beach, in the hollows between the lines of sand dunes. Two very large dark shapes are inching up the dune face toward the raptors. He knows what that sort of movement means—giant predators are stalking the raptors. And the raptors don't know it.

On a normal morning one adult raptor would be on sentry duty, sitting on the dune crest to prevent a surprise attack. Today all three adults are circling each other on the beach, ignorant of the danger from the dune field.

The old dactyl has a fondness for Raptor Red and her pack. He thinks of them as *his Utahraptors*. They've been his meal-ticket for several years—as were Raptor Red's parents before them. It's not that he views them as his family—he has a subconscious knowledge that raptors have no significant genetic ties with his own kind. But he has bonded, at a distance, to this raptor group. He views them as the living center of his territory.

He banks very steeply and dives. At thirty feet he levels out, gravity giving him sixty-mile-per-hour velocity. Sand grains are whipped into the air by his slipstream as he skips over the dune crests. A three-ton body flattens itself onto the dune as the dactyl buzzes the last crest before the beach.

The dactyl gives a high-pitched alarm call. He expects an instant response. The raptors have learned that he doesn't give alarms in jest.

The raptors ignore him.

Raptor Red's sister should be the morning sentry. On

most days she wakes up earlier than the rest of the pack, and she's naturally suspicious of any unknown sight or sound or scent. But this morning she woke up in an angry state of mind. For no particular reason—other than the fact that she still finds his presence irritating—she walked over to where the young male was sleeping and bit him.

He snarled and withdrew to the foot of the big dune. Now he is walking back and forth, half awake, growling softly. He didn't sleep well. All the strange sounds coming from beyond the dunes bothered him. Strange *Utahraptors* came and went and left scent-signals. Even worse was the faint smell of giant predators. He'd hoped they would be free of acros forever.

Raptor Red is standing between her sister and her consort. She hates being in this position. She's making soft gurgling noises, looking back and forth at the two creatures she loves most in the world.

The older chick is next to her mother, hissing loudly with all the bluster adolescents have when they mimic adult behavior.

Raptor Red walks slowly, deliberately to her sister and nudges her. Her sister stops making threatening motions and turns abruptly away.

One crisis dealt with, Raptor Red turns to the young male. He's busy testing the morning air with his snout. Raptor Red sniffs too. Her heart sinks. There it is again— the scent of female *Utahraptors*, strangers.

The young male rises very tall and sniffs. Then there's an awkward silence as he stares at Raptor Red. He comes over and gives her a snout nuzzle. It doesn't last long, and he walks away.

This complex social drama has occupied the entire pack. They're not as vigilant as they would be if they were a stable family.

A huge acrocanthosaur is sitting behind the crest of a pale yellow sand dune. Her three-ton body is hidden from the beach. Since an hour before sunrise, she's been watching the raptor family wake up slowly from their temporary nest not far from the water's edge. The wind is with her— it's blowing in from the shore.

This acro is a mature adult. She has chicks back in a nest two miles away. And there's nothing an acro mother hates more than a pack of raptors near her family. Raptors are the deadliest menace to other predators' chicks. Raptors are nest-raiders.

The acro's mate crawls up next to her. He stares down at the beach. The two acros are looking for the right moment to leap over the dune crest and attack the raptor family, but they're momentarily puzzled. Something strange is happening among the raptors.

Raptor Red stands frozen in fear, her head trembling. Tiny pathetic squeaks are coming from her throat. Her pupils are dilated even though the morning sun is bright. She's staring at her sister, who is staring at the male raptor.

The male raptor has the little raptor chick in his mouth. It's squealing.

He didn't plan to do it. The chick was getting on his nerves, playing games with his tail. Usually the male's strong attachment to Raptor Red modulates his urge to bite the chick in half. His strongest instinct is to please Raptor Red—so she'll agree to have chicks with *him*.

But not this morning. The chick has been too obnoxious. Its mother has been too bloody-minded. And the male is just too edgy. The final insult came when the chick tried to bite him, just as its mother had. The chick imitated its mother too precisely—for a second the male thought Raptor Red had not one, but two hellish sisters.

That's a thought that makes him lose control.

So he didn't *exactly* intend to grab the chick in his mouth. He snapped at it to keep it away from his tail. But the chick zigged in the wrong direction, and the male's jaws, almost by accident, closed tight on the chick's calf.

Now the chick is screaming. The male's jaws tighten just a bit, then relax.

He's fighting instinct with reason. His reflex emotions say, *Bite hard and get it over with.* His rational inner voice says, *Drop the chick and act submissive.*

Raptor Red is afraid for the chick. It's her niece, and blood ties are strong. But she's even more afraid her sister will rip the male to pieces.

Raptor Red's sister stands on her tiptoes, making herself look as tall as possible. Ripples of muscle contraction pass through her entire body until every ounce of body mass is tensed.

She's uttering a low, guttural snarl.

Raptor Red advances slowly toward her sister, keeping her head close to the ground. It's a walk of appeasement, the submissive display of a sibling trying to defuse a deadly situation.

The male looks at Raptor Red, then at her sister. He's frozen where he is, unable to move.

Suddenly, Raptor Red's sister slashes out with her left hand. Raptor Red staggers. She looks down at her elbow, where a fresh wound is beginning to bleed. Raptor Red sinks down on her knees. She's never, NEVER been struck in anger by her sister before. She doesn't know what to do.

Then a cloud of sand comes flying into Raptor Red's face, stinging her eyes. She blinks hard. She sees a blur of hindfeet churning up the beach. Her sister is charging the male.

Raptor Red tries to run to cut her off, but the sand is so soft, it's impossible to accelerate fast, and she stumbles.

Her sister is coming at the male with her arms flailing. He drops the chick, who runs away toward the surf, splashing out until the water is lapping at her knees. She focuses her eyes at her mother and doesn't notice the dark mass breaching the surface, gliding toward shore, out beyond where the waves start to break.

There's a gentle disturbance in the surface as the immense body changes course and steers directly at the chick.

The male raptor turns and starts running uphill. Raptor Red's sister tries to follow but slips and skids sideways down the sand dune. Raptor Red sprints between them. She stops, looking in panic both up- and downhill. But then she doesn't know what to do. Her sister gets up and just misses Raptor Red with a swipe of her forepaw.

Out of the corner of her eye, Raptor Red sees the body shadow of a sea-monster coming at the chick. She gives the alarm call, but her sister ignores it and begins to climb the dune after the male. In the next instant, an avalanche of sand bowls the male and Raptor Red's sister over. They lie sputtering at the foot of the dune. A four-foot-long head juts out from the dune crest and snarls. Then the neck and shoulders emerge. Then the massive thighs of the acrocanthosaur.

Raptor Red screams another alarm call. The chick standing in the surf sees the acro and backs out farther into the water, unknowingly putting herself in an ideal spot to be attacked by the sea-monster. The chick is now in water up to her hips and she's having a hard time staying upright in the tidal surge.

Raptor Red's sister is lying on her back, half buried in the dune. The male acro is crashing clumsily down through the sand. The sister looks at the acro, then at the male raptor, then back at the acro.

She twists her body around and attacks the male raptor.

Raptor Red yells in exasperation. The hoarse scream means *You IDIOT!*

Raptor Red grabs her sister's tail and drags her down the slope. The charging acro pauses. He's confused by all the raptors yelling at each other. It seems to be some newfangled group defense he's never seen before.

The female acro walks briskly along a diagonal route across the dune face. She's older and wiser than her consort. She knows sand and she knows raptors. She knows that the raptor pack is fighting among themselves.

Raptor Red recognizes immediately that the female acro is the real threat to her sister and the male raptor. But the giant sea-reptile is closing in on the raptor chick.

For a horrible second Raptor Red is sure she's going to lose her mate, her sister, and her niece.

But then the thought strikes. Her brain puts two things together.

Raptor Red charges the female acro, screaming her loudest. She brushes past the snapping acro muzzle. A mouthful of four dozen enormous ivory teeth, each saw-edged, clamps shut a few inches from Raptor Red's skin.

Raptor Red whirls and strikes. Her index finger makes a shallow but painful cut on the acro's upper lip.

The female acro blinks hard. She looks at the male raptor and at Raptor Red's sister, hissing at each other as they retreat to the left. Then the acro looks at Raptor Red, yelling defiantly to the right, at the edge of the water.

The acro runs after Raptor Red. *I've got it cornered—its back is against the sea,* the acro thinks to herself.

And the charging acro does close the distance rapidly. Raptor Red splashes noisily out into the salt water.

*I've got it—I can wade out farther than she can!* The acro's brain sends messages of confidence to her legs.

Raptor Red turns and runs through the water, parallel to shore. She passes the raptor chick, frozen in fear, and knocks it down.

The acro ignores the chick and follows Raptor Red through the surf. The long, strong acro shins and ankles slosh through the water with ease.

The distance is down to a few yards. *Another second, and I'll strike,* the acro thinks. Her sensory system preps her neck and jaws.

The acro snaps her neck backward into a tight S-curve. Muscle groups work against each other—tensing the head and neck and torso. The whole joint-muscle apparatus is a coiled weapon, ready to fire and send the jaws down and forward.

KAWOOOOOOSH! Raptor Red is knocked backward. Her head goes six feet under. Her muzzle drags along the bottom. Wet sand is stuffed up her nostrils.

KAWOOOOOOOSH! A second explosive force sends tons of water over her, rolling her body along the bottom.

Salt water clogs her throat.

Five more surges keep her from grabbing the sand with her hindclaws.

Raptor Red jabs all six of her foreclaws into a clump of brown seaweed. Then she jams one set of hindclaws in between two submerged rocks. She sticks her head and neck up as far as they'll go.

Her nostrils break the surface. She spits out green water and a mouthful of salty mud. Her right eye opens just above the surface.

Drops of hot blood spatter the water all around her. She looks around. It's a hideous sight.

Streams of bright red arterial blood are squirting up from the surface. The acro has a huge open wound in the thorax that exposes three broken ribs and lacerated viscera. A hindleg, dislocated at the knee, flaps about in unco-ordinated spasms.

A three-yard-long kronosaur snout swings viciously to the side, seizing the acrocanthosaur leg and spinning the acro body beneath the waves.

Raptor Red struggles to the shore and looks back. The acrocanthosaur surfaces again, her left thigh and shin flexing convulsively. The kronosaur shifts his jaws up his victim's body, clamping his giant tooth-row across the acro's neck. The krono's flippers on the right side tilt upward as he dives to his left, dragging the acro down again.

Back on shore the raptor chick who had been in the water rushes up to the sand dune. Both raptor chicks huddle next to their mother.

The male acro on the beach has sat down. He's staring at the water's surface where his mate disappeared. He sees the acro resurface a hundred yards farther out. This time her body is nearly limp. There's just a faint hint of movement in the corner of the mouth.

Raptor Red walks out of the surf. She's very happy. And she's proud of herself too. This is the best victory she's scored in her life as a predator. It's better than bringing down an iguanodon. It's better than a group assault on a twenty-ton astro.

This time she beat an acrocanthosaur with her brain, not her claws.

She trots up the sand dune diagonally.

The male acro has already retreated to the dune crest.

He catches one last glimpse of his mate, three hundred yards out, her body is being spun around by the thirty-ton kronosaur.

The acro male is unhurt, but his spirit is gone. He trudges away, defeated.

Raptor Red follows cautiously. She watches the acro grow smaller and smaller until he vanishes beyond the next line of dunes. She looks down. Her sister is calling to her. Raptor Red joins the two chicks in an orgy of snout rubs and reciprocal grooming. Everyone seems in splendid shape.

Raptor Red jerks her head up and sniffs. Her good mood disappears. She trots back up to the dune crest and surveys the landscape.

*There!* she says to herself. *There he is.*

She can see her male consort two hundred yards away to the north. She's confused. *Is he afraid? Does he know we won?* She calls to him. He doesn't respond. She calls again. He's moving.

He's trotting away from her.

Raptor Red stretches her muzzle high and makes a single piercing call.

The male freezes. He turns his head. Maybe he's making a return call, but Raptor Red can't hear it.

*Maybe that's not him,* she thinks. She sniffs and stares and sniffs again. No doubt about it, that's her male's distinctive smell.

The male is standing still, looking back at her. *This has happened before—he'll come back,* Raptor Red thinks.

She detects something else in the air—the scent of female *Utahraptors,* the group of strangers camping nearby.

Far to the north she can see them, tiny figures making slow body movements.

Raptor Red is at a loss.

She stands quietly and watches the young male turn and walk quickly north.

Raptor Red stays there, high on the dune crest, for five hours. His scent gets fainter and fainter. He's not coming back.

# Segno Caves

Raptor Red pauses to catch her breath. The mountain air takes getting used to. She knows that they are traveling north. North is the direction she and her original mate came from three and a half long years ago. Now she and her sister and the two chicks are going north involuntarily. It's the only direction that seems free of acrocanthosaur hordes.

A week after Raptor Red lured the female acro to her death in the surf, three more family groups of acros showed up on the beach. It was too much for Raptor Red and her sister to deal with. Winds from the north were free of acro scent, so the raptor pack went north.

And up. The *Utahraptor* family's flight leads them to

higher and higher elevations, far higher than Raptor Red has ever been.

After a long day of zigzagging up a mountain valley, Raptor Red's sister nuzzles her. It surprises Raptor Red. Her sister is not the huggy type.

Her sister's mind is usually a muddle of conflicting rages that she can barely control. She fears and hates the smell of other raptors. She's driven to apoplectic anger when she senses acrocanthosaurs nearby. And she flails her arms in frustration when the physical elements go against her—when it's too windy or too rainy or too hot.

One central purpose holds her thoughts together: protect her chicks, protect her family, protect her sister.

Now penetrating through her paranoid and frequently frantic intellectual fog is the realization that Raptor Red is sad. And Raptor Red's sister has finally figured out that this sadness began when the young male left.

To Raptor Red's sister, the young male was a dangerous annoyance. She hated him from day one. She wanted to get rid of him. She never could figure out why Raptor Red protected him.

She still doesn't understand. But she wants to make Raptor Red feel better, so she nuzzles and gurgles awkwardly. She's trying hard, but her instinctive skills of comforting a sibling are poorly developed.

Raptor Red turns away. She still blames her sister for depriving her of her young mate.

Her sister follows, making exaggerated submissive movements with head very low. She's not very good at it. She's had little practice in submission rituals.

Her clumsiness eventually causes her to run her snout directly into a fallen log. She trips, tries to regain her balance by digging her left forepaw into the ground, tumbles over herself, and lands on her back with a sour look on her face.

If evolution had given Raptor Red a full set of lip muscles, she'd smile.

She moves over to her sister and gracefully caresses her neck and shoulders.

---

Raptor Red lets her sister make all the decisions now. She's the pack leader. And the pack continues to go up, climbing the seaward side of a mountain range clothed in heavy forests of tree ferns and tall conifer trees. The air becomes clearer, fresher, and much colder, especially at night.

Raptor Red pauses to stick her snout high in the breeze. Yes indeed, there are no acrocanthosaurs here. She sniffs again and sighs. There are no *Utahraptor* males either.

The pack feasts on a dead iguanodon they find covered by fallen leaves. Raptor Red winces when she cuts the meat with her teeth. The iguanodon's flesh feels hard and cold against her gums. She tastes ice crystals in the connective tissue.

Raptor Red's sister looks up at the sky. Her keen eyes follow something small and light falling in irregular spirals. Maybe a bug.

Snap! She jumps up and bites at the whitish fleck. No taste. No crunch.

Another whitish speck comes down. She watches, stone still, to see what the bug will do.

She takes a very shallow breath. The bug zips into her nostril and dissolves immediately, leaving a cold, wet sensation for a split second.

*Cold bug. Strange,* she thinks to herself.

The night becomes frigid, but the sisters find abundant pine needles to build a temporary nest, and the older chick helps like an adult in this housekeeping chore. The scent and sounds coming from the montane forests show that there's plenty of game.

One of their local neighbors is a small iguanodon species with a spotted hide who runs in big herds and is easy to kill.

The pack wakes up to a heavy fog clinging to the ground. Raptor Red's sister is thirsty. Up ahead is a pond nestled among lichen-covered boulders. She trots ahead of the rest of the pack and squats down.

But as she stoops to drink, she whacks herself against a rock, bruising her nostril. At least that's what she thinks.

She examines the pond edge carefully. There are no rocks in sight.

Again she stoops, and again she whacks herself.

She growls at the water. She hisses. The water doesn't ripple at all.

*Weird water,* she thinks. *Bad water.*

She reaches out to scratch the pond. Her middle finger hits the surface and bounces off.

Now she stands up and screeches a full threat.

Raptor Red and the older chick rush up to help defend her.

Raptor Red's sister reacts the way she always does. She thrusts her right hindfoot at the pond. *I'll fix you—I'll rip you open with my killing claw,* she's thinking.

Her claw hits the pond and slides forward. She slips and falls on her rump. She expects a splash. She gets a knock on her dinosaurian derriere instead.

Raptor Red is very curious about this strange hard water. She takes a more inquisitive, less confrontational approach to the problem than her sister. She presses one foot hard against the water's surface where some reeds are growing. Cold water oozes up alongside the reeds.

CRACK! A jagged piece of water breaks off. Raptor Red backs up. She's never seen water act like this.

She sniffs. She nudges the water with her snout. Then she bites tentatively at a piece. She tries to drop the piece of water, but it sticks to her lip. She shakes her head and the piece of ice drops and shatters against a rock.

Late that afternoon, it snows.

Raptor Red watches, fascinated, as the wet, cold, fluffy layer gets thicker and thicker on the ground. The small chick huddles against her side, shivering. Shivering is why Raptor Red's pack can survive in this climate—it turns up their internal thermostat so heat production from body tissue increases.

Raptor Red has noticed that the ponds and rivers here are devoid of crocodiles and turtles that are so common at lower elevations. Crocs and turtles can't shiver.

Raptor Red's sister doesn't like the snow, and all her growling and hissing just seems to make the snow come down faster. She glances at her chicks. Both are now shivering next to their aunt.

*Must find a hole,* the chicks' mother thinks to herself. Raptor Red's sister has always been the best of the pack in finding holes to hide in.

She sets out with grim determination. Cold can be as dangerous to chicks as an acrocanthosaur. She needs a burrow to shield her family.

For three hours the pack searches for shelter. The snow gets heavier, and the younger chick is having a hard time as it high-steps through the freezing mixture of mud and slush.

The raptors' thighs and shins are in no danger of freezing because the blood vessels are arranged to save heat. Arteries with hot blood going down the legs pass alongside veins coming up from the feet carrying blood chilled by the cold ground. The heat is transferred from the descending hot flow to the ascending cold.

That way the upper legs don't get drained of body heat.

The foot tissue itself can operate at very low temperatures. It's a trick that the raptors' relatives, the birds, also have. But the belly tissue of the little chick has no such protection, and it's in imminent danger of frostbite.

The chick whines and stuffs its nose into Raptor Red's armpit. Raptor Red starts to worry. She realizes that the chick could die in another hour or so.

Raptor Red follows her sister as the visibility drops to zero in the swirling snow. The cold, heavy flakes whacking into her eyeballs makes Raptor Red close her eyelids so only a narrow slit remains to see through. Her sister goes up through a heavily wooded ridge and then stops when a heavy, pungent odor causes her nostrils to twitch. The smell is *foreign—and warm*.

Her sister growls under her breath and advances through the dense conifer needles.

A strange noise comes from a crevice in the rocky ledge ahead. A pair of pale blue eyes stares out from the dark interior of a cavern.

Raptor Red and her sister advance side by side into the mouth of the hole. The blue eyes retreat.

Raptor Red feels the faint swoosh of air that a claw makes. She stoops, and a trio of long, straight claws just miss her head.

Only a moment passes, and then she hears her sister attack in the darkness. There's a heavy thumping noise. Then a screech.

Raptor Red can smell blood. It's her sister's. But she can't see a thing in the cave.

She sniffs and slowly walks farther into the darkness. It's very quiet. She bumps into something inert, a big lifeless body that smells of earth and conifer roots. Her sister is already chewing on the weird carcass.

The morning breaks cold but clear. Warm red light seeps into the cave. Raptor Red wakes up and checks on the chicks. They're both still snoring little raptor snorts, half buried in a nest of conifer bark. Her sister is already up and out and feeding on the dead segnosaur carcass.

Raptor Red comes out to investigate. The segnosaur has a smell totally foreign to the raptor's olfactory memory bank. And its shape is bizarre. The long neck and small head with weak teeth are like an ostrich dino's. But the awkward-looking body with wide, spreading hindfeet is thoroughly un-ostrich-dino. And the hands—the hands have huge, straight claws for digging.

The cave is the segnosaur's home. It dug out an elaborate tunnel system to escape the worst of the snowy weather. Segnos are the only dino family specialized for major excavation. Right now, in the Early Cretaceous, segnos are montane rarities—species that can be found only at high altitudes. This mountain-loving habit has kept them from meeting the normal inhabitants of the lowlands, like *Utahraptor*.

Raptor Red's family has no experience to guide them in dealing with segnos, and no instinct either. Segno front claws are dangerous slashing weapons—Raptor Red's sister was very lucky.

Raptor Red gives the segno's body a thorough sniff-search and visual examination. Her olfactory inventory doesn't detect any sign of poison. She takes a bite of the liver that her sister has dragged out of the carcass.

Raptor Red notices her sister's wound: a deep gash over the waist, just in front of the left hip. When her sister shifts her weight, the wound bleeds.

The cave proves to be a splendid lair for the raptor clan. The two adults can go out hunting whenever it's sunny—

and that's every other day or so. And whenever the snow begins again, the four raptors can snuggle in the bark bedding that the segnosaur had gathered.

Raptor Red is aware that her sister walks with a limp. The wound has scabbed over, but Raptor Red can see that it still causes pain. Her sister refuses to stay in the cave to let the wound heal and insists on going on every hunt.

Raptor Red worries about her sibling. She hasn't seen her injured before, and it changes her attitude toward her own responsibility in life. Raptor Red takes on more of the maternal duties—grooming the chicks, making sure that they don't fight too much over food brought in for them. It's not that the chicks are especially lovable now—just the reverse. At this stage in her development, the older chick is just adult enough to be obnoxious and irritating. She can run around as fast as Raptor Red, but her mind is still a chick's half the time. She has no sense of how serious life is, how dangerous it can be.

The older chick constantly teases the younger chick. And both chicks tease the adults, nipping at tails and screeching.

In raptor years the older chick is a teenager, that time when physical energy far exceeds common sense.

The mountain fauna is full of many surprises. The dactyls are different here, smaller and faster on the wing. There are more birds. There are exotic dinosaur species—and some of them are dangerous. The scent-signals are hard for Raptor Red to decipher. There is raptor sign in many places—from deinonychs and *Utahraptors*—but the identity of the dung-signers is hard to read because the cold nights freeze the dung-marks, erasing much of the information.

Raptor Red and her sister leave their marks on tree trunks: they place a dung-sign at the base, then reach as high as they can and scratch long wounds in the bark with their foreclaws.

Any other raptor can read the message: *We're* Utahraptor *sisters, and we're* this *tall, so keep away!*

At the beginning of their second month on the mountain, Raptor Red notices a new and strange behavior being practiced by her sister. It starts with her sister snuffling the soil with intense olfactory energy, then stamping her foot, growling, pawing dirt over a spot on the ground, and running.

Raptor Red has been assuming that it's a danger sign and has been running off with her sister every time. But the sixth time her sister repeats the performance, Raptor Red gets suspicious. Instead of running away, she goes back to the spot where her sister pawed the earth.

Despite her sister's growls, Raptor Red sniff-searches the area. There's a lingering scent, a familiar one. She claws the earth, overturning the sod and releasing more aroma.

It's male *Utahraptor* sign—*her* male consort!

Raptor Red claws the ground furiously and reply-marks the spot with her dung-sign. Then she glares at her sister, who has assumed a nonchalant posture and refuses to make eye contact. She tries to look busy scanning the meadow ahead for imaginary iguanodon herds.

If raptors had complex facial muscles, her sister would be wearing a sheepish expression.

Raptor Red charges and bumps her sister so hard on the rump that both of them tumble head over tail. For the rest of the day, Raptor Red ignores her sister, refusing to return head-bobs or muzzle-rubs.

It's not the last time Raptor Red finds fresh sign from her young male on the ground and in the bark of trees.

"Eeeep . . . ssssswsh . . . bmp-bmp-bmpity-bmp."

It's a sound Raptor Red hasn't heard before, ever.

"Eeeeeeeep . . . ssssssssswsh."

They're squeals of delight, like a raptor chick playing with its mother's tail, but even higher-pitched.

"Eeeeep—" BUMP!

Something alive, something tiny—something is playing over there beyond the pine trees, where the ground slopes away for a hundred yards.

Raptor Red glances at her sister. She has a very curious expression on her face. Not a snarl, or a look of fear, or even an appearance of perplexity. Something else.

Her sister gets up from where the pack has been resting in front of the cave and walks quickly toward the noise. Raptor Red follows.

An iguanodon-herd path snakes through the trees, making a tunnel seven feet tall and three feet wide, where the underbrush has been beaten down by countless generations of herbivore hooves. Ordinarily raptors are cautious when they negotiate this passage—there's always the danger of meeting a rogue bull iguanodon. But now Raptor Red watches her sister bound through the opening and disappear.

Carefully, pausing at each step, Raptor Red goes through the tunnel. She hates this place. It gives her a weird feeling.

Noises come from the other end of the tunnel—shrill, scary, unnatural calls, vaguely like her sister's victory whoop but distorted.

Raptor Red is afraid some horrible herbivore is trampling her sibling slowly, causing inconceivable pain. She stands still for a moment, gathering her courage, and plunges out of the passage into the open space beyond.

And there she's struck dumb by the extraordinary sight.

"EEEEEEEP . . . whoopwhoop-whoooop!"

Her sister is sliding down the snowy slope on her back, gurgling and calling like a maniac. She lands at the base of the slope and continues to scoot across the meadow, coming to rest in a mound of crushed saplings. "Eeeeeep!" Still upside down and lacking any shred of raptor dignity, she calls to Raptor Red.

"Eeep." Raptor Red makes a weak reply. *What is she doing?* She begins to suspect her sibling has caught the "mad raptor disease," a malady that makes carnivorous dinosaurs run in circles, growling at themselves, until they fall over.

There's a flurry of movement at the top of the slope. Raptor Red's sister isn't the only predator enjoying the snow slide. A troop of tro-odonts, small raptorlike meat-eaters about forty pounds in weight, are running up to the edge, jumping into the air, and landing on their backsides.

Tro-odonts are slender-snouted bug-eaters and chasers of small furballs. Raptor Red has always ignored them. They pose no danger to raptor chicks, and no competition for game.

"Eeeeep . . . eeeeep . . . eeeeeep."

It's the tro-odonts who are emitting the high-pitched calls Raptor Red heard before she came through the trees.

Her sister flips herself over onto her feet and starts climbing the slope, her hand claws slipping every other step. She's still making manic gurgling noises. When she reaches the top, she makes a bobbing gesture to the tro-odonts.

They look nervous, back away, but then they bob back. Some parts of carnivore body-language are universal. The bob is understood by most species. It means *Let's play!*

Raptor Red's sister looks down the slope, flexes her knees and ankles, makes a half-turn sideways, blinks twice at Raptor Red, and does a partial somersault.

"EEEEEEEEEEEEEP!" Down the slope she goes, spinning slowly like a *Utahraptor* top. She rams into a ridge of mud, bounces once, and slides into an arroyo, where her body disappears into a four-foot-deep snowdrift.

*My sister is playing—playing.* It takes a while for Raptor Red to comprehend the scene.

*Sister—playful.* The concepts don't go together.

Raptor Red thought she knew all her sister's moods. But here's a side of her character that was hidden away, a little secret looniness. It's something her sister must have learned when she was alone, before her chicks were born.

Her sister's nose pops up from the snowdrift, followed by her hands and feet. She makes her way awkwardly to where Raptor Red is sitting.

Raptor Red feels her chest being rammed by her sister's forehead. She isn't sure what the proper response would be. She feels the two chicks huddling behind her thighs. Clearly they don't understand their mother right now either.

Her sister picks up the younger chick and swings it over the edge of the slope. Down it goes, followed by its mother. A dozen tro-odonts are sliding down twenty feet away. The air is filled with "eeeps!" spanning four octaves.

*It does look like fun,* Raptor Red thinks. The younger chick's fear gives way to childish pleasure. It scrambles to the top again, jumping up and down impishly. Raptor Red's sister returns and whacks Raptor Red hard on the rump.

*I'll try it.* Raptor Red looks out over the slope, now churned into a low-viscosity mixture of red mud and slush. She grips the edge with her hindclaws, lowers her body, and—

Whump! She's shoved by her sister and falls on her side. The mud-slush feels smooth as Raptor Red goes downhill. She rolls on her back and is surprised how trees look when seen from this position.

It's an exhilarating, scary, strange, fast, spinning, upside-down feeling.

She likes it.

# Whip-Tail

It is a very windy day when the raptor pack meets the whip-tail brontosaur. Whenever the dark clots of clouds block the solar heat, the air becomes chilly and inhospitable. But mostly the air is clear and bright, and as long as they stay in the sun, the raptor sisters feel comfortable.

The raptors see the whip-tail from two miles away—a dark mass moving alone in a mountain meadow. They try to sniff out some target data—Who is this potential prey? Is it too strong for an attack? Is it injured?

The scent that wafts up from the whip-tail makes Raptor Red pause. It is like *Astrodon* scent—but, on the other hand, it isn't. Raptor Red knows only one kind of brontosaurian—*Astrodon* itself—and she knows how to attack these immense vegetarians. If that were an astrodon down there, she and her sister could probably handle it.

But the scent tells her to be careful, to expect something new. *That is an unknown* Astrodon *variation.*

As she stands on tiptoes, trying to get a better look, she becomes aware that she is alone. Her sister has already gone downhill to begin the attack.

Raptor Red has a bad feeling about this attack. She screeches a short alarm that says, *Wait—wait for me.* But her sister doesn't wait.

Raptor Red bounds down the hill to catch up.

When Raptor Red sees the whip-tail up close through the shrubs, the big dino is staring right back at her. Raptor Red doesn't like this at all. It's a universal rule: Predators of all ages are naturally suspicious of prey who don't appear to be scared. Self-confident prey are often those who have extra skill and strength in defense.

Clearly the whip-tail is not rattled by the prospect of battling two *Utahraptors.* It sees Raptor Red's sister and swivels its head back and forth, keeping track of both raptors.

The whip-tail moves deliberately out away from the treeline, toward the middle of the open meadow, where fresh snow covers the tops of ferns and conifer seedlings.

Raptor Red feels even more uneasy. The whip-tail seems to be setting up a defense that the raptors don't recognize.

Raptor Red gives a low gurgling call to her sister, who looks back briefly, then circles around the far side of the whip-tail. The older chick stands trembling next to Raptor Red, afraid to join her mother, afraid to stay.

The whip-tail makes a quarter-turn so its shoulders are facing away from Raptor Red and its broadside is opposite her sister. At a sudden zipping sound, Raptor Red ducks instinctively. A conifer branch five feet above her nose is severed from its trunk and falls heavily on top of Raptor Red's back. The older chick crouches in terror.

Raptor Red recoils, jumping backward. *What was THAT?* her brain demands of her senses. *Let's get out of here—there are plenty of iguanodons to hunt—let's leave this strange monster alone.*

But before she can run away, Raptor Red sees a blur of tough, flexible tissue whizzing just inches above her eyes. A slab of bark is loosened from a thick conifer trunk and slides down to the ground.

The whip-tail has moved backward, closing the distance between itself and Raptor Red. It's whooshing its tail back and forth, holding the twenty-foot-long tip high off the ground. Raptor Red recognizes the tail as the deadly weapon that is cutting branches off trees.

The whip-tail has muscles of exceptional power in the base of the tail, just aft of its hips. When these muscles twitch, the wave of contractile force passes down the tail, out to the thin whiplash tip, amplifying the movement. Just a few degrees of flexure at the rump become a thirty-foot arc at the tail extremity.

It's a great weapon for hitting targets far from the whip-tail's torso. The tail tip can travel at hundreds of miles an hour, and when it hits a predator's body, the kinetic energy will cut flesh and stun limb joints.

This whip-defense gave the whip-tail clan great success in their evolutionary past. Now they're reduced to scattered remnant populations, their ancestral dynasty ruined by immigrant disease. But as individuals, the whip-tails are still the most dangerous herbivores ever to face a dino-predator.

Raptor Red grew up in environments devoid of whip-tails, and her species has no hardwired mode of behavior to deal with their tail-defense.

Wise predators are not reckless. Predators who live

long and raise many chicks are not bombastic fools who rush into every dangerous situation. Evolution has not favored raptor genes that give their owners bravado.

To be a Darwinian success, it's absolutely necessary to know when to run away.

And Raptor Red knows it's running-away time right now. She can't figure out the tail-defense and doesn't want to hang around until she does.

Her sister has reached the same conclusion. She's skulking back up the wooded slope, head down, mostly hidden in the underbrush.

The raptor sisters are halfway up the slope when they hear a high-pitched alarm call. They stop dead in their tracks and turn around.

"Screeeeeeeee!" It's a *Utahraptor,* and it's a chick.

The raptor sisters stand as tall as they can and look down. The giant whip-tail has followed them to the base of the slope. The older chick is still on the other side of the meadow, separated from Raptor Red and her sister by the whip-tail.

Raptor Red sees the chick zigzagging in panic, trying to get past the whip-tail. A quick flip of the whip-tail's whip, and the chick falls over, then gets up.

*Dumb, dumb chick,* Raptor Red says to herself. *Go the other way, go around.*

But the chick tries to come straight up the slope, ducking low to avoid the whip-tail. The giant vegetarian moves sideways with surprising agility and flicks its tail tip at the chick.

A long line of snow explodes just short of the chick, showing that the whip-tail missed by inches.

"SCREEEEEE!" Raptor Red flinches at the ear-splitting call of anger emitted by her sister. She watches in horror as her sister goes flying down the slope directly at the whip-tail.

*Don't DO that,* Raptor Red thinks.

The whip-tail backs off. *Maybe my sister was right,* Raptor Red thinks. She starts down the slope to join the attack.

The chick, befuddled by fear, runs in circles behind the whip-tail.

Raptor Red crashes through the line of conifers at the edge of the meadow. She waves her arms and hoots. Then she stops. The whip-tail is dead ahead, only twenty-five feet away. And it's moving toward her.

WHUMP! Raptor Red is knocked down on her side by a heavy, close-range tail hit. She tries to get up, but an excruciating pain in her knee brings her down into the snow. She tries again. No good. Her knee is partly dislocated.

She looks up. The whip-tail is coming closer, walking like a giant crab, keeping its broadside toward her, the giant tail twitching ominously.

Raptor Red crawls back under a conifer.

TTTTTWUNK! The whip-tail aims a blow accurately. Raptor Red is saved by a heavy branch that absorbs the hit. Gobs of sap appear where the bark has been crushed by the tail.

The whip-tail turns and moves a dozen steps away. Through the snow and branches Raptor Red sees a fast flutter of raptor feet. Her sister is attacking from the far side. The older chick hesitates, then joins her mother in the counterassault.

*Good chick,* Raptor Red thinks.

The speed of the tail strikes is amazing. Raptor Red sees the chick leap gracefully straight into the air to avoid a well-aimed blow. The whip-tail seems momentarily confused.

*Very good chick.* Raptor Red stretches her injured leg and feels the joint pop back in place.

THUMP! Raptor Red sits up when she hears that sound. The tail has hit flesh, hard.

She can see the chick, safe, running up the slope. *Who was hit?* she asks herself.

*There*— She sees her sister's head and left hand poking up from the snow. The whip-tail is advancing deliberately.

*Get up—GET UP!* Raptor Red thinks. She screams a high-pitched alarm.

Her sister gets back on her feet, but she's very wobbly.

Whump. She's bowled over and bounces against a large rock.

There's a silent pause. The whip-tail takes a few steps. Its tail muscles tense.

WHUMP—WHUMP—WHUMP. Three heavy blows fall on the spot where Raptor Red's sister lies. All three sound like close-range hits onto bone and muscle.

Raptor Red's pupils dilate with anger. She looks over to the chick, and her expression communicates the message, *We must work together.*

The chick bobs its head once and makes exaggerated steps toward the whip-tail. The big herbivore turns his attention from Raptor Red's sister and toward the chick and lashes out with its tail. But the chick has judged the distance just right—she's a few yards beyond tail range.

*Very, very good chick,* Raptor Red thinks approvingly. She limps forward, behind the whip-tail. Her knee limits her mobility, but she still can turn and kick to the right. The whip-tail sees Raptor Red and turns away from the older chick.

*We're playing the "keep-away" game,* Raptor Red thinks. It's the game she and her sister played around their own mother, years ago. Raptor Red would tease the adult from the front, while her sister would tease from behind—always keeping out of reach of the adult feet and claws.

This time the game is in deadly earnest. Each time the

older chick teases the whip-tail, she leads the big plant-eater up the slope, away from her injured mother. Each time Raptor Red teases from behind, she induces the whip-tail to make a half-turn, still increasing the distance from where her sister lies.

*Very, very smart chick,* Raptor Red thinks as she watches her niece make another deft mock-attack just out of tail range.

Raptor Red and the older chick lead the befuddled whip-tail to the top of the slope. Now the snow begins to fall so heavily that it's hard to see more than a few yards ahead. *Is it gone?—Is it gone?* Raptor Red asks herself silently.

Raptor Red squints to make out a dark shape—a clump of conifer seedlings. To the left is another dark mass of vegetation. Raptor Red sees the older chick run past her and snarl at the trees.

One of the trees moves. The chick backs away, and Raptor Red sniffs loudly and finally gets a clear scent—it's the whip-tail.

Visibility drops to zero. Raptor Red can hear the quiet crunch-crunch of the enormous, cushionlike paws coming toward her. The whip-tail halts six yards away. The wind is blowing in gusts so hard that he can't see or smell Raptor Red.

Without a sound the whip-tail charges, rearing up and coming down hard on its forepaws.

Raptor Red rolls over to her right to avoid being crushed. The protruding thumb-claw of the whip-tail's paw hits a shrub next to her and breaks it into jagged splinters.

Raptor Red isn't hurt by the strike of the forepaw, but she loses her balance on the snow-slickened ground. She tries to grab a clump of ferns, but her sharp foreclaws cut right through the branches without securing a firm grip.

She slides backward, all the way down the slope onto the open meadow.

Her leg throbs, but otherwise she feels very good. The whip-tail has finally given up and fled. She can hear it breaking tree limbs in frustration as it moves away.

The older chick bounds down the slope and slides into her. Raptor Red gives the chick an adult-style head-bump and nuzzles her neck. The chick nuzzles back as if to say, *See! I can fight like an adult! I'm ready to take my place in the pack!*

The two raptors play-wrestle for a few seconds. Raptor Red disengages and raises her head to check on her sister.

A head pops up where her sister has fallen. It's a raptor head. For a moment Raptor Red is happy—her sister is alive.

But the head bobs up and down and whimpers. It's the younger chick. Raptor Red makes a low, gurgling sound—the greeting call of sibling *Utahraptors*. There's a weak reply. Raptor Red limps over toward the sound.

Her sister lies next to the little chick, and she tries to raise her head when Raptor Red sits down. Raptor Red reaches her muzzle down and nudges her sister's body all over. There's no blood, except for a drop at the corner of her mouth. Raptor Red stares at her sister's chest. When the rib cage rises and falls with each breath, there's an awkward unevenness in the series of rib bones.

The wind picks up. The little chick tries to get underneath Raptor Red, to escape the cold, clambering over her injured left leg.

Raptor Red howls in pain. The chick jumps and huddles against her older sister. The older chick stands still, in emotional shock. She's always assumed that her mother would be there to protect the chicks. Life without her was—is—unthinkable.

Raptor Red's sister raises her torso with her hands and makes low, reassuring noises.

Raptor Red feels relieved. *It's going to turn out all right,* her brain tells herself. She tries to ignore the limp way her sister's hindlegs lie in the snow.

# The End of *Utahraptor*

The air is chilled with more spring snow. Raptor Red spends the night awake, lying curled around one side of her sister, the older chick on the other. There is a weak sound of breathing.

In the morning Raptor Red sniffs the air—it's full of dangerous scents. There are two or three species of strange herbivores moving in large groups on the plateau above. And in the valley beyond the trees there is a strong smell of deinonychs.

Raptor Red decides she must get the pack back to the safety of the cave, and she gently takes hold of her sister with forepaws and muzzle. She moves ten steps up the hill, half dragging, half carrying her sister's body. But then

Raptor Red feels her own left leg collapse and she slumps down again. She sighs and sits down. She starts to whimper, but the noise upsets the chicks, so she becomes quiet again.

Her sister opens her eyes—she has a wild, unfocused look. Her body quivers, and there's a spasm of movement in tail and neck. Raptor Red now sees that one broken rib has pushed its jagged end through her sister's skin. The older chick tries to lift her mother's head up, then drops it and stares at Raptor Red.

Raptor Red still has hope. She knows a raptor body can take a terrible beating and still recover—if the pack feeds the invalid and protects him or her from extreme cold or heat. Raptor Red has seen it before. Back when she was a chick in Asia, an uncle came to the nest horribly cut up by a rival raptor pack—and he was on his feet in a week.

*Maybe we can make a nest here—maybe the pack can protect my sister here* is her thought. She drags her sister under a tree where a pile of fallen branches provides ready-made bedding.

Her sister opens her eyes again and looks at Raptor Red. Raptor Red is puzzled—her sister's gaze is calm and steady and doesn't have that frantic energy Raptor Red is used to seeing. The older chick nuzzles her mother's snout.

Raptor Red feels very maternal. She senses an expansion of her family responsibility. She touches both chicks on the snout-tip. The younger chick snuggles closer. The older chick backs away. At least for the immediate future, Raptor Red knows that two chicks are hers to feed and protect whether they like it or not.

Raptor Red is feeling her species-heritage. The duty of raising youngsters automatically shifts to the sister of the dead or injured mother.

Her new sense of shared motherhood gives Raptor Red

a ferocious desire to live. She tries out her left leg—it hurts, but she has some confidence that she'll be able to walk and hunt in a day or so. Her right leg, body, tail, and arms are uninjured and strong.

She looks down across the valley to scan for trouble. She sees nothing. She looks and sniffs upslope. All scent of the whip-tail has evaporated. The older chick joins her in sniffing and staring.

Raptor Red's subconscious evaluates the pack's situation. Worries, hopes, and conclusions well up. She weighs the need to rest her injured leg against the necessity of getting meat to the pack: *Tomorrow morning—when my leg is better—I'll go hunting—I'll bring back food.*

---

The next day Raptor Red's leg is still stiff. The older chick is already awake, preening her mother.

*I can't do it by myself,* Raptor Red thinks as she stretches her legs and tries a series of steps. All she can manage is a quick hopping walk. Not good enough for efficient hunting. She hasn't been forced to hunt by herself in nine months. And even then at least her legs were in good shape, and all she had to do was feed herself. Now she's faced with the responsibility of providing meat for her three kin as well.

Raptor Red feels depressed and inadequate. *I'm the only adult, and I can't do it.*

Her sister hasn't moved during the night and now looks up at Raptor Red with a strange stare. Raptor Red is puzzled by the expression—her sister's pupils are dilated, and there seems to be no pain in her eyes.

Raptor Red fidgets and frets, moving away from the temporary nest, hobbling back, and sniffing the air. Whump! She gets nudged hard by the older chick, who stands tall and bobs her head twice. This is an adult gesture—it means, *Take me hunting!*

Raptor Red stands still, trying to think for a half minute. The chick rams her again, this time on the chest.

Raptor Red's mood changes. *It could work. Yes—you must play the adult role now—LET'S GO!*

Then she nudges the older chick gently, and they leave together.

Raptor Red leads the chick along the watercourses and through gullies, hoping to find the dead body of a fish or a land creature killed by the snow.

All morning the two search for food with no success. Just as Raptor Red is beginning to feel exhausted from hours of hobbling around on her bad leg, she breathes in that scent that brings joy to the heart of all predators.

Carrion!

A dead segnosaur is lying half hidden under some conifer branches. The older chick bounds over to the body and gives a victory whoop, and Raptor Red limps over to join her. It's a most fortunate find—the segnosaur is spiced just right by early decomposition.

As the chick saws off meat chunks, Raptor Red examines the surrounding ground for ownership marks. The way branches have been dragged over the carcass is sure evidence that this segnosaur had been claimed by some other meat-eater.

She finds fresh deinonych sign—dung-marks left near the carcass. And she sees furtive movement beyond the trees: a trio of female deinonychs, the original possessors of the carcass. The 120-pound deinonychs are too afraid to make any challenge to the *Utahraptor* pair.

Raptor Red's leg aches at every step as they return to the temporary nest, but her spirits are high. Inside their gullets are warm hunks of meat ready to be regurgitated to their kin. The younger chick zips back and forth in front of the nest, cooing and begging at the muzzles of the returning hunters. The older chick regurgitates meat to her younger sibling, and Raptor Red gently lays some morsels down in front of her sister.

Raptor Red's sister sniffs the meat, takes a tiny bite, swallows hard, and closes her eyes.

Raptor Red has a feeling that maybe it will be all right.

---

Raptor Red and the older chick return daily for one week, salvaging all of the segno carcass, carrying back meat in their gullets and bones in their jaws. It seems to Raptor Red that her sister is getting better.

On the eleventh day Raptor Red sits watching her sister until late afternoon, worrying when her breathing becomes labored, cheering up every time her sister opens her eyes and tries to swallow a little more segno flesh. Snow begins to fall again.

Raptor Red is so preoccupied with her sister's recovery that she doesn't see the group of strangers approaching. The older chick gives the sentry alarm.

Raptor Red hears the chick's deep growl and stares in the direction the chick is looking. A dozen dark figures are moving in a wide semicircle up the valley, across the new snow.

The wind picks up, and Raptor Red flinches as wet snowflakes fall against her eye. *Who are those animals?* Her mind tries to play tricks on her, hope overcoming her usual caution. *Maybe they're a herd of small herbivores.* She can see nearly two dozen now.

The wind shifts, bringing up the scent from the intruders. Raptor Red's olfactory system gives the identification.

The strangers are raptors. A pack of deinonychs, a very big pack. The three females who had killed the segno are part of this pack.

The deinonychs are moving slowly, following the scent of the segnosaur meat, advancing with tentative steps, heads down, staring intently at Raptor Red and her little group. Ordinarily, *Utahraptor* scent would cause terror in their minds—even the biggest alpha male deinonych is no more than 150 pounds, a tiny fraction of the big raptor's size.

But deinonychs are clever opportunists. The pack has sensed that there is something wrong with the *Utahraptors* up ahead. Healthy *Utahraptors* would never let deinonychs come so close without attacking. And they've seen Raptor Red limping.

Raptor Red rises to her feet. She tries to look tall and dangerous. The older chick too lifts her head and assumes a threatening stance. The deinonychs stop. Two of the pack retreat, but the leaders stand still.

A hot spasm of pain makes Raptor Red's left leg fold up, and she starts to fall, catching herself with her arm. The deinonychs all raise their heads simultaneously and stare. Then they all advance.

The older chick screams at them and looks back and forth from the deinonychs to Raptor Red. The deinonychs slow down, then speed up, spreading out into a wider arc.

At a range of twenty feet the deinonych pack pauses again. Raptor Red knows she must do something before the deinonychs cut off the line of retreat toward the cave. She flexes her legs and lunges half a body length. The *Deinonychus* pack recoils, fleeing to the treeline. Then they return. Raptor Red lunges again. The pack retreats, but not as far this time.

The deinonych pack tests Raptor Red. They're quick learners. They've decided that this adult *Utahraptor* is weak and crippled—a discovery that gives them courage. Now they come with heads high and clawed hands flexing and unflexing. Their eyes are fixed on Raptor Red. She doesn't move, except for her breathing.

One of the lead deinonychs makes a quick running jump and lands a few feet from Raptor Red's sister. He opens his jaw wide.

The biggest deinonych, the alpha male of the pack, steps close, his mouth open. He weaves his head backward and forward, evaluating Raptor Red, the big chick, and Raptor Red's sister. Two more deinonych males approach from the other side. Raptor Red is worried—with her injured leg she can't defend the nest from all sides. One wounded adult *Utahraptor* just isn't enough.

But just as the alpha deinonych crouches to attack, the big chick becomes a *Utahraptor* fury—screaming in a deep voice and making short charges. Two male deinonychs hop backward, and the alpha male flinches, taking his eyes off Raptor Red for just one second.

That second is long enough. Raptor Red makes her move. Her long arms shoot out and grab the alpha male. Her right leg hooks his rib cage from underneath. With all her strength she kicks.

The deinonych leader feels his body being lifted completely off his feet and hurled five yards in the air. He hits the snow and slides on his backside, colliding with three of his packmates and coming to rest upside down against a tree. The other deinonychs scurry in all directions. Their leader gets to his feet and staggers away.

Raptor Red looks down at the confusion that she and the chick have caused. For an hour the deinonych pack moves around uneasily a quarter-mile away. Two large males approach the alpha male and dispute his position of leadership—his ignominious fall down the slope has lost him the respect of the rest of the pack. He backs away and retreats to the rear of the deinonych horde.

Raptor Red tries to hide the fact that her body has been

thoroughly crippled by that last defensive kick. Her entire left side is immobilized by pain that shoots from hip to knee to ankle. She knows she cannot defend herself or her family anymore—but maybe she won't have to. Maybe the deinonychs have lost heart.

The deinonych pack does make a disorganized retreat to beyond a treeline.

The older chick hops over to Raptor Red and gives a war-whoop of victory. Raptor Red feels like cheering herself, despite her pain. *We did well—we defended our family—we did very well,* she thinks.

Raptor Red drags herself to the temporary nest—she wants to share the victory with her sister.

"Ooop-oop-oop." Raptor Red coos a happy greeting. Her sister doesn't answer. Her eyes are wide open and still. Raptor Red sits quietly for ten minutes. Her sister's chest doesn't move, and her eyes don't blink as heavy snow-flakes pile up around the eye socket.

––––––

It takes several hours for Raptor Red to accept the reality of her sister's death. Her left knee throbs terribly, but she doesn't notice. What she does feel is a near total loss of energy, as if the wind has been knocked out of her lungs and she can't inflate them again. Her sister was the one individual for whom Raptor Red would and did sacrifice her own well-being.

She looks around. She's alone. The two chicks are gone, their lingering scent trail leading upslope, in the direction of the cave. Raptor Red is unable to move. For the first time in her life, there's no spark inside, no motivation to struggle, to figure things out.

The snow blows in unpredictable gusts, and Raptor Red's body begins to shake in convulsive bursts of muscle contraction. Shivering like this will exhaust her in a hour.

And then, her metabolic reserves used up, she will freeze to death.

Raptor Red lays herself against her sister's body. Its residual heat helps keep her warm for a few minutes longer. The cold has eased the pain in Raptor Red's left knee. Gradually she loses feeling in her other limbs too.

And she doesn't care.

A dull, heavy feeling of failure falls on her. She doesn't review her life one memory frame at a time. But deep in her consciousness she is aware that she's failed in the great tasks Nature gives each female *Utahraptor*. She lost her original mate before they reproduced. Then she lost another mate, still without producing chicks. And now she has lost her sister's orphans.

Raptor Red has a deep sense that the chicks have little chance in this dangerous region by themselves. Even the older chick isn't ready to survive on her own yet without an adult to help.

Raptor Red feels pain in her head. Her ears ache from the cold, and it hurts to breathe. She can still smell, though. She smells the pine trees and the segno bones. And now she smells the deinonych pack. They're coming back.

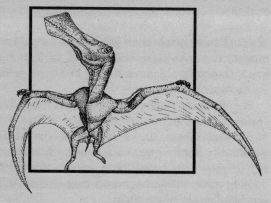

# Raptors in the Clouds

Raptor Red no longer can judge the passage of time. An hour. A half day. She has no idea how long she has lain next to her sister. It's night now, with weak light from a quarter moon. She's drawn up her legs as tightly as she can, trying to minimize heat loss from her body. And she's pressed her shoulders against her sister's body, exploiting the last bit of warmth. But even that heat source is drained after a while.

Raptor Red's mind is cloudy—her eyes are closed, almost frozen shut, but she sees bright, clear images that come and go in quick succession. These are the dreams that come before death.

She sees a mortally wounded *Astrodon* in bright afternoon sun. She sees the heavy body tilt and roll heavily on her mate. She tries to scream, but there's no sound in her dream.

A brilliant pterodactyl swoops down from the sun. Its wings are so shiny that Raptor Red tries to squint. She wants to jump up and bite those blindingly white wings. But in her dreams she can't move.

She hears the dactyl now, coming and going, and coming back again.

A crocodile breaks the surface of a pond, sending a slow-motion shower of droplets high into the air. Each droplet glows, then transforms into a point of light.

Her sister's image condenses in the center of the light, close enough to touch, then fades.

Scents come and go too—mixed in ways they never are in life. The smell of warm iguanodon meat makes Raptor Red feel safe and content. The smell of tick-birds close up, about to groom the raptor pack, is pleasant too. Even better is the smell of a warm cave, lined with bark made pungent by the nearby droppings from the two chicks and her sister.

She tries to move her body to get close to the chicks, but she can't feel her legs.

A male raptor appears, a *Utahraptor* with wings. She calls to him, and he answers. It's her young male.

Her pleasant reverie is broken by the smell of *Deinonychus* very close. She growls and thrashes her arms, not knowing whether the scent comes from real enemies or the dreamtime. She tries to open her eyes, but there's only cold blackness out there. She lifts her snout and forces her eyelids up. Hate finally rouses her brain from sleep.

She sees the deinonychs now: twenty of them, their legs and torsos outlined by moonlight, showing no fear. Five are chewing on parts of the segnosaur carcass that

Raptor Red piled near her sister. The other deinonychs are strolling around the edge of the nest, sniffing and marking the ground with their dung-sign.

Raptor Red tries to move her forepaws, but the deinonychs ignore her feeble threat. To them, she's already as good as dead. The deinonychs squabble over the segnosaur remains, having a tug of war over a leg bone.

Several deinonychs cautiously approach Raptor Red's sister, sniffing and pawing at her body with their claws.

Raptor Red can't keep her eyes open—it's as if a heavy hand is pulling her eyelids down from inside her head, and she doesn't want to resist. The sounds of the deinonych pack stamping the snow with their feet are all around, but the footsteps merge into each other and become a cacophonous mass. The deinonychs are scent-marking the *Utahraptor* nest, declaring it to be their territory, and she hates their smell—it's blocking all other scents.

The cold seeps upward through Raptor Red's legs and body. She begins to welcome the numbness. There's nothing to protect her from the wind where she lies, and each new gust spreads its anesthetizing effect further through her knees and torso and shoulders. A vague but profound feeling of defeat and resignation is taking hold of her spirit.

A series of unspoken thoughts and wishes play in her mind, making her body quieter and quieter. *It doesn't matter anymore . . . there's nothing more I can do . . . I just want the hurt to go away.* It's a combination of physiological shock that dulls her bodily responses and a final acceptance of her failure. The failure to carry out her duty as protector of those who carry her genes.

A deinonych bumps into her tail, catching the tip of his killing claw into Raptor Red's skin. A tiny message of pain travels from tail to Raptor Red's brain. It wakes her up for a second. Her right eye opens involuntarily. The deinonych stares at her for a second, decides that she's no danger, and saunters over to her sister's body. Raptor Red's eye follows his movement, but the images sent to her brain elicit no response.

The deinonych stops to sniff at her sister. He approaches her hind foot cautiously, turning his head one way and then the other, examining the deadly claw that in life had killed scores of dinosaurs far larger than he is. He reaches out with his own hind foot, pushing on the massive calf muscle.

Raptor Red's mind wakes up just a little bit.

The deinonych crouches down and extends his jaws toward her sister's shoulder. Suddenly he gets bold and tries a quick bite at her lifeless neck. Raptor Red's other eye snaps open.

Curiosity and revenge overcome the deinonych's inborn horror of all *Utahraptor*. He remembers being chased by the great raptors many times in the six years he's been alive. He remembers going hungry because this particular *Utahraptor* pack stole carcasses from his own family.

He growls and grabs Raptor Red's sister by the neck, his head twitching and jerking in vicious spasms. He's so absorbed in venting his anger that he doesn't notice Raptor Red's head rising from the snow, her arms pushing her torso up from the ground.

Raptor Red's brain sends messages to her limbs and body. Waves of muscle contractions pass up and down her hindlegs, warming the tissue. The pain from her injured limb starts to glow again, but her brain overrides those signals. A very terrible emotion is welling up inside her, something irrational, something that makes her oblivious to the throbbing in her knee and thigh.

She pushes her body backward a few feet so her shoulders are braced against the rough bark of a pine tree.

Then she drags her body into an upright position, half sitting, half standing, her hand claws digging into the tree trunk.

The deinonych sees the movement. Overcome with fear, he backs up and opens his mouth, and his fingers start to tremble. His eyes fix on Raptor Red's—her pupils dilate, contract, dilate again.

Five other deinonychs see her now, and they shift their weight back and forth from one leg to another, uneasy, unsure of what to do with this *Utahraptor* who seems to be rising from the dead.

Raptor Red staggers forward and rests her torso on her sister's body. Then she raises her neck and shoulders as far as she can, bringing her head eight feet above the ground. She clenches and unclenches her hand claws.

The entire deinonych pack watches her every move from a safe distance, beyond the reach of her still-dangerous forepaws. They want to start tearing apart the two *Utahraptors* but they're smart enough to know when to wait. The pack is used to waiting for hours while large victims collapse from their wounds. They've watched for as long as two days until a two-ton iguanodont at last sank down on knees and elbows, unable to get up again. The deinonych pack members are experts in waiting and watching.

Raptor Red has been operating on pure instinct for the last few minutes. But now she's aware of what she's doing. She knows she can't reach her tormentors. And yet she wants to prolong the time her sister's body is protected from those hateful deinonychs.

She decides to use her last weapon—sound. She fills her lungs deliberately. Her chest swells. Then she exhales, channeling the air through the echo chamber built into her nostrils. A powerful threat-noise, louder than she's ever produced before, rips through the cold air, tumbling snow from the pine branches.

The deinonychs crouch low and retreat another few yards. But they're not fooled by the threat-sound. They now know Raptor Red is incapable of charging.

And Raptor Red realizes that the deinonych pack will wait to come close until she dies. That's what she wants. She has satisfaction knowing that her sister's body will be safe as long as she herself is breathing. She makes another threat-sound, less loud this time. The deinonychs flinch.

The echo of her threat comes back from the snowy cliff face a mile away. The deinonychs turn to look at the source of the sound, but they don't retreat any farther.

Then another echo comes from the opposite direction, another *Utahraptor* threat-noise. The deinonychs bob their heads, look around and make chirping calls to each other. They're confused—the second echo wasn't like the first and it was louder.

Raptor Red's eyelids open very wide and she aims both her ears toward the new sound. She cries again, a strange combination of threat and greeting. Her call is answered immediately by a *Utahraptor* voice from upslope on the edge of the plateau.

It's a male voice.

The deinonychs crouch very low and stare intently up through the trees.

Raptor Red issues a long, low, rumbling growl. She swishes her tail explosively, sending snow into the air in a crystalline shower of white. Two young deinonychs turn and run away toward their nest near the streambed.

The deinonych pack leader stands firm, gnashing his teeth together. Six other adults come up to him and stomp on the snow, side by side.

A moan, very deep and barely audible, comes from the trees upslope. The noise is getting closer.

The deinonychs look upslope where a savage form gradually becomes visible in the darkness. The male *Utahraptor* is standing absolutely still, with his eyes fixed on the deinonych pack leader.

Raptor Red gives a low, throaty greeting. The male responds, and the two begin a duetted battle-call. The calls become faster and louder with each cycle of response and counter-response. The deinonychs swing their heads back and forth, from Raptor Red to the male. Three of their pack lose their nerve and flee.

The battle duet stops abruptly. Raptor Red watches her male consort for a half minute. He slowly flexes knees and ankles, pauses, then charges. A pine sapling breaks into a dozen pieces as his five-hundred-pound body smashes the line of small trees between him and the deinonychs. Raptor Red's nostrils are overwhelmed by the pungent scent released from the male *Utahraptor*'s throat glands.

The deinonych pack leader jumps seven feet into the air, his head banging into conifer branches. He comes down running, his feet skidding on the snow-slickened soil. He dodges the male *Utahraptor*'s hand claws by diving over toward Raptor Red.

She reaches far out with her thumb claws and snags the deinonych by the base of the tail. He fights back, swinging his hands over her face. Raptor Red closes her armored upper eyelid tight and bites the deinonych under his left shoulder. She can't reach his body with her one good hindclaw.

She lifts the deinonych up in her jaws and slams his head against the ground, throwing all the force of her neck and upper body into the blow. His hands grab at her face frantically.

She lifts him again and brings his head down onto the earth even harder. The deinonych goes limp.

Raptor Red opens her eyes and sees her male consort picking up another deinonych in his handclaws. The deinonych body goes sailing over her head, upside down. Then she sees her consort just behind her, standing very tall.

The battle is over in just a few seconds. Raptor Red can hear the whimpering defeat-calls of the deinonych pack as they gather together and mourn their dead several hundred yards away.

Suddenly, Raptor Red feels dizzy—her head becomes light, her vision blurred. She sinks down on her knees, clutching her sister's body. The exertion of the fight has used up all her reserves of strength. She wants to sleep. But she hears a soft cooing a few feet away. A wonderful sound. She answers.

She feels a warm body leaning against her, and she smells her consort's fighting scent. She's not sure that she is still alive, but she's happy. A very deep sleep envelops her brain.

———————

The light comes again inside her brain, this time an orange-yellow light from outside. It's morning light, a bright, warm spring morning. Her eyelids become so warm she blinks. Drops of hot water seep into the corner of her eye. There's a dank, heavy smell all around. She sees a mound of conifer branches heaped up on one side, with steam rising. She opens one eye a little farther and sees a clear blue sky reddened in one quadrant by a midmorning sun.

She smells meat—it's right next to her—and suddenly she's ravenous. Strips of fresh segnosaur steak and chunks of liver are within easy reach, and she gobbles down several mouthfuls.

"BleacccCCh!" She coughs up a piece of bone that got stuck in her throat. Coughing makes her sit up. She finds that she can wiggle her left hindtoes. That's a welcome surprise. And she can stretch all six fingers, flexing and unflexing the big meat-hook claws.

Feeling has come back to both legs—especially the left, which hurts terribly at the knee. Raptor Red grimaces. She doesn't know where she is.

She closes her eyes, and the smell of the young male comes back. She doesn't want to open them again for fear that the image will go away. Hot breath and a snuffling sound are right next to her ear and neck.

Something wet and hot bumps her eyelid hard, making her head recoil.

She slowly opens her eye. There, too close to be in focus, is the muzzle of her consort. She reaches out and pokes his nose with her hand. He's really there.

The old white dactyl surveys the scene below as he rises on the morning thermal currents. The dactyl sees the two adult *Utahraptors* preening each other. Two chicks are feeding on meat in a new makeshift nest at the edge of the meadow. All around the nest are the signs of a desperate battle. Two dead deinonychs have been hurled into the lower branches of a tree. Tracks show that other deinonychs have fled with bloody wounds.

All the tracks will disappear in the hot sun by noon.

# Raptor Family Values

Raptor Red eats her fill and goes back to sleep. She needs to sleep.

She wakes again later the same morning. She looks at the clear blue sky. Bright March sun is transforming snow into vapor, and the layers of white evaporate in the open spaces, leaving cold remnants only in the deep shade.

Raptor Red leaves dreamtime gradually, in stages. Her morning dreams have been soft and warm and comforting. She's seen herself curled up with her male consort on one side and her two nieces on the other. Now, as she is crossing the boundary between sleep and consciousness, she feels safe. In her last dream of the morning, she's being guarded by a huge white dactyl who won't let predators come near.

She opens one eye wide. The light is so bright that she shuts it again. She moves her hand to shade her head and opens her eye again. She sees a huge white dactyl standing motionless six feet away.

Raptor Red snaps her eye shut and reenters the dream. The white dactyl is there, taller, more massive. Raptor Red's brain grapples with this most unusual duality.

Dreamtime and reality aren't supposed to be the same.

It wakes her up completely. She opens both eyes— there's the white dactyl. Raptor Red blinks twice and moves her head back and forth, the way she does to make sure of the identification of an immobile object.

Yes—that's a white dactyl. In fact, that's *the* white dactyl, her aloof companion since her childhood.

The big dactyl jerks his head down into the weeds and yanks on some meat scraps attached to a segnosaur carcass. Raptor Red pulls her head and shoulders back.

"Eeeep!" Her pupils dilate, and she utters a little alarm call. The white dactyl jumps straight up three feet and backpedals a couple of yards. The two predators stare at each other.

The white dactyl moves away and clatters his jaws together quickly, his outward sign of inner agitation. He settles down after a minute or two and starts playing with a deinonych body.

Raptor Red sniffs—and the air around her retells the story of the previous day. There's a dung-scent left by deinonychs—a smell full of anger and fear. But it's faint and fading away into nothingness. Much stronger and much nearer is the scent of her sister's chicks. They've been next to Raptor Red while she slept.

Raptor Red tries out each of her extremities, one by one, stretching and flexing and stretching. Her injured leg throbs at her first attempt to straighten the knee and ankle. But the other leg operates smoothly and painlessly, and her arms and neck, although stiff, are in operating condition.

It's already nine o'clock, and the ground is warm around her. She sniffs at the segnosaur carcass and picks out some soft meat. Swallowing three big chunks makes her feel even better.

A light breeze starts up and brings a strong smell from upslope. Raptor Red stops eating. She hobbles to her feet, using both hands and one hindpaw to carry her weight. She shuffles up to the body of her sister.

Her sister's body looks very slender, very small. Much smaller than it seemed in life. Raptor Red sits quietly for five minutes.

Another powerful scent seeps into her nostrils from a bush twelve feet away. Raptor Red raises her head and stares and sniffs.

The bush has been scent-marked by *Utahraptor* dung. Raptor Red closes her eyes and breathes in the acrid smell. Excellent. It's from her male consort. Its message is clear to all raptors: *This spot and this family are mine.*

Raptor Red's period of mourning is over. She won't forget her sister. Dreamtime will bring her back. But her conscious life has just changed. The tangled web of loyalties that has caused her pain for months suddenly becomes simplified.

Something old has clicked off inside her brain, and a new thing has clicked on.

An hour later Raptor Red sees three figures, *Utahraptors*, coming down the slope—two tall, one short. The two tall ones are carrying parts of another segnosaur carcass.

Long before she can smell the three raptors, Raptor Red identifies them from their gaits. The short one is the younger chick, still gawky and goofy and playful. The tallest is walking with a jaunty, self-assured rhythm, even though he's carrying a heavy piece of meat. That's her mate.

The other tall raptor causes a moment of confusion in Raptor Red's mind. The long stride, the aggressive carriage of the arms, a kind of defiance in the head and neck—

For a brief moment Raptor Red thinks her sister has come back to life.

She lowers her head and rocks back and forth. No, that one is her sister's older chick. Raptor Red hadn't realized how very much the chick had grown up to resemble her mother.

Raptor Red gets up as tall as she can and bobs her head in greeting. The male responds, offering the heavy side of meat. She replies, performing the bonding dance duet as well as she can in her semicrippled state.

The male follows and spreads his hands wide. He's going into the full mate-bonding dance, with all the elaborate moves. He walks back and forth with exaggerated steps, lowering his head, presenting the meat, then withdrawing it. It's the first time he has been able to carry out the full bonding program without interruption.

The chicks don't like it, but they stand back. The smaller one snarls in a high-pitched voice. The taller one moves away, glaring and showing her teeth.

The male finishes his dance and lays the meat offering at Raptor Red's feet. She doesn't look at it. She stares at the male and bobs her head, initiating another round of the bonding dance. She wants to see him do it again.

He raises his head, pauses, then lowers his jaws, picks up the meat, and starts an encore performance.

———

The white dactyl visits every day for two weeks. The pickings are good—the pack hunts segnosaurs in and around the caves, and easy meat is so plentiful that the dactyl is allowed to help himself to nice pink flesh and innards too.

Both the male and the older chick hunt, but not together. The older chick acts more and more like an aggressive adult, and she won't let the male get close.

Every day Raptor Red gets stronger. For a while she doesn't even try to join the hunts—she knows she doesn't have to. The courtship-bonding dance is repeated every morning and assures her that the male will provide.

On the fifteenth day Raptor Red is getting uncontrollably restless. She walks around the temporary nest the pack has built from conifer branches. She tests her injured leg—it's up to eighty percent efficiency. She bites and claws at young trees, gnawing deep grooves in the bark.

She wants to get back to her role of active predator. She enjoys searching for prey-sign. She enjoys stalking. And she gets pleasure from making a kill.

She stands tall, sniffing the air. She sees the white dactyl poking his beak into a muddy pond. Raptor Red lowers her body, and slinks toward the winged old-timer. She crawls to within twenty feet.

The old dactyl stops poking bubbles. Raptor Red leaps forward, making as loud a noise as she can.

The dactyl jumps up and away and is airborne. He's pissed off. *Adult raptors acting like chicks—this is wrong!* he thinks as he flaps away, mumbling to himself.

Raptor Red turns, looks all around, and sniffs the scent-trail left by her mate. She's vaguely aware that her own rambunctious mood isn't just because she's nearly healed. It's also because it's spring.

The sunlight floods over their bodies and heads, making Raptor Red feel bouncy and playful. The days have been getting longer, and inside her brain Raptor Red unconsciously is using daylight length to mark her life's calendar. The window of opportunity for breeding is about to be announced.

This year, she's not afraid.

Here on the mountainside there are no acros. Prey is superabundant. And Raptor Red and her young male consort have proved to be very efficient hunters—when they work together.

Raptor Red whumps her consort very hard with her snout. She begins to understand the message of the sun— soon, very soon, it will be time to reproduce. He looks up, confused. His bioclock is a few days behind hers.

Four days later, a profusion of yellow and pink flowers explodes over the mountain shrubbery. Raptor Red and her mate spend a leisurely afternoon poking and chewing and pulling up the flowers. Every ten minutes or so she bumps him hard on the rump with her forehead.

Raptor Red notes that this day is marked by other changes. The white dactyl has stopped coming around, but to compensate there are new neighbors. The mob of tiny tro-odonts, the little fellows with inquisitive faces who like to slide, take up residence and sneak in to bite carrion beetles and steal carcass scraps.

Raptor Red continues her sister's tradition of welcoming the playful scavengers. The tro-odonts in return squawk loud warnings anytime a large dinosaur approaches. And they provide playmates for the younger chick. Raptor Red and her mate move the pack to the inside of the segnosaur cave, and the tro-odonts camp outside.

Two days later Raptor Red feels too lively to stay at the cave, and she rejoins her pack on the hunt. They return at midday to hear an unholy racket near the nest-cave—two dozen tro-odonts are bouncing around, beside themselves, hissing and screeching at a group of predaceous invaders.

Raptor Red advances very carefully. There near the cave she sees a pack of *Utahraptors,* all young adults.

Raptor Red lies down and stays out of sight. She doesn't know what the strangers are up to. Her consort joins her. The strangers are uneasy. They walk slowly around the cave entrance, sniffing and depositing scent-markers.

Raptor Red's older niece comes up behind her but refuses to lie down. Instead she does exactly what her mother would have done—she advances straight toward the strange *Utahraptors,* head down, teeth bared. Raptor Red moves her muzzle between two bushes so she can watch what's happening.

As her niece strides into the clearing in front of the cave, five of the strangers retreat. One stands its ground. The niece walks up to the muzzle of the stranger and bobs her head once, twice, three times. He responds.

*Courtship dance.* Raptor Red identifies the movements. Then the pheromone detectors in her muzzle give the message: *Sexually active male.*

The duet is one-sided—the female chick makes far more grandiose bows and jumps and arm gestures. Raptor Red can see that the strange male is scared at first, but then he begins to respond. The dueting young couple moves in wide circles that lead them farther and farther away from the nest.

Raptor Red sits up, resting her body on her pelvis. She sighs. An immensely heavy weight seems to dissolve away. The burden of raising this chick to adulthood is finally lifted.

The older chick and her lover move down a gully and disappear from Raptor Red's view. The chick does not look back. Raptor Red gets up and investigates the abandoned dance floor. There's a small dung-pile left by the male stranger, and Raptor Red sniffs it thoroughly. In the future she will respond to this male as if he were family.

Raptor Red scans the area—she can see another strange *Utahraptor* far away, sitting on a boulder, making no aggressive moves but just staring back at the cave.

Her own mate joins her and he finds something her nose missed—a tiny dung-marker plastered against a tree, sixty yards from the cave. Raptor Red sees her mate lingering with great interest here.

The pheromone alarm goes off again in Raptor Red's brain: *Sexually active female!* She watches her mate's nostrils as they flare, sniffing the still air. The strange raptor sitting on the boulder stands up and makes a graceful head gesture.

"SkkkkkrrrrrAWK!"

Raptor Red emits a fierce threat and raises her muscular arms. She snaps her huge, sharp hand claws up and down as she advances with long strides toward the strange female.

Raptor Red's mate looks at the stranger, then back to Raptor Red. *No contest* would be a translation of what he's thinking. *My mate is the most beautiful raptor in the world.*

He adds his voice to Raptor Red's threat. The strange female lowers her body in a submissive gesture and slinks away.

Raptor Red looks back at her mate. He's bobbing his head and making short mock-charges. He bumps her rump with his forehead. Raptor Red feels a flood of emotions—aggression, joy, anger, relief. It's exactly one year since she lost her first male consort in the lowland mud of Utah.

Raptor Red is bumped by her mate. The two *Utahraptor* lovers make a slow dance around each other. Raptor Red makes submissive motions with her head and neck. The male replies with the identical bows and head-bobs. He mounts her once, but she shakes him off. He dances and bows again, attempts to mount, and again Raptor Red shakes him off—but this time more gently.

On the third try, Raptor Red lets the male mount her unhindered.

## june

In early summer the great white dactyl returns to the skies over Raptor Red and her family, making low spirals to catch up on what's happened in the last several months. He looks down and can't believe what he sees. He swoops down closer. He's very surprised—and happy.

An unruly mob of *Utahraptors* is sliding down a slick mud slope. Adults scramble awkwardly up the incline. Little chicks dart in serpentine pathways past their elders. Everyone is coated with red muck.

The dactyl examines the raptors carefully. He recognizes three of the four adults, but the chicks are mostly new to him. The way the chicks play with the adults shows that there are two raptor packs mixed together. One is led by Raptor Red's niece and her consort, a short but powerfully built male. The other pack belongs to Raptor Red and her mate.

The white dactyl's shadow passes over the packs. Five tiny, timid *Utahraptor* faces look up at him. Two chicks lie down next to Raptor Red's niece. Three snuggle between Raptor Red and her mate.

Both families retire later to their nests in the cave. The dactyl notes with satisfaction that the combined dung-scent posts of the two *Utahraptor* packs are respected by all other predators. The deinonych packs in particular shudder with apprehension when they sniff the air at the base of the hill, and they never dare to come closer than a mile.

Raptor Red watches the old dactyl make his familiar spirals over her head. Another gigantic set of white wings joins him, and the two pterodactyls engage in spectacular dives and zoom-climbs, gurgling greetings to each other and making elaborate neck movements.

The old white dactyl has taken a new mate. Late in the summer, three young dactyls join the two adults.

---

Ten years later the plague of acrocanthosaurs recedes when the big predators themselves are hit hard by multiple epidemics that rage through their dense populations. Some acros survive, but they will never build their numbers back up to extreme levels. *Utahraptors*—children and grandchildren and great-grandchildren of Raptor Red and her sister—will descend from their montane stronghold and colonize the low-lying floodplains and river-edge forest.

The sixth generation will invade Siberia, crossing the North Pacific land bridge that their ancestors used when they entered North America going the other direction. For two million years, *Utahraptor* will reign as top predator.

---

The family of Raptor Red will leave a legacy for the modern world. Where her first mate died, at the scene of the *Astrodon* fight, geological processes will seal the record. During the winter rains, a flash flood will cut a swath through the dried lake mud, ripping up gobs of sediment, carrying mud and bones a half-mile away to a shallow depression in the floodplain. Other dried-up dinosaur carcasses will come to rest here too—the armor-plated hide of a *Gastonia* lies jumbled against the astro and raptor bones.

A hundred million years of geologic time will do its

work over the scene. First, layer after layer of mud and sand are heaped over the bones—every major flood brings in two or three feet more. During the successive epochs, a mile of sediment accumulates—some of it brought in by rivers, some by the shallow oceans that cover this part of Utah in the second half of the Cretaceous Period.

At last the oceans drain away, and the landscape rises. Hundreds of miles to the west, volcanic islands collide with the Pacific coast of North America. Then a microcontinent crushes into the coast. Repeated geological collisions release heat and compressive forces throughout Utah and Colorado, and mountains rise. The even layers of sediment, now hardened to rock, are fractured, twisted, and bent.

This parcel of real estate becomes a jagged landscape of young mountains, high plateaus, and interior desert basins. Ice ages come and go and come again, sending heavy spring and winter rains to engorge the mountain rivers that cut deep arroyos through the many-layered sediment pile. In Africa a smart species of ape is evolving into a higher primate with the ability to chip stone tools and tame fire. This primate will spread to every continent, and learn to write down its experiences, and wonder how mountains formed and what fossils mean.

By the late summer of 1991, erosion has eaten into the tomb of the raptor and the astro. Their bones are rockhard, permeated with mineral-rich water that fills every pore with brittle calcite. As the floodplain rock crumbles away under the influence of rain and frost and summer heat, broken bits of fossil bone tumble down the slopes of the gullies. Telltale bone fragments lie everywhere, signals to alert humans that a dinosaurian bonanza awaits excavation by skilled hands. The first *Utahraptor* specimens are unearthed.

In 1994 scientists will announce the discovery of more

giant raptors in the sediments of Asia. Kids who love dino-saurs, and adults too, will name giant raptors as their second favorite dinosaur, after *Tyrannosaurus rex*. A signif-icant minority—twenty percent or so—will say they like *Utahraptor* best.

# Epilogue

I think a lot about Raptor Red and the other raptor species, where they fit into the history of life, and how we've pieced together their lifestyle from the bits and pieces of evidence gleaned from the rocks. The entire history of the Dinosauria is 165 million years long, and *Utahraptor* flourished for just a thin slice of that history, a million years or so. To understand the great raptors, we must probe their ancestry and the ways of life of their descendants.

As I write this epilogue, the field season has begun in Wyoming, and I drive my beat-up 1980 Datsun pickup from the lodge to the dinosaur beds every morning. If I take the long way to our quarries, I can travel through a hundred million years of Mesozoic history, laid out in the successive strata. It was during this time interval that the forces of evolution created the raptor family from very primitive dinosaurian ancestors.

Each rock layer is a punctuation mark in Raptor Red's heritage.

The truck bumps over the dirt road, deeply rutted by last winter's rains, and my progress is marked by a crimson dust cloud as the tires churn up the red sediment of the Chugwater Formation. The Chug is from the Triassic age, 220 million years ago—the Dawn of the Age of Dinosaurs. Fossil footprints in the red and maroon siltstones record a momentous event, the evolutionary debut of the first predatory dinosaurs, flesh-eaters ranging from fox to wolf-size, the beginning of the family tree that would ultimately produce Raptor Red and her clan.

The fundamentals of *Utahraptor*'s adaptive personality were being established in Chugwater times. The fast-acting legs, hearts, and lungs were there, and so were the social bonds. Raptor Red's Triassic ancestors already had a fast-stepping style of movement that left birdlike tracks in the lake-shore sediments. Each footprint has three toes pointing forward and one pointing back—the avian pattern—and the dinosaurs always walked on their toes, keeping their ankles off the ground.

I've tramped over the Triassic redbeds in many places—Massachusetts, Colorado, Wyoming, South Africa. Everywhere the impression you get is the same— these early dinosaurs were moving at hot-blooded speeds. There's a simple equation that lets you calculate how fast a dinosaur was moving from the stride length of the fossil tracks plus the length of the leg. When you plug the Chugwater trackway data into the formula, the results are astounding. On average, the dinosaurs were cruising around at four or five miles per hour, as fast as a pack of coyotes do today. Top speeds were probably forty miles per hour or more. No cold-blooded creature walks and runs that fast.

And these earliest dinos were social predators. Many redbed trackway sites show a dozen predators—all of the same size and the same species—moving together.

Fossil skeletons of Chugwater age add more evidence that the ur-dinosaurs were operating at a high metabolic level. Neck bones and torsos have deep cavities that in life must have been filled with air chambers arranged just like those of birds. This pneumatic system gives birds the highest lung efficiency possible in any living species, far better than that of lizards or crocs or even us humans. When Chugwater dinosaurs breathed, the air passed through a high-tech ductwork system, built to an avian blueprint, that supplied oxygen to all the body tissues at a tremendous rate.

Body proportions gave the early dinos unprecedented agility. Joints and muscles were arranged so that the backbone in the neck region was coiled into an S-shaped curve, ready to strike downward and forward. Thoracic ribs were deep, to house a capacious heart. And the entire hindquarters were massively reinforced by many connections between the lower back and the hip bones, another emphatically birdlike feature that made the hindlegs capable of quick bursts of speed.

The next rock layer above the Chug is the Jurassic—the Age of Whip-Tails—when gigantic herbivores armed with fifty-foot tail weapons ruled the landscape. The somber gray and black badlands are full of bones from *Barosaurus, Diplodocus,* and *Brontosaurus,* representatives of the dominant family that would suffer almost complete extinction at the end of the Period. And we've found short-tailed brontosaurians in the Jurassic too—*Brachiosaurus* and *Haplocanthosaurus*—close kin of the astrodons who would come a bit later, in the Early Cretaceous.

Rarest of the Jurassic dinos are the armor-plated ankylosaurians. We found one skull in the summer of 1993. This clan would expand in the early days of the Cretaceous, blossoming into many new species, *Gastonia* among them.

The Jurassic predators are more advanced than their Chugwater antecedents, and closer to raptors in design. We've got splendid specimens of *Allosaurus,* including all the bones from the hand. Each bone in the forepaw has precisely formed joints so the huge claws on thumb and forefinger converge as they flex downward. The wrist bones give the entire allosaur hand the capacity to swivel quickly side to side. Raptors would inherit their basic hand structure from allosauroid ancestors.

Allosaurs prefigure raptors in many ways—overall body configuration, shorter, more compact torso, longer hindlegs, and sharper S-flexure in the neck. Allos weren't the Darwinian grandfathers of raptors, not the direct ancestors. But they were a sort of evolutionary uncle, close kin of the actual ancestors. So allosaur construction gives us a picture of the raw material from which Nature created the raptor family.

Allosaur skulls from Utah are so well-preserved that you can see where each lobe of the brain fit and how the nerves exited the braincase bones to the sensory compartments. Eyesight was superb, and the avian pattern of nerves indicates that allosaurs saw in color as hawks and eagles do today. Allosaur olfactory chambers in the snout were large, proving that the sense of smell was of a very high order too. Raptor ancestors would carry sensory equipment of a similar adaptive grade.

The first day of each field season I climb up to the Breakfast Bench, a modest ridge just above the last Jurassic layers. There's nothing in the rocks here to suggest that a tremendous biological revolution had occurred at this time. But the dark gray layer, streaked with orange, marks the greatest crisis in the middle of the dinosaurian era, one hundred and forty million years ago: the transition from Jurassic to Cretaceous, from the Age of Allosaurs to the Age of Raptors.

Breakfast Bench fossils are mostly small, and the best time to find them is late afternoon, when the low-angle sun highlights tiny teeth and bone fragments lying on the gentle erosion slopes. Here we find holdovers from the Jurassic dynasties, like teeth from whip-tails, as well as the minute jaws from the new wave of Cretaceous mammal species.

Crocs swarmed in great abundance in the Breakfast Bench times. Thousands of their conical tooth crowns litter the outcrop like spent bullets on a forgotten Civil War battlefield. I treat each croc tooth as a poignant memento of a reptilian life that was lived well.

When I was in grade school in the 1950s, we were taught that crocodiles were mindless, cold-blooded killers. But we know better now. Despite their ferocious jaws, crocs are sentient beings with the most complex family life of any present-day Reptilia. Mother crocs guard their nests with admirable loyalty and respond to the chirping alarm calls of hatchlings struggling to free themselves from their eggshells.

In some croc species mother and father join together in helping their young survive the first few dangerous days of life outside the egg. There's no doubt that croc mothers feel a bond with their young. And they are capable of feeling grief, too. When a hatchling dies before it can reach the water, the mother will sometimes hold the lifeless body in her mouth for a long time before gently laying the youngster down.

Crocs let us envision the bonds that tied dinosaurian societies together. Crocs are living fossils. They retain an

anatomical pattern close to that of Triassic dinosaur ancestors, and in nearly every way the Jurassic dinosaurs were
more advanced than crocodiles, including their backbone,
hips, shoulders, and legs. So I must conclude that Jurassic
dinosaurs were more advanced in their social structure,
too.

Two miles north of the Breakfast Bench outcrop we
have proof. Limestone beds that border a shallow lake are
full of footprints from a giant *Astrodon*-like dinosaur. These
footprints aren't scattered haphazardly, each trackway
leading off in a different direction. Instead, the trackways
are tightly organized into herds with twenty or thirty astros traveling together, the largest individuals positioned
at the edge of the herds, the smallest huddled in the center.

When I stop to fill in the pages of my field book with
the day's observations, I like to sit on the rim of one of the
biggest tracks, a footprint a yard wide. The lime mud
pushed up by the thrust of the hindpaw looks fresh even
though it has been frozen into stone for a million centu-
ries. This depression in the limestone is vivid evidence of
the enormous power in astro muscles and ligaments and
of the great beast's feelings of duty to family and clan.

Just above the Breakfast Bench is the Early Cretaceous
itself, a stratum of polished black gravel and sand known
as the Lakota, dating from the same epoch as the
*Utahraptor* beds of Utah and Colorado. The pale yellow
Lakota sandstones make towering cliffs crowned with
scrubby pines. It's an exceptionally beautiful spot where
peregrine falcons make inquisitive dives from their nests
along the ridge crests.

Scientists are supposed to be dispassionate, cool-
headed, and unemotional when they evaluate their data.
But it's hard for me to avoid a sense of awe when I'm
hunting fossils in the Lakota. Evolution was accomplishing

great things at this time and place. Thin seams of pinkish siltstone reveal carbonized branches and fragments of tree trunks, mostly from conifers. But there are broad-leaved fossils, too, signaling that greatest event in floral history— the appearance of flowering plants.

The Lakota bears witness to a revolution in the animal kingdom as well. The gravels and sandstones contain iguanodon bones and pieces of armor from giant armor-plated members of the *Gastonia* family, evidence of a new order among the giant herbivores. Fossil beds of this age from Spain and China show that birds had reached a modern level in the structure of wings and feathers. And one precious lower jaw from England documents the existence of a creature very close to the ancestry of ourselves— *Aegialodon.*

The world of the top predator had been changed from the Jurassic condition. Nearly extinct were the once supreme allosaurs; in their place were their cousins the ridge-backed meat-eaters, the clan of acrocanthosaurs.

And joining the ridge-backs were the raptors, predators whose body mechanics introduced a whole new dimension to the drama of attack and defense. Raptor claw design departed from that of their allosauroid ancestors, transforming a talon fit for grabbing and holding on to prey into a weapon for slashing. While all the ridge-backs kept massive hand claws with thick tips, the raptors adopted long, slender fingers that wielded narrow, knife-like claws.

The Early Cretaceous witnessed an escalation in brainpower among the carnivores. Raptor braincase bones were voluminous compared to the standards of Jurassic predators, and equally large-brained were the two other groups of carnivorous newcomers, the ostrich dinosaurs and the bantam-sized tro-odonts.

It was a time of ecological flux, when land bridges

opened the gates to successive invasions from one region to another. The iguanodonts and gastons dug from the Black Hills in the Lakota beds match those from Utah very closely, and both sets of American dinosaurs are nearly identical to skeletons from the south of England. Such exact resemblances between America and Europe could only occur when a free and easy avenue of biogeographical exchange had been opened between the two continents.

We will never know all the details of this grand intercontinental exchange of evolutionary products, but we can be sure that each dinosaur species that made passage across the Atlantic or Pacific carried with it a deadly cargo of viruses, bacteria, and parasites. Epidemiological warfare is a certainty whenever and wherever faunas mix across the world. In Wyoming today the threat of foreign disease is taken very seriously by my friends in the state fish and game commissions. Over the last few years, they've closed down several ranches that were breeding Asiatic deer because such exotic game can release pathogens that would devastate our native Wyoming deer and antelope.

We know that the life of dinosaurian hunters was hard. Most skeletons we excavate have clear marks of old wounds—broken and healed ribs, cracked limbs, and lower back vertebrae fused together by injury. To survive and raise their young, the predators needed more than sharp teeth and strong claws. They needed social bonds. How did *Utahraptor* choose their mates? How did they guide their offspring into adulthood? We do have clues.

Fossil trackways of acros found in Texas show them hunting in pairs, trailing herds of multi-ton astrodons, and it's reasonable to suppose that these pairs represent mates working together. Since raptor brains were far larger for their body size than those of acros, we can surmise that the raptor society was more complex as well. I like to think that *Utahraptor* emotional ties between male and female, parent and young, were exceptionally strong and rich.

Three hours north of our Lakota quarries we have sites from the end of the Cretaceous, sixty-six million years ago, when that most famous of dinosaurs, *T. rex,* played the top predator role. The great tyrannosaurs are cousins of the raptors, and the tyrannosaur data matrix helps us look into the mind of the raptor. My colleague from the Black Hills Institute, Pete Larson, has discovered a remarkable thing about the gender roles in *rex.* The biggest, most powerfully muscled specimens are female, as shown by the structure of the bones around the base of the tail.

Female dominance is a powerful piece of evidence that permits us to reconstruct the private lives of Cretaceous predatory dinosaurs. A family structure built around a large female is rare in meat-eating reptiles and mammals today, but it's the rule for one category of predatory species—carnivorous birds. Owls, hawks, and eagles have societies organized around female dominance, and we can think of tyrannosaurs and raptors as giant, ground-running eagles.

---

On late spring mornings, when the sun has just begun to warm the badlands, I like to walk quietly along a line of twisted fenceposts, their barbed wire long ago fallen away into rusted uselessness. This is where I see the golden eagles. They perch on the tallest posts, facing east, with wings half open to catch the light. Usually the two of them are together, the female easily identified by her larger size. They've been together for five years. Lifelong monogamy is the rule for eagles.

The eagles watch me from a hundred yards away, but

they seem to view me and all other humans with disdain. After their bodies have been warmed and the first thermal upwellings start to rise in the air, they take off and ascend in widening spirals.

They fly together and hunt together, and I've seen them feed their brood together at their nest on an isolated pinnacle of Lakota sandstone. I found the nest by accident one day when I was stooped over a string of eroded allosaur backbone in a gully. My paleontological reverie was cut short when I saw huge shadows pass over the ground in front of me. I looked up and saw the female eagle's face staring down from ten yards above.

She had the most amazing eyes, very clear and intelligent, and very fierce. When I imagine Raptor Red, she is looking at me with eyes like those.

dactyl

tro-odon

acro

deinonych

raptor red

croc

segno

# Dramatis Personae

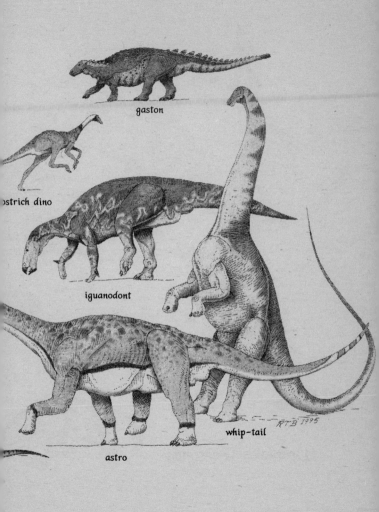

gaston

ostrich dino

iguanodont

astro

whip-tail

RTB 1995

# Acknowledgments

My mother carted me across the George Washington Bridge to see the bones many times when I was growing up in New Jersey. So mom . . . *Raptor Red* is really your book.

My agents, Ms. Kim Witherspoon and Mr. Louis Mountbatten, saw the potential in the story very early. They pursued me and *Raptor Red* with creative relentlessness, and without them it never would have come to completion.

It's been a joy working with my editor, Ms. Jennifer Hershey. She truly is a writer's editor with a superb sense of rhythm in prose that has made every revision more graceful and more elegant. Kim told me you were that good, and she was right.

Ms. Constance Clark has given me wonderful assistance in both the science and the art needed to construct this book. She has contributed a wealth of wisdom from her experience as a historian of geology, a zoo keeper, and a lover of puffins.

Most of all, I'm thankful to the Big Wonderful State of Wyoming and to everyone who lives here. I saw a room full of Wyoming dinosaurs in New York when I was a fourth-grader, and ever since Wyoming fossils have kept my imagination fired up.

The Cowboy State has filled exhibit halls all over the world with spectacular Mesozoic skeletons. But the hundreds of bone-hunters who have visited the state during the last dozen decades have given little in return.

I'm happy to devote the rest of my life to digging here and helping the expansion of our museums so Wyoming fourth-graders—and dinosaur-lovers of all ages—can enjoy our prehistoric heritage.

**Dr. Robert T. Bakker**
("Jurassic Bob" to the night man at the bar in Medicine Bow)
Tate Museum, Casper College
Casper, Wyoming
May 14, 1995

# About the Author

Acknowledged as a rebel in his field, Dr. Robert T. Bakker acted as an unofficial consultant for the special effects artists who created the dinosaurs for the film *Jurassic Park*. He is the dinosaur curator of the Tate Museum in Wyoming and the author of the groundbreaking nonfiction book *The Dinosaur Heresies*. He is most famous for proposing the theory that dinosaurs weren't the cold-blooded, sluggish, solitary creatures we once imagined them to be, but were instead warm-blooded, active, and social animals. He is considered to be one of the world's foremost paleontologists.

# THE LAST FAMILY

## JOHN RAMSEY MILLER

A harrowing novel of suspense that pits
a former DEA agent against his worst nightmare:
a trained killer whose fury knows no bounds,
whose final target is the agent's own
flesh and blood . . .

*"Fast paced, original, and utterly terrifying--true, teeth-grinding tension...Hannibal Lecter eat your heart out!"*--Michael Palmer

_____10213–3 $21.95/$29.95